IT ENDS IN BLOOD

THE EDGE OF VENGEANCE SERIES
BOOK ONE

VALENTINA VALLAY

To anyone who has ever been told you can't do it. Fuck whoever said that. They're wrong. Surround yourself with people who believe in you fiercely until you're ready to. You've got this. I believe in you.

TRIGGER WARNINGS

Hello Beloved Readers,

You are about to embark on a journey with me that can be intense, unpredictable, and unsettling. The content warnings and kinks detailed below may include spoilers. If you feel confident reading without triggers, you may not want to proceed with the rest of this note.

It Ends in Blood contains themes of organized crime and on-page violence. Certain acts, including rape, sexual assault, and the cruel death of an animal (a childhood dog), are referenced or discussed in the story (for example, the rape occurs on a surveillance video) but are not shown in scene. The Don is a fucking dick—I hope John Wick finds him.

The are sexual scenes that include FM, MFM, and MFMM, including the budding of an MM relationship in an MFMM setting. Some kinks depicted on the page include double penetration, snowballing, snowsleding, blood play, knife play, mild degradation, mild stalking, and mild BDSM, namely, Dom/sub dynamics.

Please be mindful of your triggers before proceeding, I want you to have an enjoyable experience, not a stressful one.

AUTHOR'S NOTE

To my dearest Valentines,

This story is the literary equivalent of an emotional rollercoaster ride. You may hate me just a little as we get into it, but if you stick with me—as I take you to the edge and keep you there for a while—I promise the release at the end of the series will be worth it.

We're about to begin. Turn the page for me, darling.

*You did so well, sweetheart.
Now be extra good for me, baby, and keep
going...*

CHAPTER 1

ETTORE—"TOR"

"Holy Fuck."

Seriously? This is *not* how this weapons' exchange was supposed to turn out. I look down at my hand, clutching the expanding red stain on my gut. *Holy shit*, that's a lot of blood. My head's spinning, little white dots accumulating in the air around me where I hide behind a stack of pallets. Gunfire fills the warehouse, shouts and shots ringing through the cavernous space.

"Spider!" I grit out, "On me, southwest corner, third door on the right, now." A rush of air blasts past me. I have no idea where the shooting comes from, but I know that shit was close. I slam into an office, my heart pounding from the chaos. Without hesitation, I shove a tall, black metal filing cabinet in front of the door. It's a little heavy, a little awkward, but I manage to barricade the entry despite pain exploding from my gut with every move. The sound of metal scraping against the floor echoes in the otherwise quiet room. The office is sterile, exuding the faint smell of paper and printer ink. The hum of the fluorescent lights can be heard in the space between gunshots outside.

I lean against the opposite wall, gun pointed at the door behind that heavy ass filing cabinet, struggling to stay awake. I just need to last long enough for Spider to arrive. We were supposed to be in and out, a simple routine weapons exchange with Satō's crew. We've done this exact meet so many times it should be manageable in our sleep. So what the hell happened?

I startle at the sound of a soft whimper coming from the corner of the office. My gaze scans the unforgiving, cold, concrete floor in that direction. I adjust my aim to cover the potential threat and startle as a bruised and bloody woman's face comes into focus. Are those eyes violet or black? Staring into them mimics the sensation of drowning in the depths of the ocean. As if I am staring into the Mariana Trench lit up by iridescent jellyfish swimming within. They don't look real. Huh, maybe I'm finally passing out. I push off from the wall and limp toward her, clutching my side, each step a battle I am not sure I am going to win. My shoulders tense in frustration as I move at a snail's pace. Every ounce of endurance I have left is spent staying upright. I have to hold it together. Not just for me, but for this broken woman huddled in the corner, looking feral and terrified.

"Hey. You. I'm Tor, what's your name?"

She stares up at me, eyes glossed over, blood matted in her long dark, hair so violet that it looks like midnight. She's covered in cuts and bruises. A few of her fingernails are missing. *What the fuck?* I reach my hand down to her and she flinches. I pull back, putting that hand up in surrender. "Hey, hey, it's okay. I'm a friendly. I'm not going to hurt you."

I take a deep, painful breath and inch my hand toward

her again, slower this time, and brush a strand of matted hair out of her face. She releases a sigh and I see her fighting to keep her eyelids open. Same, baby girl, same. I watch her struggle to stay alert, but she loses her fight. Her eyes close, her breathing evens out, and in seconds, she's out cold.

"I'll be joining you soon, Midnight." I sink down next to her, leaving a trail of blood smeared on the off-white walls that were once probably white. Once I reach the floor, I try to keep as much pressure as I can on my right side. As soon as I settle, she leans in my direction, her head resting on my shoulder. Who the hell is she? She's not supposed to be here. No one was supposed to be here but Satō's crew. Yet, clearly, that wasn't the case.

A crash at the door pumps pure adrenaline into my veins. I guess I have a little fight left in me. I swivel the gun toward the door, finger on the trigger. The filing cabinet screeches an unholy screech across the floor as the door swings open. I lower my weapon once I see Spider.

"Shit, man. Almost sent you to meet your maker. Or... whatever. Where's Blade?"

"Having the time of his life. It's his kind of carnage out there." The echoes of screams and bullets flying bounce off the wall. That goddamn savage lives for this kind of shit.

Spider's eyes run down the length of me. "Bloody hell, Tor, is that yours?" His eyes home in on the steady stream of blood seeping through my white button up shirt, dripping onto the concrete floor and my new friend's leg.

"Yeah, but I'm fine. It's fine, don't worry about that. What the hell should we do about her? Any idea who she is?"

"Your father did *not* mention anything about a girl. Orders were to handle the weapons deal, nothing more."

Spider's fingers reach down, gently pressing against the pulse point on her neck. "She's alive, just unconscious. Fucking hell, look at the state of her." He sighs. "Wait, your old man didn't advise you about a girl either?"

"No, no fucking clue who she is or why she's here. Sleeping Beauty was semi-conscious when I walked in, but just for a second. She didn't answer me when I asked her who she was."

Blade crashes into the room, drenched head to toe in blood, and I clock brain matter on the shoulder of his suit jacket. This fucking guy, he looks like he walked straight out of a slasher movie.

"All good out here," he says casually, like he wasn't just carrying out wholesale slaughter. "Hey fuckers, what's with the office meeting? Never mind, I don't care, I'm sure it could have been a fucking email, let's move. We should probably get the fuck out of here in case any more are on the way... wait, what the fuck? Tor, is that fucking blood yours?" Blade scans my gut before his eyes trail to our mystery girl. "Who the fuck is she?"

"No leads," Spider says as he lets go of her neck that he was absentmindedly stroking. He reaches down to untie her. Her rope-bound hands shoot outward, wrapping around his wrist and stopping him in his tracks. His eyes widen, and did his pupils just dilate? I chuckle to myself, then wheeze at the pain in my gut. Sick bastard, of course he would be turned on by a bound and bloodied girl's touch. He's the epitome of, 'it's always the quiet ones you have to watch out for.'

Blade draws his knife—this asshole's speed is terrifying. In the blink of an eye, he has it slid in place on the side of her neck. "Get your hands off my boy, little slayer. Calm the fuck down."

I can't suppress the laugh because Blade calling someone 'slayer' is peak irony. "Holy shit, Blade. 'Calm down'? When has that ever *not* escalated the situation to unfathomable heights when uttered to a woman in distress?"

Blade spares me a 'fuck you' glare but doesn't bother responding otherwise.

Spider remains frozen in place, staring at the girl softly. "What's your name, sweetheart?"

She doesn't move, just continues holding his wrist in a death grip. A grip that's disproportionately strong for a girl in her condition. She stares Spider down, ignoring Blade's presence, knife, and comment. *Interesting.* My head starts to swim, her face begins to blur. Shit, I have a minute, maybe two, tops.

"Let's go, Blade," I wheeze out before my body collapses in on itself. I must be in and out as the next thing I know, I am pretty sure I'm pressed against Blade's solid mass. I feel myself floating. Shit, did he just pick me up bridal style? Fuck me, I hope I die. I'm never going to live this down. If this dick takes a selfie, and shit I know he will, I'm going to kill him. I hear him whisper, "Say cheese." and curse under my breath. Fucking asshole.

I can vaguely hear their voices but my eyes won't open no matter how much I try to force them. It's hard to maintain thoughts, but I know I want to look into her abyssal sea eyes again. Why is she here, in this fucked up state? Who fucked her up? Who the fuck is she? And who the fuck is shooting at us? A lot of fucks to ponder.

"Tor!" I hear Blade calling for me, but I can't make my mouth spit out a response. "Fuck, Spider, call Doc Morelli. We need him to meet us at the house. Let's move. Now."

"What about the girl?" I hear Spider spit out.

"Fuck her, take care of it," Blade snarls. "Bullet to the head. Make it quick, we gotta fucking move."

"Nnuuurgh. NO!" I manage to spit out, words slurring and eyes still refusing to cooperate. "Bring her... with us," is all I manage to get out before everything goes black.

CHAPTER 2

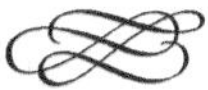

SPIDER

I sigh. Those assholes. I wouldn't put it past them to leave me here.

Frustration tugging at the edge of my voice, I do my best to keep my tone gentle despite the tension in the air. "I'm done trying to untie your wrists, sweetheart." I let out a quiet breath, managing to pull myself free from her grip. I am surprised by the strength she's still got left in her. "You're tougher than you look, I'll give you that."

I scoop her up, her body squirming in my arms; her feeble attempts to break free are adorable. I keep my hold steady, and murmur under my breath, "Normally, I'd go about this differently, maybe buy you dinner first, but there is no time for that right now. This whole fucking operation's a mess, and I'm just trying to make sure you don't end up worse off." I keep my voice as calm as I can, but I doubt it has the desired impact as I cannot hide the urgency in my tone.

I blame Blade. His 'bullet to the head' remark is unlikely to have helped this situation. But I'm not in the least bit surprised that this is where we are. Blade's solution to everything is to simply kill it; it has been since Ava... ever since a year or so after I met him when we were kids. I struggle to keep her subdued as I make my way out of that dingy office. "Shhh, sweetheart, please relax, okay? I'm trying to help you. Please hold still for me. I don't want anything bad to happen to you. My friend over there—" I nod in Blade's direction. "He's trigger happy. Keep quiet for me, and everything will be alright. We're taking you to our doctor to get checked, okay?"

She goes still in my arms and looks up directly into my eyes with the darkest, most endearing stare I've ever seen. A solitary tear rolls down her cheek, drawing a curved line through the dried blood caked on her face. Would it be weird to lean down and lick the tear off her face? Would she let me? My head starts to dip downward of its own volition, but then my brain kicks back in. She just stopped squirming, and we need to go now. I lift back up and watch the tear slowly trail down to her jaw. Her head falls back and she's out cold again. "What did they do to you, sweetheart?"

"Keep up or drop the dead weight," Blade spits out as he hurries across the warehouse, carrying Tor over his shoulder with one arm, gun held at the ready in the other. He runs out toward the car.

Twat. "Coming," I yell back. I lift her up so she would be straddling my waist, but in her unconscious state, her legs dangle to the side, making it harder to run with her. She's not heavy, but it's awkward. I'm holding my gun with my right hand, and cupping her ass with my left to keep her from falling. I can feel myself getting hard as she rubs against me. It must be the blood rush. Yeah, that must be it.

We run through the warehouse, heads on a swivel. Blade's nothing if not thorough, but more could have arrived while we were in the office. Despite years of riding with Blade, I am not prepared for the remnants of the massacre that took place here at his hands. Dead bodies are strewn across the concrete floor. It's an obstacle course to navigate around them. Blood spatter covers every available surface—plastic packing materials, wooden pallets, and metal shelving—the whole place is a red Jackson Pollock painting. Tor and I often joke that it's a miracle Blade hasn't been committed. He's always been a shoot or stab first, ask questions later kind of fella. I glance at Tor hanging down Blade's back. His face looks so damn pale. He's lost a lot of blood. My distracted thoughts lead me to almost slip on the trail of blood pooled all over the concrete. I shake my head. Bloody hell, this is not how tonight was meant to unfold.

It's eerily quiet outside other than the metal clanging sounds emanating from the nearby industrial plants. As we approach the black-tinted SUV we left parked in the alley, I scan our surroundings for any movement. Nothing. Just faded brick, the smell of manufacturing, and the steam rising from a manhole in the corner. Blade loads Tor into the backseat and crawls in with him, hands firmly pressed against the hole from which the life force of my brother is leaking out.

"Hurry the fuck up, bro." Blade's voice, usually deep, gritty, and sinister, sounds panicked. I've never heard that in his tone before. The quiver in his voice spurs me into action. Rage is his default. Blade doesn't do fear and until this moment, I thought fury was his only setting.

I buckle our new friend into the passenger seat and hop around to the driver's side. Her head lolls as I peel out. A race car driver would be proud of the way I slam the pedal to the metal and gun it to the house. I voice-dial Doc as I whip dangerously through streets full of nightlife. He doesn't ask questions, but promises to be there and set up by the time we arrive. The city flashes by in snippets. High rises, yellow cabs, black town cars, bustling bars, friends and coworkers walking to their next destination, couples out on dates, we pass by them all in a blur. The streets are filled with New Yorkers causally enjoying their night in the city that never sleeps. I don't think we will be getting any sleep tonight either.

"For fuck's sake Spider, don't kill us on the way."

"Make up your mind, you twat. Is it hurry the fuck up bro, or are you looking for a smooth fucking ride?"

When he says nothing, I slam my foot on the gas again as my heart begins to rage in my chest, worry creeping in. Blade doesn't have an off switch or a shut-up function, either. Tor must be in a right bad state back there. *Bloody hell, hang on, Tor.*

"How's he holding up?"

"He's going cold. Spider, hurry."

The lively city disappears behind us as we pull into the quiet suburban neighborhood we tend to hole up in. Beautifully manicured landscapes and expansive properties come into view on the maple, oak, and sycamore tree-lined streets. I pull into our drive, parking in front of our angular modern mansion with clean lines and open spaces that stands out among the colonials, Victorians, and grand Tudors of the area. Doc is at the ready in the driveway.

Doc Morelli always accepted late-night calls for a price, but when his phone buzzes at 1:29 AM, he knows to show up and he never complains. He's also incredibly good at what he does, not just because he's an experienced doctor, but because he knows, when it comes to working for the Don, mistakes aren't forgiven. Mistakes are a one-way ticket to a cold, brutal end.

Blade and I unload Tor from the car and follow Doc into the living room, then down the steps to the basement.

"Bring him in through here gentleman, and, yeah, right there, down on that." Doc flicks on lights as we go, navigating the space like it's his vacation home.

Blade lays Tor down on the cold sterile surface of the surgical table we keep in the middle of the main basement room.

"Now get out and give me room to work."

"Doc," I say as I clear my throat, running a hand through my hair, eyes darting around as I try to steady my voice, "How's it look? Is he going to be okay?"

"The sooner you get out and make room for me to work, the better his chances," Doc says, pointing to the door.

Blade doesn't move. Neither do I.

Doc's errand boy—I mean male nurse who also answers every middle-of-the-night call like it's normal—raises his hand to place it on Blade's chest to push him out of the room. The look Blade levels him stops him in his tracks. He swiftly raises his arms in surrender. Smart kid.

"Right through there, sir." He points to the door and slowly backs away from Blade like one would a wolf in the woods. Wise move; that's not too far off from reality.

I can't help it, the stress of tonight's events is too much. I laugh. Hysterically, like a cackling hyena. And I just keep laughing the entire way out the door. I guess we're at the unhinged portion of the night.

Blade punches me in the bicep as we make our way up the stairs to the main floor.

"Ow, fuck you, you cunt," I snap, rubbing my arm. I am losing it, because I sure as hell cannot lose Tor. I want to yell at him, punch him, something. *You better fucking fight*

Tor, leave us and I'll fucking kill you. Bloody hell, I sound like Blade.

"Stop laughing like the Joker, you psychopath. That's my role."

"Ledger or Nicholson?" I ask.

"Always fucking Heath," Blade grinds out at me amid my raucous laughter. "Go be useful somewhere. Wait, hey." He looks around the empty living room. "Where the fuck is the girl?"

I stop the cacophony abruptly. "Oh shit, the car," I mutter.

We look at each other for a beat and then both run through the house and out front at full speed. Our boots pound the concrete driveway as we rush around the SUV, coming to a stop right outside the passenger door. I hear Blade's sigh of relief coincide with mine at the sight of her. *Mmm, huh, okay, that was unexpected.* She's still lying there completely passed out, possibly dead, still bound and tied around her wrists.

"We should have Doc take a look at her, too," I say. "You know, if she's still alive there."

The glare Blade levels at me could kill a lesser man. "Doc's busy saving our brother, remember? Fuck her."

"Blade, we can't just leave her here. Tor told us to bring her. Let's take her inside and Doc can take a look at her when he gets done fixing up Tor."

"You should have fucking shot her and left her at the warehouse like I said. She'd be one less fucking problem. Don't you think we have enough of them right now?"

"Don't you think *she's* been through enough? Look at her, Blade." A balmy night breeze cools the sweat on my skin and pushes my hair into my face.

"Sure, that's why you should have put her the fuck

down. Put the bitch out of her misery. I don't give a fuck what you do, but leave Doc the fuck alone. He needs to be one hundred percent focused on Tor. I don't give a fuck about anything but that."

I sigh, push my hair out of my eyes. "He's going to make it, Blade." I don't know if I believe it, but I force myself to. He has to.

"Of course he fucking will," Blade responds. "And if he doesn't pull through, there won't be a doctor to look at your pretty little pet later."

See? Default response: kill the problem.

I reach into the car to press my fingers against her pulse again. As soon as I feel the faint beat, I exhale. I pull her out of the car and turn to see Blade ramming his fists into the oak tree out front over and over again, bark flying, blood running down his knuckles and further staining his clothes. Thank God we're the only house at the end of this street cause it's loud as hell.

"You may wanna ease up there, tiger. We'll probably need those hands to deal with whoever is responsible for tonight."

"Well, you whined like a fucking bitch when I punched you, so I had to find something else to hit. Go take care of your stray. Leave me the fuck alone."

I shake my head. "Blade, stop, bro. Seriously. Please," I beg with our little passenger tucked against my chest.

"Fuckkk," Blade yells. He turns on me and even I have a split-second where I think he might genuinely try to hurt me. "What the fuck happened, Spider? You said it was a routine drop. Easy, in and out. Easy job. That was anything but fucking easy."

"That's what Bruno told us, said it came straight from Signor Amato." I shift the girl against my chest, getting a solid grip on her, as I shove the car door shut with my butt. "I have no idea what happened, but I sure as shit intend to find out."

I walk her up the steps and into the house, leaving Blade behind to mutilate the tree to his heart's content. God help anything on the receiving end of his wrath. I lay her frail form on the couch. The deep, glossy leather is smooth and cool to the touch as I release my hold on her. The leather creaks faintly as she settles into it, and the sound of her bare skin making contact with the sleek surface feels almost unnatural. I pull out the blade sheathed on my hip and start cutting her bindings. The skin on her wrists is completely raw, the imprint of the rope clearly indented into her flesh. She doesn't flinch or stir as I carefully extract the rope from her skin. I stand up to grab the fully stocked first aid kit from the entryway closet, then walk to the kitchen to wet a washcloth with warm water. I want to try to get some of the dried blood off of her. I think she has an olive-colored skin tone. I can't say for sure; she's so filthy it's hard to tell.

I decide to start with her face. I kneel at her side, knees pressing into the wool rug that protects the hardwood floors from our exploits. As I lower the washcloth toward her skin, her hand shoots out and wraps around my throat. My dick responds before my brain, twitching suddenly with excitement. Stupid penis. My chest heaves as she applies slightly more pressure. I stare into her eyes and hold up my hands, showing her the wet cloth. My voice comes out strained under the pressure of her hand. I rasp out, "I just want to clean off some of the blood, sweetheart. You know, so the Doc can see what he's working with when he gets a chance to look at you."

She holds my gaze steadily for a beat, then releases my

throat and I take in a deep breath, my semi-hard dick still not reading the room. She lays back on the black leather, eyes remaining fixed on me. She takes in a leveled breath, and closes her eyes, but I can still see the tension in her muscles. I pause, not sure what to do next until I see she's relaxed, passed out yet again. I pull up her ripped shirt slightly to wipe the blood I can see and stop dead in my tracks. She is covered in what I think are knife marks, old and new, slashes from some kind of strip with thorns on it, puncture wounds, burn marks, and an intricate collection of ink.

"Bloody hell, sweetheart, what happened to you?" I murmur to her unconscious body. I hear a theatrical sigh and turn to catch Blade standing above us. He stares down at the carvings in her skin covered in exquisite art. He's casually rolling a bullet around between his fingers. When did he walk in here? It never stops being unnerving how silently he can sneak up on me, on anyone. He stands there completely motionless, fixating on every mark littered across her torso. While the tattoos do some heavy lifting to cover up the scars, the raised skin still gives them away.

"Blade," I say. He continues to stare, completely ignoring me, as if entranced by the view. "Blade?" Still nothing, fully immersed as if hypnotized by the sight of her, unable to look away or notice his surroundings. Hmmm, his reactions to her continue to be... different. Blade is a fine-tuned, full-body weapon, the most dangerous kind. I've never seen him distracted. Tonight appears to be filled with many firsts for him.

"Blade!" I yell, nudging his leg with my elbow. He turns to look at me. "Help me take her shirt off." I lift her up, revealing the top of a circle tattoo on her back shoulder where her shirt is ripped.

"No." He tilts his face back to stare down at our mystery girl lying motionless on the couch.

"No? What is your problem, Blade? Look at her, she needs our help."

"No, you don't know what they've done to her. Leave her clothes on. Stop touching her until she wakes up."

I pause. "You think she doesn't like being touched?"

"What girl wants to wake up to your ugly mug with your hands all over her?"

"Every girl, thank you. Better my hands than yours. The ladies happen to love this handsome face, unlike your serial killer profile."

He smirks. "Probably true." He sighs. What is going on with him? When he speaks again, his voice is gentler. "We don't know what she's been through. Don't touch her without her permission. Wait for her to wake up."

"Right, yeah. You're right." Bloody hell, how could I forget about Ava? Of course Blade would think of that. I should have, too. Waking up to strangers again will be overwhelming enough, especially with whatever the hell she's endured. "Can you watch her for a sec? I'm going to go take a shower so I can head over to Amato's compound. I need to figure out what the hell we walked into tonight. We need to start damage control, limit the fallout from whoever you just annihilated in that warehouse."

"I don't want to watch your little pet." He looks at me like I'm crazy. "You brought her here, you make sure she doesn't pee on the rug."

"Blade," I forcefully grit out. His eyes slowly drift back down to the markings still visible where her shirt remains slightly raised in the front and ripped in the back.

"Fuck. Fine, but if she wakes up and gives me shit?" He

holds up the bullet he has been steadily playing with in his hand. "You'll know where you can find this."

Demented twat. I fucking love him, but he's the most brutal man I know. Sometimes I think he's even more ruthless than the Don himself. He won't kill her, right? Bloody hell, he might. "Don't kill her," I say as I walk away shaking my head.

He doesn't respond.

CHAPTER 3

BLADE

How long have I been standing in our living room? I shake my head, trying to snap out of it. I have no idea how long I have been frozen in place, staring at her as she lays asleep on the ebony leather couch. In the dim light, she almost looks magical, otherworldly. Like she isn't real. Like her skin would burn you if you touched her. What did they do to her? What the fuck do I care? We need to get rid of her.

"Wake up," I shout. I should let her sleep. I don't actually want to fucking deal with her. It's better to get this over with though; the sooner she's up, the sooner we can get her the fuck out of here. She's a pest we don't need, especially not right now.

Her eyelids snap open and she stoically stares up at me, as if she maybe hadn't been asleep at all. Her eyes have the darkest, most innocent doe-eyed look to them, like a baby deer caught in headlights. It's impossible to look away. I watch as the tiny thing struggles to lift her torso. She can barely move an inch. I'm fascinated as she keeps trying, even as her face contorts in immeasurable pain. *So, you think you're a little fighter.* I smirk.

I hover my hand above her chest, as close as I can get without contact. "Stop."

She doesn't.

"I said stop," I bite out.

She stills, staring up at me with glassy, bloodshot eyes. Her chest rises and falls in rapid pants. Her face contorts on each inhale, yet her breaths don't ease.

I extend my hand out to her for her to grab. "Up."

Her eyes fixate on mine. She ignores my hand and remains still, motionless as a statue.

"Can't you hear me? Get up," I grind out louder.

She starts to turn onto her side and the sound she emits elicits the internal discomfort one experiences when nails scratch down a chalkboard. She sounds like a wounded animal dying in the forest. I turn to the first aid kit Spider left on the coffee table and pour out three painkillers from the bottle of Ibuprofen.

"Open." I hold them out in front of her.

She doesn't open her mouth, though she is now sitting upright fully. She continues to stare up at me silently.

I don't have time for this shit. I grab her cheeks and force them apart. "Open your fucking mouth." She doesn't move. "For fuck's sake, it's just painkillers." I force her mouth open and shove the pills down deep into her throat with my three fingers. She coughs as she struggles to get them down. I probably should have given her some water but I told Spider, I'm not in the business of caring for strays. When I pull my fingers out, they are coated in her saliva. I lick my fingers and pause when I realize what I just did. *Jesus fucking Christ.* I should have been the one to go to

Amato. She's Spider's complication, not mine. I grab her arm and lift her to her feet.

She flinches back so abruptly, I drop her arm like it's on fire.

She sways on her combat-boot clad feet. I reach out again to catch her as she starts to collapse backward toward the floor.

"Hey, hey, look." I try to catch her eyes as I hold her shoulders in a death grip. "I'm going to pick you up and walk you to the bathroom. If you fight it, I'll fucking drop you and leave you to it on your own. Do you understand?"

She stares at me wordlessly. As I scoop her up into my arms, I hear that pained whimper again. Fuck.

I sidestep her through the hallway, careful to avoid banging her against the modern metal light fixtures on the wall. I use my shoulder to push us in through the door of the first-floor guest bathroom. I drop her down on the black marble counter, plopping her butt next to the sink. Several grunts escape her lips as her eyebrows furrow.

I turn on the water in the slate grey marble rain shower. I turn back to face her. Damn, there is something so commanding about her. Yeah, she's covered in blood, and seething in pain, yet she sits up straight, unperturbed by her circumstances. Under different conditions, I'd almost respect her demeanor.

"Can you undress and shower on your own?"

She doesn't speak, eyes still staring me down expressionlessly.

This is so fucking frustrating. I exhale sharply, rolling back my shoulders as if trying to shrug off an invisible weight.

"I'm going to pull your shirt off now."

She continues to stare at me, still no movement. I go to

pull her shirt over her head and the growl she releases forces me to drop my hands.

"Fuck this."

I pull out my knife and she flinches again. She leans as far back away from me as she can and turns her face away.

"Hey, stop. Fuck. Come here. I'm not going to fucking cut you... unless you give me a reason to." I smirk.

She turns back toward me, her eyes narrowing in disdain. I pull her shirt away from her body and in one swift stroke, slash through the material. I let it fall to the counter unceremoniously.

I can't take my eyes off of her waist. The mirror behind her reveals the rest of the circle tattoo I caught a glimpse of earlier. Inside the circle are beautifully ornate Sakura blossoms and two butterflies. A katana stabs through the circle diagonally. It's beautiful ink. I feel like I've seen this somewhere before, but I can't quite place where. The style looks so familiar. A frisson of something tickles my memory. I look down at my chest, and consider for a moment but then let it go. He's dead. I look her over again. Many of the marks covering her body look fresh, but a few deep running scars look old—years old. "Who did this to you?"

She looks up at me with those pitch-black eyes and I notice tiny specs of violet in them, imitating a magical creature, like if a baby deer and a unicorn had a spawn. For a moment I am lost in them. They are filled with so much pain, yet somehow seem full of immense strength and intensity. I shake away my intrigue. I don't want to know anything about her. I want her cleaned up and gone. Cleaned up is fucking optional, actually; I'm just doing this for Spider. Yet I can't stop myself from asking, "Who gave you that ink on your back? Why Sakura blossoms and butterflies?"

She stays silent, but a tear slips down her cheek, followed by another, and another. A steady, endless stream. Her jaw is locked, eyes steady. Too steady. Her breath is languid; controlled, as if restraining something eruptive beneath the surface. Her fingers curl, gripping the edge of the counter, knuckles white, but she makes no move to wipe the tears away. The contradiction is striking, the despair crumbling her while defiance holds her upright.

I know this expression. I've worn it myself many times.

My hand draws up to push some of her hair out of her face and she flinches again. "Shhh, it's okay, princess. You're safe here. Everything is going to be alright."

What the fuck? My hand stops in its tracks. I yank it back immediately. I take one more good look at her. "Nah, fuck no." Then I turn on my heel and storm out of the bathroom, slamming the door behind me. Something about her feels wrong. Weirdly familiar, yet very wrong. Every instinct in my body is screaming that I need to stay as far away from this bitch as possible. So that's exactly what I'm going to fucking do.

CHAPTER 4

SPIDER

I am not looking forward to this at all. Visits here are never pleasant. I pull into the overly extravagant circular driveway of the Amato compound. Nothing this man touches isn't over the top. The center fountain I pull in front of, with its ornate statues, gives the Fontana di Trevi a run for its money.

Once parked, I push my seat back and fire up my laptop to pull up the security footage from tonight, peripheral vision alert to my vicinity for any movement. There is nothing of value, just a loop of the empty warehouse space. For over three hours before we arrive, up until we leave there is absolutely no live footage. It is all one continuous loop. Whoever is behind this is no amateur. I pull up the cameras around the block, checking to see if I can find any cars driving through. I look at the clock and realize an hour has passed. I've checked five square miles of traffic camera footage and all the cameras are looped. Damn. Pulling that off takes some serious skill. My level of skill.

My gut sinks as I realize I was not aware of anyone out there who has that.

With the footage a dead end, I make my way in to talk to Signor Amato and his right hand, Bruno. No matter how many times I walk into this mansion, I will absolutely never get used to this place. Marble floors stretch out in a polished sheen, reflecting the soft glow of Murano glass chandeliers imported from Venice. They hang from the high ceiling, casting an almost reverent multicolored light across the space. The walls are adorned with dark, intricately carved, rich wood paneling, interrupted only by carefully placed, obviously expensive works of art. Oil paintings in heavy gold frames feel almost like a warning, their eyes following anyone who dares to walk by. It's like they're screaming, 'I'm always watching you.' Though the Don could afford it all and then some, I'm certain more than half of the art is stolen from museums in Italy.

A grand staircase sweeps up to the second floor, its dark wood balusters intricate and imposing, leading to a mezzanine that overlooks the entire entryway. Perfect for defending against any intruders that make it past the fortress's first few lines of defense. The scent of leather and mahogany hangs in the air, mixing with the profuse fumes of too much expensive cologne. Seriously, it's hard to breathe in here. Probably by design. Across the way two arched entryways reveal a lavishly furnished lounge with a marble coffee table so heavy it took a forklift to get it in here. Everything about this space is calculated, arranged to exude a sense of awe and intimidation while doubling as a protective measure. While I wait to be summoned back into the Don's office I shoot a quick text off to Blade.

SPIDER:

Any news on Tor?

BLADE:

No, they're still in the room, fucking Doc
won't let me in.

SPIDER:

And the girl?

We really need to get her name.

BLADE:

No fucking clue. I left her in the bathroom.

Fucking hell, Blade.

SPIDER:

What if she needs help?

BLADE:

Why the fuck do I care? She's your pet, you
check on her.

SPIDER:

Stop being a twat and go make sure she's
okay.

BLADE:

Fuck you. And fuck her. She isn't my
problem. Any news from the compound?

SPIDER:

Still waiting to be seen. I'll fill you in when I
get back.

As Bruno approaches, I slip my phone in my pocket and
follow him into Signor Amato's office. I step onto the silk
Persian rug, its deep crimson hue woven with distinct,
hypnotic patterns that seem to come alive beneath my feet.
It feels like blasphemy every time I walk on it, as if I am
defiling a work of art with my filth. The Don is dressed to

the nines in a three-piece designer Italian suit, sitting behind his solid oak desk. He turns to face me in his over-sized leather executive chair.

"Do you want to explain to me why I have six injured men on my hands and a pissed off Yakuza boss telling me we fucked him out of product?" Signor Amato asks, his tone leaving no room for bullshit. "The cleaning crew is still mopping up Blade's handiwork. Where the hell is Tor?"

"Tor was shot, he's with Doc Morelli now." I stand tall, making eye contact, but not holding my chin high. Balancing subservience with confidence. Always balancing on a knife's edge. "Blade is at the house monitoring the situation. We had to abandon the guns and ammo in order to make it out alive. I've checked CCTV footage, extending to a five square mile radius and everything is looped. Whoever we're dealing with, from a tech standpoint, they know exactly what they are doing. This was planned perfectly, and executed with precision. They hit us out of nowhere and we had insufficient resources to contain the situation. Had we known it wasn't going to be a simple in and out, we would have been better prepared."

"Spider, son, is this what I've taught you? To make excuses? You should always be prepared, either to do the job appropriately or to die."

"I apologize, sir. I didn't mean to provide excuses, I am simply trying to convey that whoever we are dealing with, it's not some street thug or minor player. They're orga-nized. I will find out what happened, and rest assured when I do, they will pay tenfold."

The bastard is lecturing me on excuses while his son is laid out on a surgical table. I want to believe he did not hear me, or maybe he misunderstood, cause he hasn't once asked if Tor's okay. But I know better. Signor Amato is a lot of things; a loving father has never been one of them.

"Very well. Keep me updated on what you find. The men I sent to recover the merch came up empty. Have Tor call me when he's up. You, he, and Blade must lead a swift response to this. Someone stole from me. I want to know who and I want them made an example of. We cannot let tonight's events stand."

"Understood, sir. Ciao, Signor, Bruno," I say with a head nod to them both and back out of the room. I learned years ago never to give anyone my back, not even my 'friends.' I have the bullet wound to remind me to never make that mistake again.

I leave the compound with a steady pace, but once I'm back out on the street, I stomp on the gas and rush back to the house. My mind races with potential ways Blade has disposed of our little house guest. On arrival, the chaos of before seems to have subsided, replaced with an eerie quiet. As I walk in the door, Blade is laid out on the couch, his favorite blade, the one his sister gave him before she died, is drawn, gun resting at his side. The half-empty whiskey bottle in his hand and the empty look in his gaze tells me that there is no news on Tor. The bastard probably hasn't checked on the girl yet either.

"It's been two hours, still nothing?" I ask as he turns to look at me. His blank stare makes it clear the answer is no.

He takes a heavy pull from the bottle and replies, "Obviously fucking not."

Panic rises in my chest. *Fuck, Tor. You need to pull through.*

"Where's the girl?"

He looks off to the side, glaring toward the bathroom

door as if he is trying to see through it. He shakes his head and turns back to me. "I don't know, last I saw her, she was in there. Never saw her come out, so my guess is that's where she is."

"You never went to check on her like I asked?"

"She's not my fucking pet. You're the one that picked up a rescue. You deal with it."

I stifle a grumble. He's been acting strange since he saw her on the couch. Or maybe this is all just a reaction to Tor. Tor's a stubborn bull, but he's also the only one of us that has never been shot before. It's rattling me too, but I can't do anything about it, so I focus on what I *can* maybe do something about. I walk over to the bathroom door and knock. There is no response. I knock again, still nothing. On the third knock I say softly, "I'm coming in, okay? It's Spider, I just want to make sure you're okay." *Your name doesn't mean anything to her, you fucking idiot, cause she doesn't know who the fuck you are.* "You know, Spider, the one with the glasses that picked you up back at the warehouse."

I turn the knob and gently open the door. For fuck's sake, the water is running in an empty shower. She's sitting on the bathroom sink, passed out against the backlit mirror, wearing a bra and satin shorts, shirt on the counter, torn open by what looks like a knife. Bloody hell, Blade.

"Hey, sweetheart, are you okay? What do you need?" How long has the water been on? So unbelievably wasteful. "Blade, you're an asshole," I yell out toward the living room.

He grunts in response.

The water is cold to the touch. I shut it off and then come to stand in front of her. "Hey, sweetheart, wake up and talk to me. Can I help you get cleaned up?" Her eyes flutter open and, my god, the way she looks up at me. Like she needs me. I know I'm fucked by the whirl of excitement that dances in the pit of my stomach. She nods, putting her hand into mine. I think she wants me to help her off the counter. I pull as gently as I can, but it doesn't help. She winces and inhales a sharp breath.

"Oh, sweetheart, I'm sorry. Come here, let's get you fixed up." I wet a washcloth in the sink and gently begin to wipe away more of the dried blood clinging to her flesh just as I did before. Each wince from her beautiful mouth constricts my chest in discomfort. I can't drag the cloth across the surface of her skin any more gently. I wish I could absorb her pain. She looks too sweet to be in this state.

The entire time she is staring up at me with the most curious expression on her face. I would give anything to know what she's thinking right now.

"What's your name, sweetheart?"

Her eyes remain locked on mine as her silence persists. She reaches out for my hand with the washcloth and halts my movements. Nothing could have prepared me for the wave of bliss that washes over me at what she does next. Her arms dart around my waist and squeeze around me so tightly that it forces a grunt out of me.

It takes me a second to catch up to what is happening at this moment. My skin tingles at every nerve ending where we're connected. When my mind finally understands what's happening, I wrap my arms tightly around her and hold her.

I can't remember the last time I've been hugged. I let her latch onto me for as long as she wants, partially for her, and partially for me. This feels so damn good. Two or three minutes must pass before she sighs and loosens her grip. She slides off the counter, up onto her feet, walks past me, and turns on the shower I just turned off. She places her hand under the water to check the temperature. As she starts to remove her shorts, I clear my throat.

"I'll give you some space, sweetheart. If you need anything just call for me, I'll be right outside." I take one last look at her, my eyes tracing the curves along her body and make my way out of the bathroom, pulling the door shut behind me. In the dimly lit hall, I lean my back against the bathroom door, my head tilted up toward the ceiling, eyes closed. Hell, it's been a long time since an urge this strong to protect someone pulsated through me. I stand tall, letting the weight of responsibility rush over me. I will take care of her. I smile. I can't wait to take care of her.

Blade's voice breaks me out of my stupor. "How's your fucking pet? Can we put her down yet? Or at least set her free?"

My normally limitless patience for him is starting to wane. I push away from the wall and square up. "Listen to me really carefully, asshole. You will not touch one hair on her goddamn body. I mean it, Blade. Don't even try."

"I see you've already been put under that witch's fucking spell." He steps closer, invading my personal space. "We have no idea who she is, what she's been through. Did you see the tattoos? That shit looks Yakuza. I hate unknowns. Especially now, after tonight's clusterfuck."

My response is cut off by Doc stepping heavily up the stairs from the basement where he's been working on Tor.

"What's the verdict?" Blade voices my question. "Do I have some more kills on my agenda tonight?"

Doc laughs uncomfortably, the crow's feet surrounding his blue eyes crinkling. "He's over the worst of it. Bullet was pretty deep but he was extremely lucky. It didn't hit any major organs. He'll be off his feet for a little bit, but he should recover just fine. I've left antibiotics and instructions on the bedside. I want to see him in a couple days just to make sure everything is healing properly. We'll set it up tomorrow. Someone may want to stay in the room with him until he comes to."

I pull out my phone and quickly transfer his fee. "Thanks, Doc. Seriously, thank you."

"Yeah, yeah, just tell him to be more careful next time. This was an extremely close call. He lost a lot of blood and was touch and go there for a minute. You got the boy here just in time. I'm glad I was able to help."

"You mind sticking around for a minute to take a look at the girl?" I ask.

"The girl?" Doc's brows furrow.

"Yeah, we came across a girl tonight. She's pretty banged up."

"Of course you did." Doc laughs, shaking his head. "What sort of trouble have you boys roped yourself into this time?"

"Oh you know, murder, fucking mayhem, a random bound feral woman that Spider thinks it's his mission to save. The usual," Blade replies.

I smack the back of Blade's head; he doesn't even flinch.

"Forget I asked, I don't want to know. I'm happy to look her over, where is she?"

I answer Doc, "She's finishing getting cleaned up in the shower, she'll be right out."

"Alright, no problem, I wasn't planning on sleeping tonight anyway." He relocates into the living room and takes a seat on the couch to wait for our little visitor to come out of the bathroom. He takes out his phone—likely to confirm he's been paid—and we leave him to it.

Both Blade and I head to Tor's side, our disagreement over the girl dropped for now. We pass the male nurse-slash-errand boy on the way; he squeezes against the wall to let us pass.

Tor's passed out, but it doesn't escape my notice that we both reach for his wrist. Blade beats me to it. I love these moments, the ones where tiny hints of care and concern bleed out from Blade's normally psychopathic tendencies. It reminds me he's still in there somewhere. Blade lets go of Tor and I grab on; feeling his pulse beating steadily calms me. I realize for the first time tonight how on edge I have been. It all hits like a freight train the minute my nervous system settles. Exhaustion consumes me, but I can't sleep, not yet. We still need to get our mystery girl sorted.

My steps are heavy as I trudge up the stairs, down the hallway, and into my bedroom to grab her some boxer briefs and a t-shirt. When I pull out the t-shirt, I accidentally get blood on it and the shirt underneath. Huffing in frustration, I pull out both and toss them directly in the hamper. I push open the door to my bathroom with my elbows. Once at the sink, I squirt two pumps of soap onto my hands, turn the hot water knob twice and the cold water knob once. I wash my hands meticulously, making sure I get all the blood and dirt off my hands and out from under my fingernails. Turn off the knobs in the exact reverse order then rush back to my dresser, align the t-shirts underneath back into a straight line and pick out a new shirt for her. I open the drawer underneath and pick up a pair of tightly-rolled boxer briefs. My clothes will likely envelop her, but at least they're clean and she'll be comfortable. We don't have any underwear for her so this will have to do.

By the time I reach outside the bathroom I left her in, I can hear that the shower is no longer running. I lightly knock, and she opens the door and peeks out. She's wrapped in a gray towel that I'm annoyed at for existing, yet somehow still grateful for. My eyes are drawn to her legs, a snake tattoo peeking out on one thigh, and a garter belt tattoo peeking out on the other. My gaze lingers a moment longer than it should until I hear her clear her throat. "I brought you this, sweetheart. I know they're a bit big, but they're clean."

She reaches out and grabs them from me. Her hand brushes against mine as she takes them. There are those fucking tingles again. Blade might be right, I may be bewitched.

The door shuts in my face and I stand around like an idiot with my hands in my front pockets waiting for her to come out. A few minutes later, she exits, absolutely swimming in my clothes. I am taken aback by how much I love the sight. My chest expands with pride, my clothes look amazing on her. I never want her to take them off. Well. Maybe not *never*.

"We've got a doctor here," I say after clearing my throat awkwardly. "He'd like to make sure you're okay." I gesture toward the living room and follow her over to where Doc and his nurse boy wait. Leaving them to it, I grab the whiskey bottle Blade made an impressive dent in and sink into the cushy side chair. Doc murmurs and she nods silently while I focus on whiskey and staying awake.

I have no idea how much time has passed when Blade walks in, stopping to stand in the juncture between the living room, entryway, and hallway. I wonder where he was this whole time. Probably with Tor. Doc packs up his bag and turns to us.

"It's mostly surface level wounds. I've applied antibiotic ointment and wrapped them up. Keep the bandages dry and clean. She should be good in a couple of days."

As Doc makes his exit, Blade side-checks the nurse boy's shoulder. He scampers past, avoiding eye contact.

"Can you not unnecessarily taunt the man? We need people to be willing to show up here when we need them."

Blade ignores me, grunts, and walks away.

I turn back to the girl sitting on our couch donning my clothes and can't seem to look away.

CHAPTER 5

KAI

hy is he looking at me like that?

He quickly averts his gaze, pink staining his cheeks. Wait, did I say that out loud? I shake my head. No, no I didn't.

"You hungry?"

I nod. Spider. Twenty-eight years old. Of Irish descent. One of the best hackers in the world. His mom died of a drug overdose when he was twelve years old. He was placed in the foster care system. Shortly after, he met Tor—Ettore Amato—in junior high. After three years in an abusive as fuck household, he was taken in by the Amatos at the age of fifteen. He and Tor grew up like brothers. He's the easiest mark. The least distrustful of the crew. He's not what I expected, but honestly, I have no idea what that was. This is playing out a bit differently than envisioned. But that's okay. I'm nothing if not adaptable.

"Follow me." He leads me back through the living room toward the kitchen. There is a black marble island, lined on one side with large, black leather barstools. He pulls one out for me. I follow his lead and take a seat. Marble coun-

"

tertops, expensive leather furniture, designer everything, everywhere; these boys are living large.

"What do you feel like, sweetheart? We're fairly well stocked."

I bet you are.

I stare up at him from my perch on the stool. He seems so fucking nice. It's irritating me.

He leans over the other side of the counter, arms extended, bracing his weight. He looks exhausted. "Oh right, um, you don't speak. Okay, you good with pasta? The Amato family Bolognese recipe is to die for."

I nod.

He lets out a sigh and turns to the fridge. He sets each ingredient down meticulously on the counter. I watch him carefully align the carrots and celery into a perfect line. He alternates the carrots until each is facing in the same direction before pulling out an onion. He takes out canned tomatoes and turns the cans until each one has the label aligned perfectly. Fuck, if he is this detailed with food prep, it is probably going to be a pain in the ass to navigate around his OCD ass. His attention to detail in computer codes is starting to make sense.

Once he orders everything on the counter to his liking, he grabs a cutting board and places the knife down perfectly parallel to the edge. He reaches into his pocket and takes out his phone. Softly-playing music hits my ears, and tears well up in my eyes. *Jesus Christ, get a hold of yourself.* I've shed more tears in the past twenty-four hours than I have in over a decade. It must be because I'm close. Relief is within my reach.

He grabs the knife and the first carrot. Impressive. He dices it with a level of skill that would make even Gordon Ramsay proud. It's as if he's entered his own world and I'm just an observer, watching from the outside in. I guess that's not too far off from the truth. He begins to sing and a flood of memories rushes to the forefront of my mind.

"You're the first light. The first light that I see. When you hold me in your arms I feel the sunshine on me."

My father's face burns into my soul. I can't hold back the steady stream of tears as I see him singing the song to me and my mom while they are tucking me in for bed.

"The first glimpse in your eyes. The first thought in my mind. Don't want to turn the next page or ever read the next line."

His smile, my mother's, mine. I can't remember the last time I smiled like that.

"Hold me closer, teach me to breathe. Stay with me."

The last memory kills the tears immediately. Rage bubbles up like lava looking for an escape from the confines of a volcano. The familiar sense of anger embeds itself in my core. He's lying on the sidewalk, gripping my hand as I sob outside the restaurant. Blood seeps from his gut, and some trickles from his mouth.

"No Daddy, no, don't go. Daddy, no. Daddy? I'm scared, what do I do? Tell me what to do." He sings to me one last time.

"Cause time is no longer a thing, no longer a thing, for you and me. Oh why, can't this always be, this always be our reality. Stay with me."

I try to smile. I want him to see me smiling. He needs to see me smiling. That has to be what he wants. Why else would he be singing Mom's and my song? But I can't. No matter how hard I try, I can't force myself to do it. He only wanted one thing from me, and I failed him.

His hand goes cold, the grip non-existent. *"Aishiteru, K —"* barely audible, leaves his lips. And then he's gone.

I'm abruptly brought back into the room as Spider drops the pasta into the boiling water before asking, "Are you okay?"

I nod. Fuck, hasn't even been more than a few hours and I'm already slipping. *Almost, Daddy. I'm almost there.* I can feel how close we are.

"Is it my singing?" Spider asks. "I know I'm not great, but my mom used to play this song all the time before she died. The song calms me, and I can use a bit of calm after tonight."

Huh. What are the fucking odds?

"Wine?"

I nod at the 1982 bottle of Mazzeo Reserve from Sicily. He places a fancy crystal glass in front of me. Jesus, he pours with a heavy hand. Good. I need this. He watches me intently as I raise the glass to my mouth and take a sip. Fuck, it's divine. I look up to find him staring at me again as I lick my lips.

Oh. I see. So that's my in.

He places a bowl and fork in front of me. He keeps his bowl on the opposite side of the island, as if he's going to eat standing up. As soon as the aroma of butter, tomatoes, and herbs hits me, I realize I'm famished and dig in. Fuck, it tastes so good. I'm halfway through the contents of my bowl when I look up and realize his eyes have never left me. He has a big, goofy smile on his face.

"So I guess you like it?" He chuckles.

I can't help it. I start giggling, too. I nod profusely. This guy missed his calling as a Michelin-starred chef.

"My mom taught me how to cook when I was younger. Before she got..." he pauses, "...sick. Once her health deteriorated, I started cooking for us. Until she passed."

I try to communicate my apology with my gaze. I can

feel the shared pain of losing the only ones destined to love you unconditionally so young reverberating between us. That shit changes you. No way anyone who hasn't lived through it understands. He goes quiet and finally looks away. I think he takes what is his first bite as the one called Blade crashes into the room. Though we found endless information on the atrocities he's committed on behalf of the Don, digging up info on his past was impossible to do. It's like he didn't exist until he became the Don's youngest executioner.

"He's awake," Blade declares. He turns to look at me. "Oh, you're still fucking here? We're fucking feeding the strays now? Spider, come on, man. Fuck, is that Bolognese? Ugh, later, he's up."

"Blade, stop being an asshole," Spider retorts as he follows Blade out of the room toward the basement where the other one, Tor, is recovering.

I'm not sure what I am supposed to do. My heart races, and my chest is so tight, this is different than what I imagined. I don't know enough yet to know where to look. The air is thick with tension, a mix of brutality and unfamiliar warmth. I can feel the weight of silence pressing down on me. The soft creak of the oak floorboards beneath my feet is the only sound as I stand up from my stool and awkwardly move to the middle of the room, still trying to piece everything together.

My mind is foggy, like a dream state, struggling to form clear thoughts. The house appears larger than life, yet unbearably quiet. I hear the thumping of their footsteps as they move downstairs, leaving me alone. The door to the basement is ajar, tempting me to follow. I have no answers right now; I prepared for this yet somehow I am completely unprepared.

My heart picks up its pace, a soft but insistent pounding in my chest. Sweat clings to my back, and I suddenly realize how small and unprotected I am in this unknown space. Where do I go? What do I do now? I want to move, to follow them, but a strange pull keeps me rooted to the spot. The weight of their kindness—well, Spider's kindness, let's be honest Blade is being a dick— pushes down on me. The beating I endured disoriented me more than I expected, otherwise why am I hesitating?

I look to the staircase, then back at my unfinished bowl of Bolognese. My breath catches in my throat, and I force myself to inhale slowly, to stop my hands from trembling. I grab my necklace firmly in my hand. I don't know where Spider's setup is yet, so I can't yet place what Han gave me. Fuck, I want to make this quick and get the hell out of here. No need to spend a second longer than necessary in the wolves' den. Spider and Tor seem manageable enough, but Blade is definitely one breath away from ending me.

I grab my wine glass—there is no way I'm letting this exquisite shit go to waste—and steel my resolve. I'm going down the stairs to the basement of three insanely dangerous criminals, unarmed, cause yeah, that is the logical best move. Fuck. I descend the stairs and halt when I reach the bottom, stunned.

It looks like a full-blown hospital. There's a steel surgical bed in the middle of the epoxied floor, a real fucking hospital bed with an IV tower and all the monitors and shit tucked into the corner. Overhead is a big steel light fixture that would likely be brighter than the sun when it's turned on, but warmer, softer light comes from lamps and sconces all around the room.

Fuck. Tor looks bad. Shit. He winces as he tries to sit up slightly in that propped-up plastic hospital bed. Fuck,

fuck, fuck. He wasn't supposed to get shot, not yet. Blade sure did clean up the mess left behind, though; Han is a fucking genius. Predicted his nature to a tee. I love it when we kill two birds with one stone. Or, in this case, snakes.

"Don't fuck up your stitches. I don't want to deal with Doc's attitude." Spider sighs as he helps adjust Tor's pillow. Blade moves closer to the other side and I hover in the shadowy stairwell watching him. For a moment he looks like a child that doesn't know what to do. The way Tor smiles at him is almost adorable. Almost. I thought they had a bit of a rivalry going, I guess not all the intel Han collected was right.

"Stop hovering man, I'm fine." I'm not sure which of them Tor is talking to, but they both back away. "What's your name?"

It takes me a second to register that he is talking to me. I look him in the eye from across the room, but don't respond.

"She doesn't talk," Spider answers for me. "Doc got a chance to check her out. She looks okay, most of her wounds were superficial."

"Can I have a sip of that?" Tor nods at the wine glass in my hands. I cautiously walk it over to him.

"You're on antibiotics, Tor," Spider scolds. "And pain meds."

"Spider, I love you, but stop mothering me. I don't want to have to ask Blade to kill you." Tor smiles.

Spider backs away slowly and lowers his head.

So there is a hierarchy here. I reach over to hand the glass to Tor, but he grabs my hand with the glass in it instead. I startle and try to pull away, but his grip is vice-like.

"Bro. Chill the fuck out," Blade voices my exact thoughts.

Tor downs most of the wine as I half-heartedly try to pull away. Dickhead; I was enjoying that. Once he's drained the liquid delight from my glass, he releases his grip on me and I scramble backward, scowling at him.

"Midnight, can you give us a minute? We have some things we need to discuss. Wait in the living room. When we're done here, we can set you up in our guest room, okay?" He also seems nicer than I expected. Blade seems to be the only one living up to the hype. But I know better than to underestimate anyone. *Ever.*

I nod slowly and back out of the room. Midnight? That's like the second time he's called me that. Was that the time when they found me? I don't know, I lost track. I walk up a few steps, making sure to stomp and shuffle as I ascend. Then I stealthily sneak back down and press my back against the wall.

"Can you please tell Spider to get rid of his new fucking puppy? We don't need the complication right now." Blade is a real fucking dick. He's the biggest threat, which is what we expected.

"She stays," Tor responds, with no room for argument in his tone. Helpful. Thank you, sir. "At least until we start putting this puzzle together. We need to know what she knows and how she fits into all of this. What do we know so far?"

Spider chimes in first, "Nothing, we know absolutely nothing."

Good.

"Whoever they were," he continues, "they must be working with an experienced crew. All the cameras in the vicinity were on a loop. They used ghost guns. They were all masked. They got away with all the merch during the fight. It has to be Satō's people. No one else knew we would be there."

"Say the word, and I'll fucking kill him." Blade only has one mode and it's apparently *beast.* How boring. Talk about a one trick pony. I wonder if there are any thoughts other than murder in that tiny, underdeveloped skull of his. Probably not. He doesn't seem too bright.

"For heaven's sake, Blade," Spider jumps back in. "I have a few ideas on how to track down who was behind all of this, but it's going to take some time. I still think Satō is the most likely culprit."

"That doesn't make sense; the buy was his." There's a long pause and Tor asks hesitantly, "Has anyone spoken to my father?"

"I just got back from the compound," Spider says too evenly. "He's livid and he expects us to get answers yesterday. He wants you to call him for instructions."

There is silence for a beat. "Does he know I was shot?" Tor's voice wavers as he forces out the question. It's almost as if he is hoping the answer is no. Fuck, that shit is sad. I almost feel bad for him. *Almost.*

"Yes," Spider replies.

The silence is longer this time. I wish I could see their expressions. Tor sighs and says, "Alright, which one of you dicks is going to help me get up to my room?"

I ascend as quietly as I can the rest of the way up the steps.

"Blade, if you try to pick me up bridal style again, I'm going to order you to kill you for me. And delete that fucking selfie."

The last thing I hear is the men's laughter as I run, not walk, to my heavenly bowl of pasta. I'm not letting that shit go to waste. And wine, I need more of that wine.

CHAPTER 6

TOR

"Ow, shit." Holy shit man, being shot sucks. How did Blade manage to make it look like it was no big deal last year?

"Sorry, princess," Blade gets out through his laughter.

It's pure hubris that forces me to slap the back of his head, despite him being all that stands between me and a crash to the ground. He doesn't flinch, not even the slightest reaction. He simply braces more of my weight as we slowly make our way up the basement stairs. The air feels thin, like no matter how deep my breaths, I cannot seem to fill my lungs with enough oxygen. Each creaky wooden step is akin to the climb up Mount Everest, except there is no breathtaking view at the top. All I have to look forward to is more exhaustion and legs that are struggling not to give out. The only thing keeping me going is the soon-to-be-experienced sensation of my cold sheets against my skin. The promise of sleep to wash away the stench of this trash ass day.

"Fuck." Blade pauses on the second to last step with me,

supporting my weight. "Just let me carry you bro. I'll stop laughing I promise."

"No chance in hell," I bite back.

"Fucking stubborn ass bull, I already did it once tonight, what's one more?"

I level him with a look that makes it clear my ass isn't getting carried bridal style twice in one night by this dick. I need to delete that goddamn selfie he took. I can't forget.

"Fuck, okay, you ready?"

I nod. "Yeah, man, I'm ready."

I don't remember our hallway being this long before.

"I'll go get your phone," Spider says with some exasperation while shaking his head. "Your father asked that you call him as soon as you were conscious." Spider walks off and Blade and I continue our way down the hall. I've never noticed how barren our decor is. Repose grey walls with no paintings, fixtures, or art. Endless plain space with nothing but modern, angular sconces breaking up the monotony. The space lacks warmth, as if it isn't lived in. I wonder if Mia would be willing to help decorate it.

Once we cross the threshold to my bedroom door, my king-sized bed, donned in black sheets, a dark grey down comforter, and oversized pillows calls to me. They fuel my final few steps. I carefully position myself on the side of the bed and lower my body as gingerly as I can. Though no amount of care seems to suppress the pain. I allow myself to groan for several long, agonizing seconds.

"Hey fucker, you need anything? I'm going to go grab your antibiotics and shit."

"Nah, I'm good," I grit out and he leaves me to my groaning and shifting around, trying to get comfortable.

Spider strolls in, my phone in hand. "Tor, do you want me to stay in here with you?"

"I don't need a goddamn babysitter, Spider. I'm fine." Shit, I hate the look on his face as his eyes drop to the rustic hardwood floors so I add, "But thanks."

Blade returns, pill bottles and water in hand. He sets everything down on the sleek black side table and silently heads toward the door alongside Spider. They both turn around at the threshold and start speaking at the same time.

"Don't ever get shot again, you stupid fuck," Blade gets out at the same time Spider says, "I'm glad you're okay, Tor."

I roll my eyes and laugh shallowly. Very shallowly. "Good night, assholes."

They close the door behind them and I take a deep breath as I stare down at my phone. No missed calls. No messages except from the crew asking what the next move is after confirming the guns and ammo and the drugs they were to be exchanged for are nowhere to be found.

I dial my father, every muscle in my body tensing and bracing for a conversation that will surely further fuck up my already sour mood.

"What the fuck happened out there, Son? How did you lose control of such a simple assignment?"

Hi, how are you? You feeling okay son? Glad you're not dead. Ha, I don't know why I expected any different. He's only ever cared about one thing, and it's not me.

"I don't know. There were a ton of gunmen, they came out of—"

"So, both you and Spider are under the impression that excuses are acceptable in this life. How is Blade the only one of the lot of you that grew up into a man? I raised you all the same."

He's really just going to completely ignore the fact that I

was shot, huh? While praising his precious goddamn favorite, Blade.

"No excuses, sir, we are looking into it."

"I want to know who was responsible. I want to know your planned response within twenty-four hours. I expect results, don't disappoint me again."

"Yes, sir, we're on it, sir—"

I hear the *beep beep beep* of the dropped call before I get the chance to finish my sentence, let alone utter a goodbye. Oh, okay, I guess that conversation is over then. I put my phone aside and force myself back out of bed. Holy shit man, I just got here. Today blows. I ease my way to the door. I need to make sure Spider gets us something useful and fast. I shuffle across the hall with tiny, painful steps, and see him getting our unexpected guest situated in the guest room.

"Hey, Midnight, how are you holding up? What's your actual name?"

She stares up at me in silence as Spider asks, "What are you doing out of bed?"

The look I give him stops him in his tracks.

"She doesn't speak, remember?" He pivots. "But you understand us perfectly, don't you?" He looks back in her direction. "Wait, maybe she doesn't, do you speak English?"

She nods.

"You lose your voice?" I ask.

She shakes her head no.

"You mute?"

She shakes her head no again.

"You afraid to speak?" I'm running out of ideas and getting bored with this.

She just stares at me. What the shit? Fuck this, it's

tomorrow's problem. "Do you have everything you need to get some rest?"

She nods.

"Okay, we'll leave you to it. If you need anything I am right across the hall and Spider's next door on the right. I'd avoid the door on the left, that's Blade."

Spider chimes in, "I left out some sundries for you in the bathroom. If you need anything just swing by okay, sweetheart?" Great, Spider found someone to take care of that won't fight him on it. Good for him. Hopefully that occupies his time enough that he leaves me the hell alone.

"Spider, come on, she needs to rest and we got shit to discuss."

She follows us to the door, and grabs it with her right hand at the same time I do. My hand engulfs hers. The static shock startles me, and she quickly pulls her hand away.

"Sorry, Midnight, good night." The hell. Sorry? "Get some rest."

The door shuts behind us. I don't even have the energy to try to figure out what to do about her right now. We need answers fast before my father loses his patience.

I speak low and urgent, knowing how thin the door is and that she could have her body—*ear*—pressed against it. "My father gave us twenty-four hours to find the intel on who was behind tonight and present a plan of action."

"Okay, so sleep's out of the question." Spider sighs.

"I can help." I start to follow him to his office.

"No, you can get back in your bed and get some rest." He stops suddenly and turns to put a hand up in front of my chest, blocking my path. I stifle a groan at the stabbing pain as my abs shift against my sudden stop. "You got shot tonight for god's sake, Tor. Go to sleep, you'll just be in my way anyway."

I let out a sigh; he's right. I can't contribute anything here. Intel gathering is his wheelhouse. "Alright, but wake me up as soon as you find anything." I make my way back toward my bedroom.

"Will do."

He heads off and I shuffle my way back to my bed. As soon as my head hits the pillow, tonight's events come rushing back to me.

We walked in and started taking fire on entry. Whoever it was, they knew we'd be there. I don't even think I saw any of Satō's men. Shit man, were they even there? I mean they could have been, the shooters were masked. I did hear Japanese.

And the girl, why was she in that office banged up like that?

We were there to exchange weapons for drugs, just like we do every month. She sure as shit doesn't look like a weapon. A mule maybe? We need to figure out who the hell she is and why she was there. Why she's here now. Maybe that will lead us somewhere.

I sit back up, swallow down the pills Blade left at the bedside. My mind slowly stops racing and my singular focus is on the triangular black metal chandelier hanging above my bed. The last thought I have is of her dark eyes, with specs of violet iridescent light, staring at me in that office, and the warm sensation of my hand on hers on the door as I drift off to sleep.

CHAPTER 7

SPIDER

Bloody hell, it's 10:00 AM, I've been staring at my four screens for five hours and I still don't have shit. It's like we were hit by fucking ghosts. I have no idea what I'm even looking for. Every lead turns into a dead end, a loop, a goddamn black hole. I've been in this chair since I put the girl in the guest room, staring at code and files that refuse to make sense. Fuck. My hands won't stop shaking. I guess that last energy drink was one too far. I've now been awake for—I do the math—thirty-one hours. The empty cans litter my desk like trophies of failure, mocking me with their crumpled silence. The noise from the strokes of my fingers on the keyboard is starting to irritate the hell out of me, but I can't stop. Not yet.

I push back from the desk and stand, my legs stiff and uncooperative. Stretching my arms over my head, I try to shake off the fatigue, but it clings to me like a wet t-shirt. My brain feels like it's coated in honey, slow and sticky, refusing to work the way I need it to. Before I realize what I'm doing, I'm outside the door to the guest room. My feet must have brought me here on autopilot, drawn by some part of me I don't want to admit exists.

The door creaks slightly as I push it open, and I wince, freezing in place. She doesn't stir. The soft rise and fall of her breathing is the only sound in the room; I can't see anything from here, due to the light of the hall behind me and blackout curtains on the window in this room. I step inside, the shearling area rug muffling my footsteps, and make my way to the bed. Standing over her, I can't help but study her face. Calm. Peaceful. So oblivious to the storm she's dragged into this house. Or the shit show she's walked into.

I pull out my phone and snap a picture, the screen and flash lighting up the darkness for a brief moment. I pause worried I may have woken her. The last thing she needs is to wake up to a man in her space, taking pictures of her. When she doesn't move, I exhale the breath I was holding. Maybe we should start with her. The tattoos have to lead somewhere. Blade swore he'd seen them before. Maybe I can find her name, dig something up. If we know who she is, it might lead us to whoever the hell wants her badly enough to not only make our lives this complicated, but also pick a fight with the most ruthless man in the city.

The blanket has slipped down, exposing her womb tattoo. My shirt is bunched up around her waist, and my pulse does this stupid, traitorous jump when I realize she isn't wearing my boxer briefs. For a second, just one second, I want to pull the blanket down a little more. Just a couple of centimeters. Just enough to... fuck. No, you pervert.

I grit my teeth and force myself to look away, taking a deep breath to steady the war raging in my chest. Stop being such a goddamn creep. Shaking my head, I pull the blanket up and tuck it around her, trying not to think about how soft her skin looks, how vulnerable she seems under the soft morning light shining around the tiniest edges of the curtains; not so blackout after all. She's beautiful, yeah, but she's also trouble. She must be. As insane as Blade is, he is right. She's at the center of this in some way, and it's my job to figure out how. If I let myself forget that, it'll be my funeral. I need to leave this room, now.

Back in my office, I upload her photo. My fingers move automatically, dragging it into the facial recognition software I designed. The scan starts running, lines of code flickering across the screen like a digital heartbeat. While I wait for the system to sift through databases, I start pulling up files from our friends at the ATF, FBI, and DEA. If there's a new player in the game, one of them might have caught wind of it.

Thirty minutes crawl by before I get a hit. Bhutan. An airport security camera caught her image eight months ago. What the...? Bhutan? I sit back, rubbing my temples. Was she a monk? A tourist? Something else? I run another program, pulling up the passenger manifest and customs data.

While the manifest loads, I turn my attention back to the law enforcement files. I skim through the usual bullshit, names I've flagged, operations I've interfered with, and stumble across my own file among the FBI's most wanted hackers. Cute. They're still chasing breadcrumbs I left behind on purpose.

But something else catches my eye. A name: Han Yoshinaga. Code name Override. That rings a bell. I open his file, scanning the details. Los Angeles native. Parents ran an electronics shop in Akihabara, Japan before moving stateside. He grew up on Sawtelle, hacked the League of Legends servers at age thirteen. Changed every champion's name to

Sora Tora for twenty-four hours. Seems like a lot of effort for such a weird modification. Random as hell. He spent a week in juvie, then vanished while out on bail. Eleven years off the grid.

And then, Bhutan. Eight months ago. Same airport, same day as our mystery girl, or as Tor called her, Sleeping Beauty.

The manifest pings. Three hundred and ninety-six names. Somewhere in that list is a connection. It's thin, sure, but it's something. My gut twists as the pieces click together. Every road seems to lead back to her.

I think back to my view of her from the door to the guest room. She's going to need to start talking. Sooner rather than later. Better it's me than Tor, or, god forbid, Blade. At least I'll keep my temper in check. At least I'll keep her safe. I decide not to share any of this with the boys just yet. If I tell Blade, he'll definitely kill her. If I tell Tor, he'll tell his father. Both options will lead to her execution. I need to know more before I sign her death certificate.

I sigh, leaning back in my chair as the screen glows with unfinished business. Morning sunlight leaks in through the curtains, throwing streaks of pale gold across my cluttered desk. Sleep is out of the question now. I need to find something on Han that I can give the boys and fast so I have more time to look into her.

CHAPTER 8

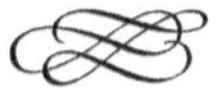

KAI

The silence is eerie as I make my way down the unfamiliar hallway toward the kitchen. Fuck, it's bright in here. The fucking millionaires can't afford black out curtains in the whole house? They keep nocturnal hours; it would be a good investment in their sleep health to have them everywhere instead of just in the bedrooms. I open and close the sleek black cabinets. I slide my fingers along their smooth surface until I come across the drinking glasses, and pour myself a glass of water from the fridge dispenser. The crisp condensation on the glass feels good against my raw hands. I didn't realize how parched I was until the liquid lubrication evokes pure ecstasy as it trickles down my throat.

I scan the area looking for signs of life. Where is everybody? I see light coming from the door down the hallway and stalk my way over. I knock lightly on the half-open door and hear Spider as he calls out, "Come in."

I push the door the rest of the way open and see him at a desk, his eyes still glued to his work. I make my way over to him and take in the four large, hi-tech monitors displayed on his minimalist slate desk. Though the desk is an immaculate representation of an OCD sufferer's wet dream, the room is a mess. Empty beer and water bottles are strewn across the floor, interspersed with a dozen or more energy drink cans. Worn clothes completely envelop a lounge chair in the corner of the room. Empty snack wrappers and chips bags overflow from the wastebasket on the right side of the desk.

My eyes are drawn back up to the screens. The top right monitor displays what looks like a quiet side street. Shit, I think it's one of the streets surrounding the warehouse. The top left looks like footage from an airport. The bottom right appears to be some sort of code. I can't make any sense of what he's doing there; I should have paid more attention to Han when he was walking me through what to look for. On the bottom left there appear to be some files I wouldn't mind seeing, but there is a black command prompt box covering important parts of them.

He still hasn't looked back to see it's me that entered the room. His attention is immersed on the bottom right screen as he types furiously.

I wish I knew more about computers.

I look down at my body and I'm wearing what I think is Spider's oversized t-shirt and boxer briefs. I'll work with what I've got; I saw how he looked at me last night. This shouldn't be too hard. Or... I guess I hope it will be. I chuckle to myself. I swear I spend way too much time with Han and the boys. Their adolescent sense of humor is rubbing off on me. Ha ha... rubbing off on me. Fuck. I need to focus. I absentmindedly grab my necklace. His computer is under his desk, so that's where I need to be.

As my eyes trail down the length of his form, a knot of anticipation forms in my gut. His muscles perfectly fill out the form fitting black button-down shirt encasing his torso. He's in the same clothes from last night. Poor fuck didn't sleep. Ideally, that works in my favor. The top three buttons of his shirt are open and his golden tanned skin looks simultaneously buttery and rough. I can see the outline of his cock resting on his right thigh inside shockingly tight pants. Alright then, this will be a fun game of, "How will we make it fit?"

Fuck, he really is a specimen to behold. Why is it always the bad boys that are blessed with the ability to make you salivate at the sight of them? Makes my job easier right now, so I'll take it.

I approach on silent bare feet, then run my hand along his left forearm until my fingers align with his.

He jumps slightly, hits a button that quickly opens some windows to cover his screen, and leans back, touching his chest in an apologetic gesture. "Oh hey, sorry, I didn't know it was you. I'm sorry, sweetheart, I didn't mean to be rude. Did you sleep okay?"

I nod slowly, maintaining eye contact. I watch his throat work as he swallows. Hard.

"Sorry, we—I should have checked on you. It's been an insanely busy morning. The pressure is on me from all sides, and everyone wants to know what the fuck happened when we found you." He's rambling. This boy is surviving on sheer will and caffeine. He looks down to his left hand, mine still lingering there.

I tease his fingers as he pulls my hands toward his chest. He stares down at where we are connected. I attempt to suppress a shiver as he gently brushes his thumbs along mine, down to my wrist, careful to avoid the raw skin damaged by the rope. He pauses, staring at our hands rising and falling on his chest in sync with his breathing. He looks up at me.

"Fuck, you're so beautiful."

As he goes to pull his hands away, I take the opening to side straddle him on the chair and look up at him. I firmly take control of his hands and bring them to my chest, just above my breasts. I feel him hardening beneath my thighs as his pinkies trace the swells of my tits. He continues his path down my side until his hands land at my waist. He pulls me in slightly closer and a rush of heat fills me as the movement rubs me up against his erection.

It's now or never.

I lean into his neck, softly wiggling my ass against his rock-hard thighs and hard-on to get a bit more comfortable. I hear him hiss out a shaky breath, but he doesn't stop me.

He smells like bergamot, tobacco, and spice. I can't help but inhale the rich scent as I pepper his neck with soft, sensual kisses. I trail down his pulse point and smile to myself as his heart rate accelerates. I startle as he grabs my upper arms and pulls me back to look at him.

Fuck. I need this to work. I have to get away from that fucking psychopath Blade before he actually follows through on his threats to kill me. I have no interest in betting my life on that crazy fucker's mood. I imagine driving my blade into Blade and smile slowly. I have been itching for a good fight.

Spider's smooth voice laced with desire brings me back to the moment. "Sweet girl, you don't need to do this. I'm going to help you, we're going to help you. I don't expect anything from you. You don't owe us anything."

I place my thumb on his lower lip and watch, mesmerized, as his plump, blush-pink lips slowly part. His pupils fully dilate, and he releases another unsteady breath. Maybe he's not such a bad boy after all. The look of awe on his face is endearing.

I press my thumb against his lower lip and slowly trace out toward his jaw, then lean in and seal my lips to his. His soft lips are an intoxicating contrast to his stubbled skin. He tastes just as sweet as he is, making me wonder how he ended up here with them. His hands tighten once again on my arms and I'm determined to help him relax. I lower my hands from his face, down his neck to his chest. Shit, he's built like a brick for a guy that spends most of his time behind a desk. This is nowhere near as hard as I thought it would be to go through with. I smile to myself again; the task might not be hard, but he sure is.

I leisurely slide down his legs and drop to my knees beneath his chair. I run my hands up along his lower legs, up his thighs towards his zipper. His hands fly down to mine, encasing them and I jolt. I look up into his eyes. Does he not want this?

We gaze deeply into each other as he breathily rasps out, "Sweetheart, are you sure this is what you want? You... don't have to do this. You don't have to do anything you're not completely ready for, or sure about, or..."

Aww, definitely not a bad boy. How cute, he's worried about me. So fucking sweet. I nod eagerly, and slowly resume lowering his zipper. He releases my hands, continuing to stare at me, the question still pending in his eyes. I continue nodding, maintain eye contact as I reach into his pants and pull him out. He lifts off the chair paving the way for me to pull his pants and boxer briefs down to his mid-thigh.

I nestle in closer and thirstily lick the slickness beading off his tip. "Mmm," the sound unexpectedly escapes me as I relish the taste of him, a bit salty, yet sweet. Still looking up into Spider's eyes, I see his lips are pursed and a swoosh of air escapes them. His breathing picks up as I wrap my lips around his cock and steadily take him into the back of my throat. His strangled breath, followed by a soft whimpering moan spurs me on to let him sink in deeper. I hold him there, engulfed in my throat, holding my breath. It surprises me that my need to breathe is overpowered by my desire to hear him moan for me again. I need to hear that sound again more than I need air. *Moan for me, baby.*

When I finally start to feel lightheaded, I slide my lips back toward the tip of his dick and gasp in a deep breath. His hands are fidgeting on his thighs, like he isn't sure where to place them. I inch one of mine onto his right hand, trying to calm his movements. My other hand wraps around his girth, guiding him back into my mouth. He lifts his free hand hesitantly and brushes a strand of hair back behind my ear. His touch is so gentle, it sends chills through me as he tenderly strokes the back of my head.

As I work his dick like a popsicle on a hot summer day, my eyes are transfixed on the dribble running down his cock. It's as if my saliva, coating his dick, binds me to him with strings akin to a spider's web, and I have him right where I want him. I take in another gasp of air, preparing to devour him when a scuffling sounds near the door. I immediately freeze with my lips around his tip. I release him as quietly as I can and crawl backwards slightly, slinking further under the desk. Spider shifts his chair forward, covering me from view. His hands release my hair and lightly slam on the table.

Blade's voice sends a jolt of excitement through me as he steps partially into the doorway. "Anything?"

I wrap my hands around Spider's cock and brazenly

take him into my mouth once again, suppressing a chuckle as he hisses out a breath. "No." I pause my movements, my tongue resting underneath the crown of his head. Was that for me? "Yes." I suck him in again, this time all the way down to the hilt. I suppress another giggle as I hear him force out, "No, nothing yet."

"Which the fuck is it? Yes or no?" Blade barks out, clearly annoyed.

"No, nothing yet," Spider grits out again. I inch my free hand forward, stroking his balls, gently squeezing them as I continue to take him into the back of my throat. I slowly run my tongue over every ridge on my way up, savoring the taste of him.

"Fucking figures, shit's all going sideways. Let me know when you have something, Signor's on my ass. Tor really needs to wake the fuck up, diplomacy isn't in my skillset," I hear Blade say as Spider's balls pull up into his body. I throat him as deep as I can, alternating between sucking and swallowing, and hollowing out my cheeks. I feel him swell impossibly hard inside me. Fuck yes, he's about to cum. "Oh, yeah and, Spider, where's your fucking pet? Did you get her to use that pretty little mouth to give us what we need?"

The only thing preventing explosive laughter is the fact that my mouth is completely full of Spider's impossibly hard cock on the verge of eruption. Blade's such a fucking prick. I don't know if this is what they all need, but I am fairly certain it is exactly what Spider needs.

"I'm working on it," Spider growls. "I'm literally pumping her for information, trust me."

I struggle to keep the giggles threatening to erupt at bay as Blade scoffs again. The urge to release them forces me to choke harder on Spider's dick. As soon as the door closes behind Blade, I feel Spider's legs tense around me as his cum floods my mouth. Fuck, he tastes so good. I hear Blade's stomping steps retreat down the hall, and Spider carefully rolls his chair back and stares down at me. His hand cups my cheek and we look into each other's eyes, my mouth still wrapped around him. Spider lets out the sexiest, throatiest moan I have ever heard as ropes of cum continue to cascade onto my tongue. Fuck, it's a lot. I can't seem to hold it all in.

He heaves a sigh and sinks back and down into his chair. Still staring into his now-drowsy gaze, I release his dick and lick him clean. I lick my lips and use my fingers to take in the drops that escaped. I reach forward to tuck him back into his pants. He grabs my hands, stopping me; I'm not sure I love this habit of his. He lifts his pants up, leaving them undone. He leans forward, face hovering faintly above mine. He looks at me in silence for a moment, as if studying me. His hand strokes my cheek as he whispers, "You're so fucking pretty on your knees for me."

I drag the back of my hand across my mouth and he picks me up and pulls me back onto his lap. "Why didn't you stop, sweetheart? You didn't have to keep going. I didn't want to make you uncomfortable, or draw attention to you, or get you caught up in anything..." He tenderly brushes the hair out of my face and leans in to kiss me. "Fuck, sweetheart," he says in between kisses. "That was so incredible." Kiss. "I couldn't have held back if I tried." Kiss. He leans back to look at me. "I feel like I should thank you, or something, but then that's kinda weird, isn't it? 'Thank you for sucking my dick and swallowing?' I'm relaxed now, but I guess I'm still nervous, too. I really wish I knew your name."

My heart lurches.

He keeps going, "Where did you come from? I hate how we found you, but I'm also so fucking happy you were there. God, I'm actually flustered." He continues to stroke my hair. "All of that doesn't matter anymore, okay? I'm never going to let anything like that happen to you ever again." He leans in and kisses me with such gentleness that I can feel myself tearing up.

I don't know what comes over me as I whisper, "Spider..." against his lips.

His entire body freezes. He stares at me, our noses millimeters apart for what feels like a full minute before he says, "Fuck, sweetheart, you spoke. My name. The first word out of that perfect fucking mouth of yours is my name." He takes a deep breath, kisses me with such fervor that my body has no choice but to melt into his. "Sweetheart," he sighs. His expression softens, and the butterflies I feel confuse the fuck out of me. "What's your name, sweetheart? Tell me, please?" he pleads as he continues to stroke my hair, showering kisses on the edge of my lips.

I should keep my mouth shut. I should have fucking kept my mouth shut before, but it's like I cannot stop it as it flows out of me. "Kai." I grab my necklace, fuck, what have I done? Spider: 1, Kai: 0. I gave him my name, I gave him head, and I didn't even accomplish what Han needed me to. I'll have to create another opportunity and fast. Get your shit together, Kai.

CHAPTER 9

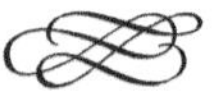

TOR

"I'm here. Etto, where are you boys? More importantly, where is your beautiful house guest? I have a mountain of goodies for her to look through."

On any other day, I love hearing Mia's cheerful, sultry voice, but today everything still hurts and the sound feels like needles poking my skin. I grab my mug of coffee and one of the crazy delicious pistachio croissants that Blade picked up from Crumbly Bakery. The flaky, golden layers shatter as I down the entire croissant in one bite. The delicate buttery aroma, combined with the crushed pistachios and sweet filling hits every time as it swishes around my mouth. I'd get shot every day if it means dozens of these would be waiting for me the next morning. I lick the buttery flakes that cling to my fingers and make my way into the living room, pain stabbing through me with every step. Maybe not *every* day.

Mia always floats into a room like an absolute goddess. Legs for days, stunning, long, flowing, dirty blonde hair, and the most beautiful hazel green eyes. It never ceases to amaze me that the little girl who used to chase me around and annoy me with her dolls grew into the most remarkable woman I know.

I've always loved her, but man every time I see her, she looks more beautiful.

She places two quick kisses on my cheeks while her hand rests on my chest. She flashes me a dazzling smile and shoos me toward the door. "Etto darling, can you and the boys fetch the rest from my car?"

"The rest?" I don't bother hiding my confusion as Blade and Spider step out the front door ahead of me. "How much did you bring? I asked you to grab her some essentials and one outfit so we didn't need to take her home in her torn clothes."

The sun stabs me in the eyes and I flinch as I trudge toward her car.

"Whoa," I hear Blade say. I squint up to see him and Spider both pulling suitcases out of the trunk of her purple SUV.

"Whoa," I echo as I take in the sight of a half-dozen more bags and boxes that need to be carried in, in addition to the suitcases the other guys already grabbed.

"I thought we just needed to dress the bitch so we can send her on her way, not prep her for a fucking beauty pageant," Blade grits out. He lets the suitcase drop to the driveway.

"Don't call her a bitch. There is no reason to be disrespectful to our guest," Spider retorts.

"Our guest? She's a feral animal we need to release back into the wild. Fuck, Spider, what's with this obsession with her? You think if you save her it'll make up for the fact that you couldn't save your precious drug addict of a mom?"

I'm trying to figure out if we can make one trip out of

the pile of stuff still in the trunk as I hear Spider's fist connect with Blade's face and Blade's grunted reaction. Jesus fucking Christ. Blade's right; we need to get rid of her. I can't afford her causing problems between my brothers. Especially not now, when we need to focus on the real problem: whoever the hell stole from us and shot me.

"Knock it off, you two," I snap at them. "Help me carry this shit in. A pissed-off Mia is the last thing any of us wants to deal with."

They shoot daggers at each other but both nod and start loading up on boxes and bags.

Spider hands me a pink rolling suitcase. "Tor, you're going to mess up your stitches, just roll this in, we got the rest."

"I can't risk leaving you two out here to kill each other," I reply.

"We're good." Spider gives Blade a pointed look. "Right, Blade?"

"Fucking peachy," Blade spits out as he stomps toward the house, loaded down with department store and luxury designer bags, and a few sleek matte black boxes with fancy gold writing in his hands.

I feel useless as I roll this fairytale princess-ass-looking suitcase into the house. The wheels catch on a pebble and my muscles overcorrect to keep the thing moving forward; I hiss in pain involuntarily. I can't believe I got shot. I need this shit to heal ASAP.

"Mia, where do you want this?" I ask, my voice sounding more strained than I want it to.

"Well, you tell me, darling, where is she? Lead the way." Her voice is so soothing, angelic almost. I need to make sure she doesn't figure out I was hit last night. The last thing I want to deal with is a doting Mia. Spider is the max limit of mothering I can handle right now.

"This way." I nod in the direction of the room she's staying in. Blade and Spider are still wrestling with bags and boxes at the front door. I gently knock on the guest bedroom door.

I am in no way prepared for the sight I see once it opens. Midnight is wearing nothing but the grey towel Spider gave her last night. Wet strands of inky dark hair stick to the side of her face and her collar bone, a small tattoo peeks out from underneath. She seems to have quite a collection. I shake myself. "Midnight, this is Mia. She brought some clothes and supplies for you, is it cool if she comes in?" This is my goddamn house, why am I asking her? I push my way in and roll the suitcase into the center of the room.

Mia extends her hand out to Midnight, and as she goes to shake, the towel starts to fall from her body.

I catch a brief glimpse of her breasts before I quickly look away. Damn, she's hot. "Sorry," I mutter. The hell? It's not my fault. Man, I need to get out of here. Better yet, we need to get her out of here. "You ladies good? Spider and Blade are bringing in the rest. I got shit to do."

Midnight's eyes dart from the suitcase, to me, to Mia, while tightly holding her towel back in place. "The rest?" She looks up at me, bewildered. Did she just fucking speak? Before I get a chance to register that, Mia is already talking a mile a minute.

"Of course, I heard you've recently been through a bit of an ordeal. Nothing gives confidence back more than a heavy dose of self-care."

"Mia, you brought an entire department store, we just needed one outfit and a few things." I shake my head.

I exit the room as I hear Mia say, "Boys, am I right? If it

were up to them they'd give you a toothbrush, a clean pair of underwear, and call it a day. I doubt they'd even remember a bra."

I pause outside the door. Midnight just *spoke*. I didn't know she was doing that. My eyes drift over to Midnight, and I realize I am watching with bated breath to hear her speak again.

"Alright then, let's get you sorted, what do you say?"

Midnight stares at Mia and nods her head.

I'm guessing she isn't going to speak again. Or maybe I misheard it. Maybe she never spoke at all. Spider and Blade jostle into the hallway behind me with the remaining bags.

"Why are you creeping outside the door like some low-level lovesick stalker?" Blade says with the stealth of a Yankees announcer.

"Shut up, Blade. Spider, does she speak? I swear I just heard her respond to Mia." I glare at him, daring him to lie to me.

"Yes." Spider looks like a bellman at a five-star hotel the way he's weighed down.

"When the hell were you going to tell me?" I don't know if I'm more pissed or confused. I don't like that he kept that from me. I don't like the effect this girl has on him at all.

"It happened this morning. I haven't had the chance yet; this is the first time I've seen you all day, and we're kind of busy." He gestures to what he's hauling with his head.

Still, I don't trust him around her. Blade is onto something; she does seem to have a bewitching effect on Spider. Maybe even on me. I push the door to the room open again to see a look of disgust on Midnight's face as Mia holds up a long, silky lavender dress. Midnight slowly backs away.

"Go on, it'll look so beautiful on you." Mia drapes the dress over Midnight's shoulder and turns to us.

"Hey, Mia, where do you want all this?" Spider asks.

"Oh, perfect. Lay it out on the bed please. I'll take this one." She darts past Spider to Blade and seizes one of the matte black boxes from him. There's an awkward tussle as she extracts one box, leaving him to balance the rest before setting them all down. She pulls out a matching lavender lace bra, thong, and garter. The silky material looks soft and delicate.

I can't help but imagine how incredible it would look against Midnight's tanned skin. I vividly picture how it would cling to her curves, tracing the lines of her body in all the exact right places. The elaborate floral pattern of the bra, cupping her supple tits that I caught a glimpse of. The matching thong, sitting low on her hips, the perfect barely-there tease to what lays beneath, and the garter belt, hanging down to her intricate tattoos. A perfect map to trace up her thighs with my... Blade knocks into me as he heads out to bring in more bags, knocking me out of my stupor. I adjust my pants uncomfortably. How long have I been staring at Midnight? Mia is still holding the lingerie out to her, yet Midnight doesn't extend her hands out to take it. She looks more frightened than she did when I found her last night. It's actually kind of adorable.

"Go on, gorgeous, take this. It'll be perfect underneath that dress," Mia says in that sultry voice of hers. "Get out, boys, I can take it from here."

I shake my head. Mia is a queen in her own right. Tough, thoughtful, patient, caring. She's one of the best people I know. She can definitely take it from here.

"Alright, we should give Mia some space to work before she puts us to work," I say as if it was my idea.

"You always were the smartest man, Etto." She smiles as she continues to shoo us out the door. This time, she closes it behind her once we exit. We all instinctively file into Spider's office to discuss our next move. I can't seem to shake the image of Midnight in that lingerie set from my mind. I need to get my shit together; it's time to focus.

I look around at the empty energy drink cans littered all over the floor. "Spider, did you get any sleep last night?"

"Don't worry about me, I'm solid." Spider pulls up some files on his computer. "I didn't find much, but I think I discovered a lead we can track."

"Before you dive into that: since when does she speak? What did you learn from her?" I sit heavily on the cot he keeps in here for the nights he doesn't want to be away from his work.

"Nothing really yet, we didn't get a chance to talk. All I know so far is her name is Kai." He can't seem to stop himself from letting loose a little smile. Holy shit, now I'm sure of it. Blade's right. Spider already has some weird sort of 'I can fix her' fixation on her. And I still can't extract that image of her out of my mind.

"We know she has fucking ties to the Yakuza," Blade blurts out.

"We do? And how do we know that?" I ask him. I don't remember Blade and her ever being in a room together, let alone speaking.

"The tattoos. Her ink is from an old Satō clan artist. I haven't seen his ink on anyone in over a decade, but I'd recognize it anywhere."

"Not that I'm doubting you, but that seems like a weird detail for you to know."

"The artist was my mom's friend. He did the tattoo on my chest after..." He trails off, rubbing absently at his left pectoral. He clears his throat. "He hasn't been seen since a few months after Ava and my parents died. Disappeared right around when the last oyabun was executed." The anger in his voice tells me it's time to change the subject. I have nowhere to channel his rage right now.

"As soon as Mia is done with her," I say, "we need to sit down and have a little chat. It appears there is more to our little house guest than she is letting on." I turn to Spider. "So, hit me. What did you find?" I look past Spider's shoulder at the bank of giant monitors and catch the image of a young Japanese man traveling through an airport.

Spider closes the file behind the image. "Han Yoshinaga. Japanese American hacker, goes by the codename Override. I'm not sure what the connection is yet. I do know the FBI flagged him as having reentered the country eight months ago. He's wanted for running away while out on bail for charges he picked up as a minor. He's been MIA for over a decade. No guess yet as to what brought him back stateside. That's what I am working on. The only thing I have so far is a potential safe house. Do you remember the old Sarbar nightclub, down on 10th near Avenue B?"

"That place has been shut down for years." Though we had some good times there before shit got so complicated. Tables, women, countless one-night stands; it feels like a lifetime ago.

"I know, but recently it's been using up a shit ton of electricity from the grid, check this." He excitedly pulls up what I assume is electric grid information. I have no idea what the hell I'm looking at, but Spider's the absolute best at what he does, so I know it's something. I don't need to understand. I trust him completely; the guy should have been a detective. Between his deductive skills and Blade's bloodhound nature, there is no one that stands a chance to remain hidden from us. "If Override is in town, this is the best place to start."

As Spider finishes his sentence a soft knock sounds on the door.

"Yeah," I grit out.

"Mind your manners, Etto." Mia enters and raises an eyebrow at me as she chastises me. "That's no way to greet a Lady." She holds the door all the way open, and into the room steps Midnight—I should think of her as Kai, I guess—donning that lavender dress she'd been terrified of earlier. The soft pastel silk drapes around her body revealing voluptuous curves. The slit reveals her toned, muscular thigh and a hot as fuck rose garter tattoo. Then that image springs to my mind again, and all I can see is her in that lavender lingerie set. An animalistic part of me wants to rip that dress off of her and fuck her against the door. I'd probably be doing her a favor anyway; she looks like she wants it ripped off as she fidgets in the doorway.

"You look beautiful," I hear Spider from behind me.

Beautiful is an understatement; she looks like a work of art. "Mia, thank you so much for everything. I trust she's set up for the day?"

"She's set for life." Mia chuckles. "I couldn't help it. You gave me an excuse to shop on someone else's dime. Thank you." She bends down to give me another kiss on the cheek. She runs her soft hands down my arm and smiles at me. Her movements are regal, delicate; the polar opposite of Kai's defiantly harsh aura. "I'll get out of your way." She turns to Kai. "Take care, sweetie. It was a pleasure to meet you." She pulls Kai in with a hug. Every muscle in Kai's body appears to tense up. She doesn't even lift her arms. They stick rigidly to the sides of her body. "Bye, boys." Mia takes her exit.

As Kai starts to walk out, I call after her, "Not so fast, Midnight, have a seat."

Blade knocks all the clothes off of Spider's lounge chair. I can see the muscles tense in his jaw in annoyance, but we can't worry about his shit right now. We need to know everything she does before my father loses it.

She carefully walks over to the chair and takes a seat. Her posture is impressive for someone who's been through whatever it is she has endured.

I look into her eyes, ready to start a standard interrogation, but those deep, dark pools unnerve me and I end up rattling off questions at her, one after the other. "What were you doing in that warehouse? Who tied you up? Why were you there in the first place?"

She tenses up and Spider stands, stepping between us.

"Tor, chill." He turns to her and speaks softly. "This isn't an interrogation, sweetheart, we are just trying to understand what happened last night. Can you please tell us what you know?"

It sure as shit *is* an interrogation, but whatever gets her to talk, I don't fucking care.

She fidgets, her fingers playing with the slit of the dress.

"What are you so nervous about?" I inquire.

"She has us three ominous fucking men standing over her barking questions at her," Spider says with a pretty insubordinate tone in his voice. "Well, two ominous fucking men; Blade's just glaring in her direction like he wants to kill her or eat her, I'm not sure which."

"Both." Blades smirks darkly.

"Bloody hell, Blade." Spider shakes his head. "What girl wouldn't be nervous?" Spider responds for her, again. He needs to stop that shit.

"Those Yakuza tattoos tell me she's not a fucking stranger to 'ominous men' standing over her, and you can let the stray speak for herself, Spider," Blade bites out.

She levels him a glare that I can't quite decipher.

I'm not sure which of them wants to kill the other more. Enough of this shit. "Kai, speak. Now," I grit out as I adjust my position on Spider's cot. I fucking hate this. I feel totally useless. I can't stand, or shift, or exist without excruciating pain. No one other than Spider gives a shit that I've been shot; life just continues the fuck on. And I have to pretend this shit doesn't faze me. I learned at an extremely young age that weakness means death, though not always yours. I'm in a miserable state, and we still don't know anything about who shot me.

She hesitates for a moment. Right before I am about to demand she speak again, she starts. "My father was Yakuza. He's dead. I got these tattoos in his memory. I don't know who took me. I was in my apartment, minding my own business when the lights went out. I can't tell you who, or how many men barged into my place. All I know is I fought as hard as I could, but obviously it wasn't hard enough."

"Who were these men? What did they look like?" I ask.

"I just said: I don't know. It was dark. They caught me off guard. There were too many of them for me to fight them off. They were speaking Japanese, which despite my appearance I don't understand. All I remember was feeling a blade against my chest before I was knocked out with something heavy and hard as fuck. The next thing I know, I startle awake when some bloody guy—" she points at me "—holding his side barged into that office. I assumed it was you all who took me. So you can understand why I thought it better to keep my mouth shut."

"You said they were speaking Japanese," I blurt. "Why the hell would you think I speak Japanese? Look at me."

"First of all," she says in an absolutely withering tone, "I never assume what languages someone speaks based on what they look like, that's a dumb move. I don't know, I figured out pretty quick once I heard the gunshots that you clearly weren't with them. Your eyes were kind and mine were impossible to keep open. So I let myself pass back out. I swear I don't know anything. My best guess is they were rivals of my father when he was alive. I don't know. I need to get back to my apartment."

"Just a few more questions and we'll take you home. What's your father's—" I'm cut off by Spider's phone pinging.

"We need to go." He taps the screen. "The man I sent to surveil Sarbar just messaged me that there is movement. It looks like they are clearing out of the space. It's now or never." Spider grabs his jacket, and pulls his gun out of the drawer.

Blade—to absolutely no one's surprise—is already armed and ready to go.

"Alright, let's head out," I say as I struggle to get up from my place on the cot. Our mystery girl darts up and sticks her hand out to help me and I push her away as I stand. "I don't need your help. Get off me."

She pulls her hand back and looks up at me with what almost looks like concern mixed with pity. I fucking hate it. I'm not weak. I don't need anyone's goddamn help, especially not this girl's.

Spider puts a guiding hand on her lower back. When the hell did this happen? "Stay here, okay, sweetheart? We'll be back in a bit and we can take you to your apartment when we return. Wait, do you live in New York?"

"Yeah, on 91st and 2nd."

He leans down and kisses her on the cheek. What the *actual* hell?

"We'll be back as soon as we can, okay?" Spider says gently.

I hate how he's talking to her. Like she's his. My mind starts rampantly cycling through so many thoughts I completely miss the first half of Spider and Blade's bickering. I shake my head to clear what I can. I can't afford to be distracted right now. Especially not by this random, albeit inarguably tempting, girl whose story doesn't quite add up.

CHAPTER 10

SPIDER

"We can't just leave her here in our fucking house," Blade barks out. "We don't know anything about her."

"She won't be by herself, Tor will be here," I reply.

"Yeah, let's leave the feral animal we don't know with our friend who is hanging on by a thread and can't defend himself. Brilliant, Spider, fucking brilliant."

"Fuck off, man, I can defend myself. What the fuck, Blade?" Tor snaps.

"Blade, what do you propose?" I say, annoyance leaking from my voice. "You want to bring her with us?"

"No, I want to get rid of her. Why the fuck is she still here? Doc patched her up, he said she's fine, let's cut the bitch loose. There is no reason she needs to be here. She told us what she knows, she's of no use to us anymore, if she ever was. I get we need to go, have one of the men take her home and get her out of our fucking way."

My eyes dart to Kai, who is impassively watching this all unfold.

"I'll decide what we do with the girl and when we let

77

her go," Tor says from next to the cot in the corner. He's slightly bent over, clutching the bullet wound in his gut. "We'll drop her off at her place after we follow up on Spider's lead."

"Get back in bed," I say, "you aren't going to heal like this." My concern for his wellbeing is clearly a point of agitation for him based on the way his eyebrows raise and his mouth cuts to a thin line in disdain.

"I'm fine, *mom*."

If looks could kill, I'm pretty sure I'd be dead right now. I get a lot of looks like that.

"Let's go," Blade says. "Tell the rest of the men to meet us there. I'm not getting caught off guard by these assholes again."

"Blade and I will head to Sarbar and check it out," I continue, pretending I don't notice Tor's glower. "It's a long shot, but it's our only lead."

"Was I not clear? We're all going," Tor commands.

Blade sneers. "Great plan. Let's take a nice family road trip. Why don't we take Spider's pet, too? Maybe if you bring some treats, she'll do some tricks for us while we scope out the place."

Kai doesn't react. Her head just swivels back and forth between us as we attempt to decide her fate. Her presence feels heavier than her slight frame would suggest.

"We're taking her," Tor says, voice like steel. "End of discussion."

Blade throws his hands up in mock surrender, mumbling under his breath about babysitting wild animals. I shoot him a warning glance and grab the keys to the SUV. I know better than to argue with Tor once he's made a decision. Blade should, too.

As we arrive at the remnants of Sarbar, something feels off. This is a strange place to establish a safe house. Nestled among quiet, retrofitted residences in the heart of Chelsea is not where I'd set up a hideout. Probably wouldn't be where I'd open a club either, so there's that. We park a block away in front of a bodega and move in on foot, Kai lagging behind us, her movements slow but deliberate. Tor is limping, clearly still in pain. They both shouldn't be here. At least she changed out of that dress Mia gave her; she's still distractingly sexy in a pair of black jeans and a black long-sleeved t-shirt that hugs every curve.

As we turn the corner, the vibe noticeably shifts. The area feels deserted. I didn't know there were any corners like that left in Manhattan. It looks so different in the dusk light, the warm evening wrapping around it. I never noticed how grimy this place was when we used to spend our nights here. Shadows stretch long, swallowing everything in their path. The SUV is barely out of sight when Tor groans again, hand clutching his side.

"You sure you're up for this?" Kai asks, her tone razor-sharp. "Your boys seemed real adamant about nothing slowing them down. You and I can wait here if you want."

He shoots her a look that's equal parts venom and heat, his lips twitching into a grimace. "I'll manage. Don't worry your pretty little head about me. Just make sure to stay out of the way. Don't make me regret not letting Blade kill you. There is still time for me to change my mind on that before we take you home."

Her eyes narrow, flashing in the dim light. "I wasn't worried. Just making sure you don't die and take me down with you. I've had more than enough close calls for the week."

Blade cuts in with a snort, his gun slung casually over his shoulder. "She's charming, isn't she? You sure we shouldn't just tie her to a pole and leave her for whoever finds her first? We can keep watch, we all know Spider loves a good show. It may bring who we're hunting down straight to us. Two birds and all."

Kai's head snaps toward him, her voice icy. "Careful, Blade. You might be the one who ends up tied up if you keep running that mouth."

So, the starry-eyed girl has some balls on her. I laugh to myself. The more she talks, the less she's what I expected. She's full of surprises and doesn't seem wounded or docile at all.

Blade steps closer, looming, his grin full of teeth. "Is that a threat, princess? Or an invitation?"

"Enough!" Tor growls, stepping between them, his presence crackling like a live wire despite his current condition. "Shut the hell up and fucking focus. Keep it the hell down, it's like you are trying to announce our arrival." As we enter the backdoor of the warehouse, his gaze flicks to Kai, lingering a fraction longer than necessary. He shifts to a hushed whisper. "Stay sharp. Both of you. Kai, wait right here, we won't be long. You're almost free of all this shit."

Once we turn the corner into what looks to be the former dance floor, figures emerge from the shadows. Our men aren't here yet, but I guess we aren't waiting. Weapons glint under the low-lit blue light of the former nightclub. If Override is here, he isn't alone.

"Ambush!" Blade hisses, dropping down behind a stained, red velvet couch as bullets whiz past, striking the concrete walls with sharp, echoing cracks. We scatter, seeking cover behind booths and velvet chaise lounges.

Pandemonium. Here we go again. Shadows explode into motion, gunfire lighting up the darkness like a strobe. I sense something behind me. As I turn my gun to shoot I stop dead in my tracks when I see Kai. "Kai, Tor told you to wait in the hallway, what are you doing here?" Her answer is cut off by a bullet that whizzes by. Kai moves with surprising fluidity, diving behind cover as bullets tear into the furniture around her.

The battle is chaotic, a blur of muzzle flashes, shouted commands, and the acrid scent of gunpowder. I catch sight of who I think is Override retreating deeper into the building past the red rope of the VIP section. "He's getting away!" I shout. Tor fires from the left, his shots precise but hurried.

"I think that's Han in there!" he shouts, nodding toward the VIP section.

If we both think it, then that must be him.

Blade is farther up, firing with wild abandon. It's clear he's enjoying himself. "Nice of them to leave us a welcome mat." He fires off more rounds.

Kai crouches, her breaths shallow. She peeks around the corner of the bar we inched toward, just as Blade advances. "You're going to get yourself shot!" she hisses, but he waves her off. Shattered glass starts flying everywhere as bullets pierce the half-empty bottles displayed behind the bar.

These assholes always seem to be better prepared than us. It's as if they knew we were coming. And where the fuck are our men? A hail of bullets forces Tor to duck, clutching his side with a wince.

Kai glances at him, seemingly torn between staying put and moving to help.

He notices. "Relax, I'm fine. Stay where you are," Tor says, his voice tight. He fires off a shot to the right and looks back over at her. "You worried about me, Midnight?"

"Don't flatter yourself." Her retort is sharp, but she slides closer, pressing against the same area of the bar as him. Their proximity sparks a strange tension, his breathing rough against her ear as he reloads. I'm not sure how I feel about that.

"You should have sat this out." She nods toward the blood seeping into Tor's shirt, his wound clearly reopened. "You're in no position to be in a gunfight right now."

"You always this bossy, or is it just me you want to order around? I give the orders around here, Midnight. You're supposed to be in the entryway where we left you." Tor smirks, despite the pain in his side.

"Shut up," she bites out. "While I appreciate the initial rescue, it's not quite a safe harbor you're providing, is it? It's the worst ride home I've ever been offered, and I've been in some questionable rides. Plus, no one orders me around, *especially* not you."

That's an odd way for her to put it.

I can hear the enemy reloading and take the opportunity to advance toward the VIP section when a gunman steps out of the shadows, weapon raised.

"Spider, look out!" Kai shouts, breaking cover. She lunges toward me, shoving me down hard. The bullet misses me by centimeters. Kai lands on top of me, hitting the ground with a thud. For a moment, everything stills.

"Kai!" Tor's voice is sharp, but he releases a breath when she rolls off of me onto her side. She is breathing hard, brushing liquor bottle glass off of her. Her outfit is covered in alcohol and grime. Jesus, Mia would kill us if she saw the state of her.

"I'm fine," she snaps, scrambling on all fours to grab the gun the assailant dropped as he ran out. The way she picks it up, almost on instinct has me staring at her for a moment too long. I can't shake the feeling that she and the man who dropped this gun exchanged a glance. For a second it looked like they knew each other. Maybe it was one of her captors?

"You recognize him?" I ask.

She shakes her head fervently, looking up at me from the floor.

Blade glances back. "Of course, the damsel had to fall. Real convenient. Thanks, princess, you helped them get away."

Kai glares at him but bites back a retort as another wave of enemies emerges from the back room. Their numbers are overwhelming. I almost miss the cell phone that the guy dropped as he made his way out. I bend down to pick it up.

"We're outgunned, we need to go!" I shout, dragging Kai up.

Blade sneers as he covers our retreat, firing wildly as Tor curses and yells, "Get to the car!"

We scramble back, bullets chasing us as we run the block and we all fling ourselves into the vehicle. I shove Kai into the back seat and jump into the driver's seat as the remote start kicks in.

Blade slams the door, barking, "Go, go, go!"

I hit the gas.

The tires squeal as Blade shoots cover fire out of the sunroof like a maniac, the vehicle swerving. Not my best driving, but evasive maneuvers aren't as slick as they look in the movies. The bullets keep coming, sparking against the metal, but somehow, we make it out unharmed. Fuck. Yet again, that didn't go as expected. I fucking hope there is something I can pull from this phone. Otherwise, we're all in for another uncomfortable conversation with the Don. You can only have so many of those before it ends in blood.

We travel back to the mansion in tense silence. Well, relative silence. Blade reloads and mutters a constant string of curse words, Tor breathes heavily and unevenly, and I tap a nervous rhythm on the steering wheel. Only Kai is truly silent.

Blade provides cover as we all dart inside, though we'd lost our tail miles before in the Manhattan streets.

The quiet continues to blanket the room like a heavy fog as we all drop down on the sofas once we arrive home. Everyone is battered, bruised, but mostly intact. Kai sits apart from us, her expression inscrutable, hands folded tightly in her lap. Tor is holding a towel against his stitches, checking his phone, and I text the Doc, who's about to be furious those stitches are reopened.

"Our men were found dead at the safe house where they were standing by. No intel on who, how, or why." Tor sighs.

"Fuck." Blade slams his fist into the arm of the sofa he's sitting on.

"All of them?" I ask.

"Yes." Tor throws his phone down on the coffee table and runs his hands through his hair.

"Wasn't this crew made up of Signor's top men?" I ask.

"The ones that he's had with him for decades." Tor sounds dejected.

"How the hell did—" I start to ask, but Blade interrupts me.

"Fucking great. So we have nothing, know fucking nothing, and more of our men are dead. The only fucking thing we learned tonight is that the stray's got some bite to her," Blade mutters, wincing as he inspects a graze on his arm. "Nice job, by the way," Blade says to Kai, his tone dripping with sarcasm. "What was that, some attempted noble, sacrificial act for him saving your ass from the warehouse last night? You know they likely fucking got away because of you."

"Maybe I just didn't want to watch Spider get shot. One guy with a hole in him feels like enough, don't you think?" Kai snaps back, her glare sharp enough to cut.

"Next time, try not to fall on your fucking face. No wonder you were kidnapped, so fucking oblivious and clumsy," Blade retorts.

"At least I hit what I aimed for. For someone who never shuts up about killing things, you sure seemed to suck at hitting the mark tonight." I suppress a chuckle; I don't need to piss off Blade any more than he is. Blade's expression and upright posture is screaming that he is on the verge of eruption.

"Why the fuck are you still here? We were supposed to finally fucking be rid of you after the Sarbar detour." Blade's agitation rises further. I sit up straight, I know what's coming.

"Between the roller coaster ride Spider's driving delivered and your bullets flying out the sunroof, it didn't really feel like there was a right time to interrupt and let you know you missed my turn." She rolls her eyes at him.

"So you're oblivious, clumsy, incompetent, have nothing useful to say, and are incapable of speaking up when it matters. Spider, your pet's a real fucking prized pig. You sure know how to pick 'em. She's utterly fucking useless, net negative in every way." I'm about to defend her when Kai cuts in.

"At least I'm wanted. Anyone give a shit about you?

Obviously not, or you wouldn't have turned out like a broken toy that has to kill everything to suppress whatever fucked up damage is hiding in that twisted psyche of yours," Kai responds.

Tor watches them from the couch, his hand pressed to his side. Blade unsheathes his knife and gets up, charging toward her.

"Blade, sit the fuck down," Tor says, his voice rough but commanding. "And both of you, shut the hell up." He meets Kai's gaze, something unspoken passing between them. She doesn't look away, her jaw tightening.

"You should rest," she says, breaking their standoff, her tone softer than before.

Tor smirks, leaning back against the cushions. "Don't act like you care. Stay out of this, Midnight. It's none of your concern. *You* go get some rest, and we'll take you to your apartment in the morning. Blade's right, you're a nuisance we don't need getting in the way any longer than you already have."

Her lips press into a thin line, but there's no retort this time, just a flicker of something she doesn't let him see, but I see it.

"Did you know the shooter who dropped this?" I ask Kai as I hold up the cell phone I picked up. I don't miss that her entire body tenses at the question.

Her mouth opens but nothing comes out, almost as if she is trying to formulate the words.

"Was he one of your captors?" I ask. She looks up at me with what appears to be relief in her eyes and nods. I nod back and she smiles at me. Fuck, she's so pretty. "Alright, I'm going to go get cleaned up and try to figure out what the fuck just happened. Again. See if I can pull anything useful off of this."

I need to wash this day off with a shower immediately, especially after falling on that disgusting floor. I probably shouldn't leave her here with the two of them, but after what I saw tonight, I have a feeling she can hold her own.

STEAM ROLLS THROUGH THE BATHROOM, curling along the edges of the mirror and fogging it completely as I step under the hot spray. The water pelts my skin, washing away the grime, the blood, and the chaos of the last few hours. I brace one hand against the tiled wall, bowing my head as droplets stream down my face. The heat eases the tension coiled in my shoulders.

Kai's face flickers in my mind, her quick movements, the push, the way she'd gone down hard right after and didn't seem fazed, the way she picked up that gun. It didn't seem calculated, but there was something in the way it happened that sticks in my mind like a splinter.

She tripped, right? I think, replaying the moment. It wasn't smooth. Her legs tangled, her body hit the ground hard. But then again, the timing was perfect. Too perfect? No, it had to be instinct, adrenaline, she didn't want me getting hurt, right?

I scrub my hand through my hair, dismissing the thought. All of these unknowns, the new players, it's making me paranoid. She was just reacting, wasn't she? Not everyone is trained to handle gunfights like me and the others. She shouldn't have even been there. We should have left her here like I said. Being abducted from her place. Waking up to a bleeding Tor, me hovering over her, a shouting Blade, and gunfire in a warehouse. Then getting stuck with us, kept against her will yet again. She's probably just overwhelmed.

But the hesitation when I asked about the shooter... my jaw tightens, water sluicing over my face as I exhale. She'd paused, sure, but anyone would if they were trying to sort through that kind of trauma. She said he was her captor, and that makes sense. Of course she'd recognize him. He's one of the guys who hurt her. But she said it was dark when they took her and she didn't see any of them.

There'd been something about the way her shoulders had stiffened. How her relief at my assumption seemed almost... exaggerated. Her eyes had softened too quickly, her answer a little too convenient. Stop overthinking, I tell myself, shaking my head. She's been through hell. It makes sense for her to be hesitant, distrusting, and nervous.

The memory of her smile creeps in, and my stomach twists. She's so damn pretty. There was something so hot about the way she was glaring and spitting venom at Tor and Blade. It shouldn't matter, but it does. That smile had disarmed all of us in Sarbar, just for a second. But seconds can be the difference between life and death in our world. Something inside me is nagging at me that she is involved somehow.

I can't stop thinking about the way she looked in that lavender dress Mia brought for her. As I picture the slit running up her leg, and visualize her sexy as fuck curves on full display I find my hand gravitating towards my cock of its own volition. I wrap my hand around my dick and I can't help myself, I start pumping. The memory of her lips around my dick underneath my desk speeds up my strokes. Within minutes I'm cumming to the thought of her. A sense of calm washes over me, but my mind remains a mess.

I lean forward, letting the water pound against my

back. This is why you don't bring strangers into your mess, I remind myself. But what were we supposed to do? We couldn't just leave her there at the warehouse. Plus, Tor ordered us to bring her with. Who am I kidding? I would have done it anyway. The thought of her not being here, of letting her go, doesn't sit right. And we're just supposed to take her home and drop her off tomorrow? I don't want to. What if they come after her again? She's safer here with us.

With a sigh, I turn off the water and grab a towel. I can't afford to think about her too much. Not now. We're under a full-fledged attack. This is a war. Override is still out there, he's our only lead and it's growing colder by the second. As I step into the cooler air of my bedroom, her face is still there, lingering like the steam from my shower. I put on a pair of fresh boxer briefs and flannel pajama pants. My pace picks up as I approach my office. I have a shit ton more work to do.

I need to stop thinking about her. The boys are right about one thing: she's a dangerous distraction.

CHAPTER 11

KAI

*B*lade's scowl makes me want to gouge his fucking eyes out. I genuinely hope he's on the kill list when all is said and done. I would enjoy every fucking second of it. Tor, on the other hand, I almost feel sorry for him. There is so much blood on his shirt and his father's men are dead. Usually, I'm not there for the aftermath of our destruction. I sense a tightness in my chest that's unfamiliar. Guilt, I suppose. I can see why it's best to avoid being in the presence of what you're taking down. It is kind of hard to watch. After all, he asked his girlfriend to bring over clothes and dress me up like a doll. While misguided, it's kind of sweet. Not something I would have expected someone like him to think of. Spider, sure; he's the gentler one. But Tor doesn't strike me as the caring type.

"Why the hell are you still here? I told you to go get some rest." The words are sharp as Tor asserts them. Without Spider in the room, I have no allies.

I start to bite back, but as soon as I see the exhaustion in his eyes and the hesitation lingering there, my voice dies in my throat. I swallow back the retort, feeling the weight of his silent struggle. This poor fuck has been shot, his father clearly doesn't give a shit about him, and they are no closer to figuring things out than they were before our little group excursion. That's a lot for anyone to take on, especially in less than twenty-four hours and honestly, it's almost all my fault. I can give him this illusion of control.

"You're right," I say, trying to sound contrite. "Thank you for agreeing to take me home in the morning."

He stares at me, clearly dumbfounded. "You're welcome. Good night, Kai."

"Good night, Tor." I stand and start down the hall to the guest room they've stashed me in. As I go, I say over my shoulder, "I hope you don't get any sleep, Blade."

"Ha, ha. Don't forget my room is right next to yours, princess, if I'm up, I'll make sure to keep you up, too." He smirks as he pushes past me on his way to his room. "I lost my sheath in the fight, I need a new one. Your gut will do nicely."

I glower at his back before ducking into my temporary abode. I strip off the jeans and long-sleeved t-shirt that Mia gave me and start digging through the drawers she filled earlier.

Fuck. For all her talk about 'the boys not knowing what girls need to wear' she sure fucked this up. I don't have any pajamas. I don't even have anything pajama-adjacent. Everything is skintight and slinky and expensive looking. I don't even have proper underwear. It's all thongs and lace. A noise of disgust springs out of my throat as I slam the drawer shut.

A wad of dark blue fabric catches my eye. Spider's t-shirt, crumpled on the floor where I left it earlier. I pretend to have a debate with myself before slipping it on. T-shirt and thong. Not the worst sleepwear.

But I know I won't be able to sleep. Not yet. I have a job to do.

My heart pounds with nerves as I twist my necklace in my hand. I have to do this now. There won't be another opportunity. I have beyond overstayed my welcome. This is my last chance. I open the locket and pull out the USB thingy Han gave me to plug into Spider's computer. A rootkit, that's what it's called. I hear him clearly in my mind, frustrated and insisting, it's a rootkit Kai, a rootkit, not a thingy. I peek out the door into the hallway to check for any movement. I take a deep breath, attempting to steel the nerves overtaking me. I can hear the showers running in both Spider's and Blade's rooms, so the only potential unknown is Tor. But he was still pretty exhausted and beat up last I saw him; he wasn't getting up off that couch any time soon.

This is as good a time as any.

I carefully open the door to Spider's office as quietly as I can. The quiet creak of the door startles me. I stop in my tracks and close my eyes. Idiotic fucking move. Playing a game of 'if I can't see you, you can't see me' is not what's called for here. I push the door back closed, stopping it at the point where the creak happened; it's still mostly closed, enough to not look suspicious. Hopefully.

I tiptoe over to and then hover over his desk. The screens and tiny LED power indicators from his computer don't provide enough light to see anything. No matter how hard I squint, my eyes don't adjust enough to find what I need. After counting to ten, taking a deep breath, and praying to espionage gods, I point the mini desk lamp as best as I can at the very edge of the desk so as not to be seen from the hall, turn it on, and crawl under the desk. As soon as I slide under, memories of last night with Spider rush through me. My pulse picks up and I'm not sure if it's from the fear of getting caught or the memory of my rendezvous with Spider. Fuck, I need to focus. The cables are meticulous back here. Black cable organizers around every cord ensure it is the exact length needed to be plugged in. They all plug into a circular black surge protector. I try plugging the little gadget into the tower's open USB slot, but I need to flip it over and try it a second time. Once it's in place, I get back up and click the space bar to wake up the monitors. The *clack* of hitting it is much louder than I anticipated. After what I register as an eternity—though it is likely mere seconds—a chat box pops open on the bottom right screen.

HAN:

Sora, finally. That was fucking close. We underestimated how quickly you'd arrive. You could have let us know the timeline shifted.

KAI:

Sorry, I was a little preoccupied trying to survive the wolf's den lol

I wait a moment and type again.

Do you have what you need? I want to get the fuck out of here. The Blade one is even more unhinged than your file suggested. Plus, I think they're starting to put two and two together.

HAN:

Yeah, we're good. I'll send Ren to grab you at the meet point. Can you be there in an hour?

I let out a sigh of relief and respond.

KAI:

Yes. See you soon.

As soon as I hit send, my chest constricts, every breath feels like a desperate gulp for air. I quickly add.

Hey, this Spider... he's sweet, but your intel is solid, he is insanely good. He won't be able to see this will he?

HAN:

Sora, oh ye of little faith, you wound me. Remove the USB, and just get yourself to the extraction point.

KAI:

Copy

I exit out of the window and go to leave when I hear that same fucking creak in the door. Shit. Fuck.

I open the browser in a panic. I type a few letters and delete. The pressure on my chest feels even tighter. What the fuck should I do? Fuck. I type in a semi colon, a zero, my fucking god, where the fuck is "p"?

The sweat beading on my neck and sliding down my back is like a flame burning its way down my skin. My cheeks must be so red, the heat in them builds as my heart beats at an impossibly rapid speed.

I sense someone approaching behind me.

He smells like Spider, like tobacco and honey.

Finally, I manage to type the word 'phone.' That must

be believable, right? It's 2025, no one can live without a fucking phone for as long as I have.

I take a deep breath and brace myself. This either works or I fight my way out of here. I prefer not to cause him pain. He has been nothing but kind to me.

Be a good boy for me Spider, don't make me have to hurt you.

CHAPTER 12

SPIDER

I'm so fucking tired. As soon as we figure out who the hell is fucking our shit up, I'm taking a four-day nap. My legs seem unbearably heavy as I walk to the kitchen in my pjs to grab a glass of water. I need to crack this phone before we are inevitably hit with another shit show, as we seem to be in no shortage of those lately. Once I'm done with this thing, I can finally get some sleep.

I look up mid thought to see a soft light emitting from beneath my office door.

A pit forms in my gut. Shit. I must really be out of it right now. I cannot remember the last time I left a light on in there when I'm not working. It takes a second for my sluggish brain to register that the door's cracked open, too. I'm more careful than that.

I need rest. I can't afford to be so sloppy just because I'm running on fumes.

I shuffle into the room, forcing one foot in front of the other, ready to tackle this fucking phone problem.

As soon as my eyes land on her, my heart starts beating

violently, as if it is trying to escape its home in my chest and hand itself to her.

Fuck, I was not expecting to see her. My eyes catch on Kai's bare legs and travel up toward her ass peeking out beneath my shirt. She looks so fucking delectable. Fuck cracking the phone, the only thing these hands want to do right now is roam every inch of her body.

I stalk up and position myself directly behind her as she's bent over my desk and absentmindedly ask, "Is there something I can help you find?" I swallow down my hesitation and let my fingers gently caress her ass, just the lightest touch possible.

The way she startles but doesn't pull away is so damn cute. "I'm so sorry." Her eyes dart nervously in every direction but mine. "I should have asked. I was trying to order a phone. I need to reestablish some sense of normalcy." Her voice lowers, becoming husky as my fingers inch their way forward, nudging the tiny scrap of lace fabric out of the way, and tenderly stroke her pussy from behind.

Her eyes finally find mine and an understanding passes between us, supercharging the blood in my veins.

Without breaking eye contact, she pushes back onto me and I can't help myself; I stop playing with her and then suck my finger into my mouth.

Relishing the taste, I teasingly slide my finger back inside her. "I can take you to go get one tomorrow morning. Is there anything else you want?" I rub my finger in tantalizing circles against the soft flesh of her g-spot.

She doesn't answer. Instead she leans back onto my hand, pushing my finger in deeper. My dick stands at attention as she grinds down on my hand, chasing every bit of friction she can get. She pushes back onto me harder, her back flush against my chest. It's as if she is trying to make contact to as many points of my body as she can. I feel a rush of heat travel throughout my entire being. Fuck, she's so damn sexy.

"Don't worry, sweetheart, I'm going to take real good care of you." I run my other hand up her back underneath my shirt. She looks so hot in it, I'm almost sad to take it off of her. She lifts her arms to help me remove it. "Good girl," I coo as I reach around to fill my free hand with her supple tits. My brain short circuits. I can't remember what I came in here to do, but I know exactly what I'm going to do next. Fuck, she is so fucking enticing.

The way she sinks into me, letting the full weight of her body press against my chest, engorges my cock with what feels like a renewed rush of blood. She tilts her head to the side, baring her neck. Inviting me to ravish her. I'm not sure I've ever been as hard as I am right now. I feel the heat from between her legs as her hips grind up against me, her pussy pulsating with need. Need for me. Her hand glides to the back of my neck pulling me in closer to her. The way she arches her back against me is the final straw.

A shiver cascades down her spine as my tongue traces a path along her neck. She releases a gasp as the sharp nip of my teeth digs into her flesh. She looks over her shoulder at me and my eyes meet hers as I sit back into the chair behind me. I watch her as she hooks her fingers into the sides of that tiny purple thong. I free my length from the confines of my pajamas and boxer briefs. She bends over, putting her glistening pussy on display as she drops the thong on the floor at her feet.

I pull her back and onto my lap. I look up to confirm if she wants this as bad as I do. She nods enthusiastically. After a breathless pause, she sits, guiding herself onto me. My hands slide down to her hips just above her bubbly ass that I can't stop staring at. The sensation of stretching her inch by inch consumes me. I have never been happier that I opted for a chair with no armrests, she is the only thing I need to hold onto right now. A ragged moan escapes her lips. She sinks down excruciatingly slowly, until we're pressed so tightly together that I can feel my pulse deep inside her.

My brain is blank, I feel completely lost in her, yet somehow at home. She stills, trembling as heat rushes between us, dripping down both of our thighs. She leans her head back, arching far enough that I can watch her eyelids flutter shut. I can't stop staring at her. I'm mesmerized by the micro expressions of pleasure on her face. The way her lips part ever so slightly, her tongue darting out to wet them. The lowering of her eyelids as she looks back to hold my gaze. The way her dilated pupils obstruct the glittery flecks that normally dominate her eyes. The flush of pink spreading across her cheeks as I slide my hands up and down the side of her body.

Her breath hitches as I savor the perfect, maddening warmth of her.

"Fuck, Spider, you feel so good," she whispers, her voice shaking with need.

A smirk tugs at my lips as her words hang heavy between us. With a slow, tantalizing roll, she lifts herself until only my head lingers at her entrance. She teases me with a deliberate pause before she sinks back down, enveloping me completely. I'll let her have her fun for a moment. It's adorable she thinks she's the one in control. I want to give her that, if only temporarily. She's clearly had a rough few days.

The calculated motion fuels a moan that bursts from my lips. There's an electricity sparking between us, surging like lightning in my veins. She has to feel that, too. It can't just be me. Every shift, every collision is a catalyst, building until our movements teeter on the edge of a powerful explosion.

The rhythm quickens, our bodies pressing together in chaotic harmony. The erratic pace raw and urgent as she grinds down harder. It's like she's determined to draw every last drop of me into her. Our breaths are ragged, merging with the wet, rhythmic sounds. The soft, plapping sound of skin on skin is hypnotic as she rides me.

Her thighs begin to shake with the strain. Pleasure coils tighter in me with each pulse and shiver. The minute she gasps my name, "Spider," I can't hold back any longer. I need her. I need her now. Without warning, I snap my hips upward, driving deep and drawing a sharp cry from her throat. I clamp my hands onto her waist, fingers biting possessively into her skin. I guide her movements with enough force to leave a mark. I want to see myself all over her tomorrow. The day after, and the ones that follow.

I stand up and position her over the desk, still inside her. And I break. Thrusting into her like a wild animal.

"Don't stop," she moans, her voice soft, almost desperate.

"Oh, sweetheart, I don't intend to," I grit out amid thrusts.

She tilts her head back toward me and her gaze locks with mine. I see the exact moment she surrenders to the unrelenting wave of bliss. Her eyes screaming that she's lost in the perfect, frenzied chaos that binds us together. Watching her cum for me takes me over the edge with her. The moan I release as I cum sounds foreign, as if it doesn't come from me. I take a second to catch my breath, eyes closed. When I open them, her expression fills me with pride. Relaxed. Sated. I did that. That was me. And fuck if she isn't now mine.

I turn her around by my hold on her waist. Pick her up, and walk her over to the cot in the corner of the room. I lay us down and pull her into me. She's completely pliant in my arms. I slide my hand down to her left leg as she starts to unwrap it from around my waist. I hold it in place. She looks up at me as she snuggles deeper into my hold. I pepper her with kisses along her forehead. Her nose. Her cheeks. Her neck. She sighs as she relaxes further into me.

"You took me so well, sweetheart. I didn't mean to lose it at the end there."

She smiles at me. And is she blushing as she giggles? She is. Goddamn, she's so cute. She looks away and her eyes close. She lets out a deep breath and is out in seconds. It fills me with pride to know I tired her out. Giving her one last kiss on her soft, plush lips, I close my eyes, too. The last thing running through my mind before sleep takes me: I love the way she molds into me. I never want to let her go.

LIGHT PEEKING in from the window wakes me. I feel Kai's warmth before I see her. I brush a strand of hair out of her face so I can have access to those lips I've become obsessed with devouring. As soon as I kiss her she scrambles up out of bed.

"Fuck. What time is it?" She avoids my gaze.

"I don't know, are you okay?" I start to panic. "Is this about last night? I..." My chest inexplicably tightens, and my heart begins to race a mile a minute.

She regrets it.

"Yes. No. No, last night was…" She pauses, staring off into the distance. I can almost see the replay of me inside her as she's bent over the desk in her eyes. Her shoulders relax, her expression softens. "Amazing. Last night was amazing. I—I have to go, though. Get home, you know. Get back to my life." Why does she look so tense again?

"And get a phone," I add.

She looks at me while shaking her head slightly, puzzled. Then, after a beat, she nods and says, "Oh yeah, yes. And replace my phone."

God, this is so awkward. I want her back in my arms again. The way she's acting, inching her body further and further away from mine without turning her back to me, I don't think that's what she wants right now.

"I'll take you. Let's go grab you a phone, I'll give you my number. Then I am happy to take you back to your place."

She looks back at me, deep in thought. Though she is staring in my direction, she isn't looking at me. She's looking through me to somewhere I don't know if I'm welcome. I don't know where she is. The only thing I do know for certain, she isn't here with me. Not anymore. "No, it's okay. I can manage," she says as she backs up toward the door. "I'll figure something out, you all have done more than enough for me."

"Nonsense. I'll take you. I need to make sure you get home safe. This isn't up for debate. We still don't know exactly who took you or why. I don't feel right just releasing you back onto the street while these guys are still out there."

Her expression tightens.

What am I supposed to do? I can't keep her prisoner here. The image of her tied up in rope and bound to my iron plated headboard, completely under my control, flashes through my mind and I smile. I stop myself, biting down on the smile before she catches sight of it. Does she even want me to think of her like that? She clearly wants to leave. I want to give her what she wants. Even if I hate everything about the idea. Tor and Blade agreed we take her home today, too. No matter how badly I want to keep her here. I can't.

"Go get dressed and pack up what you need. Meet me in the kitchen. Let's get some breakfast in you. Once you've eaten we can head out."

She straightens her spine, as if she's about to argue.

I shake my head, slow and deliberate.

She huffs and grabs my shirt that I ripped off her last night from the floor. The instant it's over her head and dropped down around her body, I struggle to take in air. This could be the last time I'll ever see her in my clothes. The thought causes knots to form in my gut. I almost wish she would argue, but instead she remains silent. She closes her mouth and walks thru the door toward her room, leaving me with that same view from last night as my last image of her as mine.

I grab my jeans off the floor. Fucking Blade, knocking my stuff all over the fucking place yesterday. I bend down and pick up the rest of my clothes and place them back on their perch on the lounge chair. Once I'm dressed, I saunter over to the kitchen to put on some coffee. Guilt creeps in that I haven't yet broken into the phone we recovered last night. It's fine, my mind is clear so I'll be more efficient today. Is it really clear? Fuck, she pulled back hard. She seemed like she was really enjoying it last night. She felt just as into it as I did. Fuck, I lost it when she moaned my name. Maybe I was too much? I probably came on too strong. I tend to do that.

Footsteps, lighter and quicker than either Tor's or Blade's catch my attention. My head snaps up, and she's there. Standing in my kitchen.

She's there in knee-high boots, tights and a microscopically short violet sweater dress, knocking the air out of my lungs. "Hey," I manage to get out awkwardly as fuck as I hand her a cup of coffee. "Sugar or cream?"

"No thanks," she replies. She won't even look at me. Yeah, she definitely regrets it. Fuck. Okay. It's fine. I'll get her a phone. Take her to her apartment and that'll be that. I ignore the pit forming in my stomach and turn to grab myself some milk.

At least some things never change; Blade and Tor are arguing as they enter the kitchen.

"It has to be Satō and his men," Blade exclaims. He's ticking evidence off on his fingers as if he's counting. "They were speaking Japanese, they knew our drop schedule, they were way too organized to be a new player. We'd have heard of someone at that level moving in."

Tor is shaking his head vehemently. "Nah, my father and Satō have been working together for years. There's been no sign of tension, no indication that anything is off. It doesn't benefit them to disrupt our operations. It has to be..." Tor trails off as his eyes catch Kai drinking her coffee quietly while leaning over the counter.

After drinking in the view for a minute, he shakes his head—looks like there's a lot of that going around—and looks her in the eye. "Let's get you home, Midnight. Vacation's over."

'Vacation' is an interesting choice of words to use to describe her kidnapping and subsequent captivity here where we dragged her to a gun fight she didn't ask for, but sure. I live with a couple of assholes, I fucking love them, but they are absolute assholes.

"I'm taking her," I say. "We're going out to pick her up a replacement phone now, then I'll drop her off at her apartment. Shouldn't be too long."

Tor's raised eyebrows seem to imply he doesn't like that idea. "No, we'll take her. We all need to check in at the compound once we drop her off."

"Cause the last family road trip went so well, let's start this day with another one," Blade chimes in, glaring at Kai.

"Fine." I exhale sharply, not hiding my annoyance. "I guess we're all going."

The sun grazing my skin provides a warmth I didn't know I was missing since Kai went cold on me earlier this morning. I open the back door of the SUV for her so she can get in. As I reach over her to grab her seat belt, she yanks it from me, keeping her hands as far away from mine as possible. My heart sinks from my chest. I lean back out of the backseat, close the door, and release a sigh before walking over to the other side of the car to hop in next to her.

Every time I glance in her direction, she is turned away from me, staring intently at the passing brownstones as we crawl through traffic. Blade stops outside the electronics store, parallel parking so fast it almost gives me whiplash.

"I'll be right back." I jump out of the car, grateful that the curb is on my side so I can beat her to the punch and go in alone. I purchase her a phone and—I know I shouldn't but I can't help myself—I place one of my sims into it. I hesitate for a moment, my hand hovering over where I need to place it. I tell myself it's to make sure she was telling us the truth about who she is. I tell myself it is to keep her safe. I almost convince myself, but I know there is a pull inside me that simply refuses to let her go. Even if she is currently acting like I'm the last person she wants to be around.

I slide back into the car and hand her the phone. "Here. I set it up for you already. Number's saved. Along with mine in case you need to get a hold of us."

"Thank you." She takes the phone from me, making sure not to make contact with my fingers as she grabs it.

My gut twists as I realize I preferred it better when I thought she couldn't speak. I hate these short answers, the stoically quiet presence. I was inside her last night. I filled her with my cum. I slept with my arms wrapped around her. Yet she feels further away than before all that happened.

She doesn't even look at me for the rest of the drive. She just types incessantly on the new phone I gave her.

After a forty-minute drive, we park out front of her apartment. I think I'm going to be the only one that walks her up. So I pause when I see Tor and Blade both get out of the car.

"Let's go, princess." Blade ushers her out of the back seat.

"I got it from here. Thank you," she replies.

"I'm sure you do, Midnight. Let's go." Tor's tone leaves no room for argument. We follow her up the stairs of her walkup. The modern aesthetic of the building's interior is a stark contrast to the Art Deco façade.

Before I can even finish wondering how she's going to get in without keys, we reach a door that has been broken in. A chill slithers up my spine as we approach the destruction. Chips of navy blue and exposed wood litter the linoleum floor on the other side and the lock has been completely broken off. She pushes open the door fragment and leans against the frame. Her eyes scan the apartment and I see a hint of a smile break out on her beautiful face. Not the reaction I expected, but who cares? She looks so radiantly beautiful.

"You can't stay here," I blurt out.

"The hell she can't," Blade bites back. "We got her home. That's what you wanted. Now let's get the fuck out of here. We've got shit to do."

"Tor, we can't leave her here on her own." I turn to him, pleading, and not caring that I'm pleading. "Look at the fucking door. Whoever took her will obviously come back for her. I see three break points in this apartment. It can't be secured. We can't just leave her here. There is a high chance they'll come back for her. She isn't safe here." My head starts to spin, I can feel my heartbeat in my ear. We can't leave her here. Not a fucking chance.

Tor remains silent, scanning the apartment.

"Tor, you can't be fucking serious." Blade's a minute, maybe two tops, away from fully losing his temper. His hand is already on his knife. "She isn't our problem. We have enough problems as it is." He turns on Kai. "I swear to god, I should have fucking killed you when I had the chance. Worst omission I've ever made in my entire life."

"Now's as good a time as any," she retorts back defiantly, puffing her chest and stepping up to him, "or are you all talk?"

Blade makes a move toward Kai and is stopped in his tracks when Tor simply places his hand on his chest pushing him back. "Down boy." Tor laughs. Blade looks like he is about to defy Tor for a moment before he breaks out into a smile.

"I'm just happy to be rid of the cunt, let's go," Blade replies with a hint of excitement in his voice.

I look to Tor, but don't miss out of the corner of my eyes that Kai's walked deeper into her apartment. She carefully navigates around destroyed chair legs and cautiously steps over the broken pieces of a Himalayan salt lamp strewn on the floor. She's completely ignoring the fact that the three of us are in her war zone of a home discussing her fate as if she doesn't have a say in the matter.

Tor's command pulls me out of my head. "Kai, pack a bag. Until we figure out who kidnapped you and is fucking with our business, you're staying with us. Spider's right, if you're what they want, you're our best lead, and this place is far from safe."

Blade huffs so loudly it's almost hard to hear Kai's reply.

"You said it yourself, I get in the way. I'm okay here, thanks," Kai yells back from a back room.

"Kai, it wasn't a request. Pack a bag or we'll pack one for you. Actually, we'll just make do with the stuff Mia put together for you. Let's go, we have places to be."

Kai walks back into the living room in leather pants, a ripped-up Ice Nine Kills t-shirt, and a leather jacket with metal studs on it. She looked beautiful in that sweater dress, but fuck if she doesn't look delicious right now. Her hair is pulled up into a high ponytail at the crown of her head, her hands are covered in rings, a leather metal bracelet adorns her wrist and she has on a new necklace, one with a slightly larger pendant than the one she was wearing at the house. Her ankle boots clack on the vinyl flooring as she walks back toward us in the hallway.

I can't even begin to fathom how she changed so fast.

"I said, I'm okay." Her shoulders constrict in annoyance. "Look, I appreciate you guys breaking me out of there. I appreciate you putting me up for a couple of days, and even the Doc for patching me up. But I'm good. Let's not pretend we're anything more than strangers who briefly crossed paths. My train wreck of a place isn't your problem. My safety isn't your problem. Just like Blade said. I am not your problem, so thanks for the phone. And for the ride. You can give those clothes back to Mia. I'm good. I got it from here." Her voice seems grittier than it did before. It has more bite and authority to it than I am used to.

"See, we're good, let's—" Blade starts, but Tor cuts him off mid-sentence by shoving Kai into the wall by the chest.

From where I stand, I can just barely see the hesitation in his eyes, and I see the moment his father's voice starts playing in his head, shutting it down. Pushing him to be someone different.

"And I said, this isn't a request," he says through gritted teeth. "Right now our best chance at finding out who these people are is you, and Spider's right, this place is not securable. They kidnapped you. It's safe to say, whatever they wanted, they still want. They will come for you. And I intend to be there when they do."

Kai tries futilely to push herself away from the wall as Tor towers over her. He slides his hand up to her throat and pins her against the wall, stepping forward. As soon as she opens her mouth to speak, his face is within inches of her mouth, his thigh pressed between her legs, holding her in place.

"The next words out of your mouth better be 'let me get my things' otherwise I'll be the one that ties you up and drags you out of your apartment this time."

Her chest rises and falls rapidly as she stares him down contumaciously.

"How dare..." she starts, but before she can finish her

sentence, Tor dips his head down and bites her. His right eye twitches at the sight of a drop of blood on her lip, but he quickly steels himself and pulls his head back.

"I'm sorry. I didn't catch that. Were you about to say, 'let me get my things?'"

She licks off the trickle of blood that beads on her lower lip and takes in a deep breath. She stares him down like a tiger ready to pounce.

"We can either do this with you coming willingly, or we can get rope. You choose, Midnight."

"Fu—"

"Blade, get the rope from the car," Tor orders.

"Fuck yeah, finally she gets what her attitude has been begging for." Blade smiles darkly as he turns to acquiesce to Tor's order.

Kai stares him down, gulps in a deep breath, and grits out, "Let me get my things." The grainy, guttural way the words escape her makes it clear this isn't going to be a pleasant experience.

"Good girl." Tor releases her throat and backs away, grabbing his phone from his pocket to shoot off a text. He turns his back to her. Kai doesn't know him, so she probably thinks he doesn't give a shit.

But if she knew him like I did, she'd know his back is to her right now because he can't look at what he just did. The boy who nurtured little animals as a kid and loved with the intensity of a soulful poet is buried in there somewhere, rendered deaf and mute by the Don's cruelty and rage. I miss him.

The smile on Blade's face is unnerving. As if a sinister level of pleasure was evoked by watching her squirm in Tor's hold.

She disappears into the back room again.

I turn to Tor. "This isn't how we should be doing this."

"We get it, you want to keep her happy. But I don't have time for her shit. We take her willingly or by force. She remains our best lead, and will make great bait."

"Bait?" I don't like the sound of that one bit. Tor has a wild look in his eyes and I'm pretty sure whatever comes next I'm going to hate.

"Crack the phone, Spider, don't worry about the rest," Tor says in a strained voice.

His father texted something. I'm sure of it. I know Tor and this is not him.

Kai emerges with a black leather duffle bag. I notice she's put a case on her phone; she must have had one laying around in her place. Without uttering a word, she stalks past Tor, Blade, and me, shoulder swiping Tor on the way out, and stomps down the stairs.

THE RIDE to the compound is silent. The air in the SUV feels heavy, laced with an undertone of animosity. The sun below the skyline but not yet really setting, making the whole city look hazy and dream-like.

The engine shuts off, but we're not at home.

I look at Tor in the driver seat as he turns to Kai and says drily, "Do I need to have Blade tie you up, or will you stay in the car without a fuss?"

Kai glares at him. If looks could kill, the bullet wound in his gut would look like a paper cut in comparison. She turns away from us and stares out the window.

"Activate the child locks when you exit, Spider."

I'll reluctantly obey, but I wait for Blade and Tor to

make their exit before I turn to her. "I'm sorry, sweetheart. I didn't mean for—"

"I'm not your sweetheart. I'm your fucking captive. You guys didn't 'rescue' me. I traded one set of kidnappers for another. Run along now, your master is waiting for you, don't forget to activate those child locks or daddy Tor will sic Blade on you." She never turns to look at me.

She's right.

I hang my head and slide out of the car. The fountain plashes, drowning out the sounds of the city beyond the estate's gates. Bloody hell, how did we get here? Not just this fucking house, but the whole mess. I can still smell her on me as if I'm nuzzled into her neck. I need this week to give us a fucking break.

We all trudge into the Amato residence and march straight to Signor Amato's office.

There is that fucking Persian rug again. Somehow I feel even filthier than usual stepping on it.

"What took you so long?" he bellows from behind his desk. "Did you not get my message?"

I knew it.

The bellowing alone almost makes me freeze. He never yells. Never has to. A real monster rarely needs to roar to be horrifying.

"We found a girl." Tor's tone is clipped. "She was kidnapped by whoever the fuck disrupted the drop. I'm thinking we take her to the Lotus. I can smooth things over with the Yakuza, rearrange the shipment, and let whoever is involved know we have her all in one move. If they'll have eyes anywhere, it's there. I want to use her as bait to draw them out."

I'll never get over the jarring juxtaposition between the commanding, in control, bullheaded fuck we interact with on a daily basis and the nervous kid that hesitates, speaking faster than usual, fidgeting his fingers at his side, and shifting back and forth when he opens his mouth around his father.

Don Amato takes in his son for a moment. Looks to Blade—who nods curtly—before he speaks. "Do it and keep me posted. Blade, Spider, stay, I have something else for you two. I assume you can handle this alone, Tor?"

"Yes, Father."

I want to tell him to keep her safe. I want to tell him not to do this. I want to go back to last night when I was buried inside her, or even to this morning when she was in my arms. Instead, I watch him exit.

I fail to hide a sigh as I turn to the Don to await our next set of marching orders.

CHAPTER 13

KAI

I scope out as much as I can from my metal prison. I've already sifted through the center console. At least I know they keep a piece in there; I file that information away for future reference. I can't climb over to the front cause the stupid cage they have there is blocking the way; I only managed to reach under it to conduct my search. Years of training and I'm conquered by fucking child safety locks. Christ, that fountain is gaudy as shit. It's like an Italian imposter vomited classless opulence onto the oversized circular driveway. I thought the boys' place was huge, but this place is a fortress. Surveillance cameras are visible at every turn. The spiked metal fence surrounding the compound is ten feet high with bushes obstructing the view from the outside. Trees provide overhead cover, I assume as protection from any kind of aerial surveillance. I count eight guards armed to the teeth on patrol and that's just what I can see. There is no way in here without an invitation.

Fuck, I'm melting in here. Sweat and leather don't fucking mix; I sound like a squeegee every time I make any slight movement. Even if they do see me as a pet, these fuckers must know they're not supposed to leave a pet in the car unattended on a hot day. How long do I have to wait here? And how the fuck am I going to get away from these dicks? My stream of thoughts is interrupted by my phone's vibrations. It's Han, replying to the text I sent off the second they left me alone.

HAN:

What do you mean they're holding you captive? We staged the apartment, you said you were taking them there after you missed the first extraction. I sent Ren there to pick you up, he's starting to feel like you're standing him up on purpose.

KAI:

I did, apartment looked great by the way, I can't believe you pulled that off so quickly, and thanks for the go bag. Apparently Tor isn't just daddy's little bitch. Fucker grew a pair and decided I stay with them til they figure out who was behind the warehouse, who was at Sarbar.

HAN:

That can't happen wtf. Should I send in a team to extract you with force?

KAI:

No. They don't know anything, right now these dumb fucks think I'll make good bait. Let's see how this plays out. May learn a thing or two. Find anything on your end?

HAN:

Not yet, I'll give it to him, he's good.

KAI:

Please don't tell me it's another dead end. I can't take another disappointment.

HAN:

Relax. I'm better. I'll let you know when I have something. I don't like this. Let me send in a team.

KAI:

I'll be fine. Focus. We're close. I can feel it.

HAN:

Ok boss. But the minute shit feels off, sound the alarm. I have a team on standby. You've done enough, don't be fucking stubborn to the point where you get yourself killed.

KAI:

I love you too.

Tor opens my door and I scramble to open the bubble game on my phone.

I should have been paying attention. Of course their pimped-out SUV is soundproof.

"Didn't take you for a recreational game player." He smirks.

"Didn't take you for a kidnapper, I guess we're all full of surprises aren't we."

He grabs me by the shoulder and directs me out of the car. "Hop up front. I'm no one's chauffeur. I need to make a stop. You're coming with me."

I reluctantly walk toward the passenger side door and get in. "Where's Spider and your leashed serial killer? Let me guess, he's safely tucked away in his kennel."

Tor fights a losing battle to let out a laugh, his shoulders raised, before gathering himself.

"Don't worry about them. Buckle up."

"Is this the part where I'm supposed to get Stockholm Syndrome and fall in love with you cause you care about my safety enough to make sure I have on my seatbelt," I say, sarcasm seeping through the harsh undertones of my voice.

"No, this is the part where I don't want to listen to the stupid fucking *ding ding ding* of the seatbelt sensor. Shut up and do it."

By the time we arrive at the venue, the sun is set. We're parked in a two-story parking garage across the street looking down at the spot, a full view beneath us. The neon pink sign hanging on a pole above the pitch-black building reads Lotus Lounge. It seems unassuming enough. The microphone art plastered on the front of the building signifies it's a karaoke spot, though we're far enough away and above the place that I can't actually read the fine print of the signage. Which is fine because I don't need to.

At first glance it looks like a wholesome establishment, but I know what this place really is. A car arrives immediately after an identical one has just pulled away. Beautiful young women in their early twenties load out of it like it's a clown car. A runway of lingerie ranging from traditionally seductive to the latest sexy anime-inspired Moeflavor fit. Passersby see the harmless karaoke lounge front. The reality of the brothel catwalks by in full view from the elevated vantage point of our parked car.

Tor shuts the car off and turns to me.

I lean back in the passenger seat, arms crossed, while Tor taps his fingers impatiently against the steering wheel. The low glow from the karaoke bar's towering neon sign spills through the fogged glass, casting a soft pink hue over us both.

"You're staying here," Tor says, his tone clipped and no-nonsense.

I arch a brow, watching him out of the corner of my eye. "Oh? And if I don't?"

Tor's gaze slides to me slowly, holding for a beat too long. "You will."

A part of me wants to listen to him. That's the problem. There is something about the way he says it, like it wasn't just about right now. It's like he knows I want to do what he says. Not because he demands it, but because of the hesitation in his demands. His voice asserts a commanding and dominant tone, but his eyes plead. It's the pleading that makes me want to do whatever he asks.

And I swear he somehow senses that. I shift, suddenly too warm despite the evening chill seeping in from outside. The air feels too thick, the blood traveling through my veins too present.

"I'm not gonna cause trouble," I offer, letting my lips tug into the hint of a smirk. "I'm just bored. You're keeping me against my will, at least let me have a little fun. What is this place anyway?" The Yakuza stronghold obviously. Uncle Satō's base of operations, because unlike dad, he has no self-control when it comes to women, and no concept of the notion of love. Dad's base revolved around family and food. Uncle Satō's base revolves around power and sin.

Tor runs his thumb along his jaw, ignoring my bait. "You almost got shot last time."

I roll my eyes, stretching out my legs in the passenger seat. My knee brushes his thigh just enough to be noticeable. "Keyword: almost. Plus this is a lounge."

"And the other one was a club. Your point?"

"It was an abandoned club. This looks like a fun, vibrant place. Let me come with you. I've had a rough week."

His grip on the steering wheel tightens. "Stay in the car."

"You're no fun."

"Kai, I mean it. Stay here."

My gaze lingers on him as he swings the door open and steps out. I wait for him to be in the stairwell of the parking garage before I get out and quietly shove the car door closed. I step to the edge and peer down at the street beneath.

The rain that's beginning to fall catches in his dark hair, dripping down the collar of his jacket, as I see him emerge across the street toward the lounge.

For a brief moment, I almost do what I was told. Keyword: almost.

The moment Tor disappears through the entrance, I follow behind him. The raindrops feel soothing on my skin as I emerge from the shelter of the parking garage. Goosebumps form on my skin but quickly disappear as I yank open the door to the lounge. I wonder if anyone will recognize me. I almost hope they do.

Keyword: almost.

Lotus Lounge is a karaoke bar that's been a staple in this neighborhood for almost thirty years. It's a collection of private rooms of varying sizes filled with seedy men, insanely beautiful women at their beck and call, and a steady stream of drugs and alcohol. I've never been here, but I always wanted to come. I loved to sing with mom and dad and I used to beg him to bring me here. I didn't understand at the time why he kept insisting this wasn't a place for me. How could a place where I can belt out my favorite cartoon songs not be a place for me? It's a shame not to make a little girl's dream come true.

Inside the karaoke bar, the air is thick with cigarette

smoke and off-key singing muffled by the glass doors that lead into each private booth. A burly man in a half-buttoned silk shirt sways dangerously in the room in front of me, belting out a screeching rendition of some old ballad that I can't quite place. Several other Yakuza members sit around, clapping with varying levels of enthusiasm while scantily clad girls wrap around them dotingly. The man in the corner is waving a lighter in mock tribute.

This is even better than I could have imagined.

Hushed conversations take place in the dark corners of the lounge. In the room to my left, no one is singing. The men appear to be having an intense conversation. I fucking hope it's about the weapons shipment my crew confiscated. I wouldn't be able to carry on a conversation in here. Too many distractions in such a tiny space. Maybe I'm outmatched. I laugh to myself. They wish.

I keep to the shadows as I creep along the edge of the room. This is new for me. I have no plan. I always have a plan. Guess there's a first time for everything. I have this nagging feeling that whatever Tor is up to, I don't want to miss it.

Tor slides into a private room at the far end of the lounge. I creep up close and find him deep in conversation with a tall, thin man wearing too many rings. I play with the collection on my own hands; I guess I'm not one to judge. The conversation seems tense, hands gesturing sharply between them. I stay out of earshot but close enough to catch Tor's occasional glances toward the wall, the direction of the parking garage, as if he is trying to see to the other side of it, to where I am supposed to be.

I stalk closer. And I see him.

Uncle Satō. My entire body freezes as I stare at him through the glass.

Does he recognize me?

That's when things go sideways.

I feel the hand on my shoulder before I see him. My pulse quickens. Fuck, my ass is getting rusty. A stocky man with a tattoo snaking up his neck hovers over me. Fuck. Ken. Uncle Satō's right hand.

Fuck, fuck, fuck.

Well, I guess now is as good a time as any. *Recognize me, you fuck.* If he's going to be the reason I have a womb tattoo that covers up the mark, at least he could have the decency to recognize me.

"Lost, girlie?"

I shift slightly, offering an easy grin. "Just here for the show. May even put in my name for 'Bohemian Rhapsody'."

His grip tightens. "This show's not for you."

What the fuck? Nothing? I stare directly into his eyes. Not even a single ounce of recognition.

"I didn't realize karaoke night came with attempted assault on both my shoulder and my eardrums."

Tor's head snaps toward us, as if he senses something is wrong. Good instincts.

I can see the way his posture stiffens despite the door to the private room standing between us. Ken pulls me closer, clearly trying to make a point, but my elbow is already moving before anyone can intervene. The crack of it connecting with his ribs reverberates through the room.

"Oh, she's got bite," one of the Yakuza men laughs. A shorter man in glasses. I recognize him; Hiro, a low-level guy, not sure where he is in the ranks now. I wonder if he remembers me. I stare him straight in the eyes, hoping for even a hint of recognition.

I am that fucking forgettable. For fuck's sake.

I twist free just in time for Ken to swing. His knuckles catch my cheek, sending me staggering backward. Oh fuck no. This slime ball is not about to leave another fucking mark on me. I see red, and go to swing but before I make contact, I am shoved aside.

I look up and see Tor, there before I can even recover from the hit. One punch, two punches, by the time I blink, that piece of shit Ken is groaning on the floor. Tor looms over him for a second longer, just to be sure he won't get up. I like the fucking view but I'm pissed as shit he took my moment away from me.

"I told you to stay in the car," Tor says without looking at me, yanking me toward the exit by the arm.

As annoyed as I am, it's kind of sweet, him jumping in to save me like that.

I wipe my mouth, feeling the sting as I brush along my lip. Great, first it's this asshole's bite mark, and now a split lip. "I really should have. I was prepared for violence, not an emotionally scarring rendition of 'Total Eclipse of the Heart'."

The intro for that old *Titanic* song plays in the background from one of the rooms. Tor shakes his head as he pulls me out and toward the parking garage across the street. Rain still drizzles down, and the stairwell of the garage smells of wet concrete. His legs are way longer than mine. I have to double my paces to keep up. Our footsteps echo in the cavernous garage space; his grip tightens and his speed quickens as I try to yank free.

Tor doesn't stop dragging me at full speed until we reach the car. He slams his palms down on the hood, breathing hard, rain dripping from his hair.

I lean beside him on the nearby pillar, watching as he presses both hands to the metal. "You know," I say, unable to stop myself, "I was really hoping to hear your version of Ariana Grande's 'pov'."

Tor doesn't even look at me. "I'm about to throw you back in there."

I laugh, rubbing my bruised cheek. "Nah, just kill me. I'd rather die than hear one of those men try to tackle 'My Heart Will Go On'."

Tor scrunches his lower face in a way that is clear he's fighting a laugh as his phone buzzes; he's standing close enough to the car that the metal reverberates, interrupting whatever chastisement I am sure was headed my way.

The laughter he was fighting with all the strength he could muster finally erupts as he fishes his phone out of his pocket.

Then comes to an abrupt halt as he views the incoming message.

The mood completely shifts.

CHAPTER 14

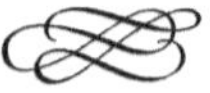

TOR

My father's text stops me in my tracks.

DON:

> I sent you to diffuse the situation and you
> started a fight with Satō's main man? Do I
> need to put the girl down like Duke? Don't
> touch anything else, I'll send Blade to
> clean up your mess.

I'm not remotely surprised; after all, Blade is his golden boy. I'm certain he wishes Blade was his real son. The asshole is implying I'm getting soft again. No matter what I do, I can never do anything right in his eyes. I will forever be his only failure. The obviously incapable son. The disappointment. The weak, pathetic, excuse for a man.

Kai and I are bathed in weak yellow safety light, our breathing ragged from the chaos we just escaped. The tension from the fight at the karaoke bar lingers between us like static electricity, and adrenaline still pulses beneath my skin.

My chest feels tight, pulse hammering in my ears. I keep

stealing glances at Kai, my eyes flicking between the angry bruise forming on her cheek and the wild determination in her eyes. She manages to look both fragile and fierce. She didn't listen to me; I don't think she ever will.

The memory of the Yakuza men surrounding her in the lounge burns in my mind. My body had moved of its own volition, pushing through them and rushing in to shield her. Even now, my hands tremble at the memory of her cornered. She'd nearly gotten herself killed. Again. And for what? To prove she could handle it alone. To be defiant for defiance's sake.

"You never listen, do you?" My voice comes out as a low growl, rougher than I intended, but I don't try to soften it. Anger simmers beneath the surface, tangled with something darker, something I can't name. "I told you not to go in there, Kai. I told you to stay in the car. You almost got yourself killed."

Kai tilts her head, her eyes narrowing before her lips curve into the faintest hint of a smirk. Defiant. Unbothered. Infuriating. She's just one more thing added to my life that I can't control. "I had it under control," she murmurs, but the flicker of uncertainty in her eyes betrays her. She always seems to have something to prove. Seemingly to herself, but it appears even to me.

I take a step forward, towering over her, fists clenching at my sides. The space between us feels too narrow, too charged. My heart continues to pound against my ribs. I want to shake her, pull her against me, or maybe kiss her, and remind her just how fragile she really is. I want her to *obey* me. To see me as the one who can keep her safe. I want it to feel like I can do something right. I want to feel like— for once in my fucking life—I have things under control.

"You think you're tough?" I breathe, voice dropping

further. I don't miss the way her chest rises sharply, the slight hitch in her breath. "You're not. And you sure as hell aren't invincible. You can't take on the world by yourself and come out unscathed."

Kai doesn't flinch, her pupils dark and wide. I can see the thrum of adrenaline is still running through her veins, too. The words hang in the air between us, thick with unspoken truths.

I move in, pinning her back against the cold concrete pillar behind her, bracing a hand beside her head. Her scent tangles with the faint metallic trace of blood and rain.

"You scared me, Kai," I murmur, the words burning on my tongue. "That's the second time you've thrown yourself into danger despite me trying to keep you out of it. It makes me fucking crazy. It's like you don't give a damn about what happens to you. You think I can watch that and feel nothing? You think I want to?"

She doesn't answer, but she doesn't look away either. Her hands drift to my chest, fingertips barely brushing the fabric of my shirt, sending heat rolling through me. For a moment, everything else fades away, the blood on her lip and on my knuckles, the fight, the chaos, and it's just us, standing there in the quiet garage, listening to the patter of rain on the asphalt below.

"I don't need you to save me, Tor," she says softly. Her fingers trace the line of my jaw, lingering there as if she wants to memorize the shape of me. "I can take care of myself. I always have. But that doesn't mean it isn't nice that you're here."

My breath catches; I like the way her fingers feel on my skin. I want to believe her. But the fear of almost losing her back there coils tight in my gut. I cover her hand with mine, squeezing gently. I brush my thumb over the soft skin of her wrist.

"I know you can take care of yourself," I rasp, pulling her closer by the waist, her body molding to mine. "But that doesn't mean you have to. You have no idea where you were just now. They could have... I don't want to lose you to those assholes."

Her breath hitches again, sharper this time. The weight of those words shifts the energy between us into something else, something intoxicating. Dangerous. Her lips brush my ear and she whispers, "Then don't lose me."

My body reacts before my mind can catch up. I need her. I need to feel her, to know she is alive, that she is safe, that she is still here with me. Everything I have ever been in awe of has been taken from me. I don't want anyone to take her. But I also want to punish her for being so fucking reckless. Kai is slowly etching her way into my being, becoming a weakness I can't afford. But whatever I care about ends up destroyed. I can't let myself care about her. I go to pull back.

Her fingers brush the back of my neck, stopping me. Her touch is light but electrifying. She knows what she is doing. She knows the effect she is having on me. But she doesn't pull away. Instead, she leans in, her lips brushing against mine in a kiss that is both tender and hungry.

I groan, my body pushing against hers, and for a moment, everything is forgotten. All the danger, the fear, the anger. It is all just background noise to the overwhelming pull between us.

As the kiss deepens, reality hits. We are still in the parking garage. We are still caught in a world of violence and chaos, and we can't afford to be distracted. I can't afford to have any affection towards her. It will sign her death certificate. I pull away again, breathless, my forehead resting against hers.

"We need to get out of here," I say, my voice rough. "Now."

Kai nods, but she doesn't let go of me. "I know." She tightens her hold.

I grab the back of her neck, tilting her head so she has no choice but to look up at me. I fully intend to demand that she get in the car. It's right there, waiting to be said. After a beat, though, I can't stop myself.

"Get on your knees." The command rolls off my tongue, heavier than I expected. I shrug off my jacket, folding it neatly on the ground beneath her, as if this moment demands reverence.

Her eyes flicker, but she doesn't hesitate. She kneels in front of me as if waiting for communion. I'm not sure if I manage to mask the pure shock from displaying on my face when she complies. The sight of her below me makes my breath catch. She looks up, sparkling midnight eyes locked on mine, waiting.

I unzip my pants, freeing the aching hardness that presses uncomfortably against the fabric.

She leans in, tongue flicking out to taste the precum already leaking from me. One slow, deliberate lick, her eyes fluttering closed as she does so.

My hands sink into her hair, guiding her closer. She takes me in deeper, her lips wrapping around me like silk. The heat of her mouth, the pressure, sends a shiver down my spine.

I let her work me for a moment, savoring the way her tongue moves, the way she hollows her cheeks as she takes me in and out of her mouth. She swallows my dick down so deep into her throat I know she can't breathe, but I can't stop her. Not while the movements of her mouth and tongue transcend me to an ethereal realm of bliss.

But this isn't her show. She needs to learn to surrender. And I need control like I need air. I fist her hair, pulling her off me just enough to force her gaze upward. "Look at me." I wait for her gaze to lock with mine. She looks fucking magnificent staring up at me, lips already swollen. "If it gets to be too much, tap my thigh twice."

She nods, eyes never leaving mine.

"Use your words, Midnight. I need to hear you say it." My grip tightens, not enough to hurt, but enough to remind her who is in charge.

"I understand," she says, voice hushed but certain. Heat floods through my veins at the sound of her submission.

I drive my cock into her mouth, deeper this time. I hold the back of her head to prevent her from slamming into the pillar with the force of my strokes. Her throat tightens around me, the soft gurgling sounds escaping her making me shudder. She desperately claws at my thighs, nails digging in to gain any purchase she can, but she doesn't tap for me to stop. Tears gather at the corners of her eyes, sliding down to mix with her mascara and the faint smear of blood on her cheek.

The sight makes me snap. I fuck into her mouth harder, hips rolling mercilessly, driven by the frustration and fear still simmering in my veins. The tears, the bruise, the reckless way she'd thrown herself into danger, I need her to feel this. To know what she did to me.

Her fingers dig deeper, but she takes it. All of it. Without any of her usual defiance. Without even a hint of protest. The way she remains malleable for me, the way she surrenders to my every movement pushes me over the edge.

My release hits hard, spilling into her mouth and down

her throat as I groan her name into the dimly lit space. "Kai." When I finally ease back, she opens her mouth, tongue flicking out to show me the mess I've left behind. Pride swells in my chest, primal and possessive. The sight almost makes my knees buckle. She looks so fucking hot with my cum covering her mouth. The way she fucking displays it for me... fuck.

She stares up at me patiently, frozen, waiting for permission. For the first moment ever in my entire life, I am in complete control. I have complete submission. The high is beyond intoxicating. Like nothing I have ever felt before. I never want to stop feeling this feeling. I want to thank her. I want to shower her with everything she wants. I want to protect her. Fuck, I will do anything she wants me to do, whenever she wants me to do it, as long as she always makes me feel like this.

"Please swallow," I whisper. She obeys instantly. *Fuuuc-cckkk.* Whatever you want, Kai. Fuck.

Still cupping her face, I lean down and kiss her gently, savoring the taste of her lips. "Good girl," I murmur. "You did so fucking good for me."

She smiles, wiping her mouth with the back of her hand as I help her up. I stuff myself back into my pants, then grab my jacket and throw it around her shoulders. I lean in and kiss her one more time before walking around the car. Well, fuck, that just happened.

"Come on. We need to get out of here." I open the passenger door, but she pauses, that familiar spark of defiance back in her eyes that are glittering with mischief.

"Awe, come on, can't we go back and put in our names for 'Mr. Brightside'?" Amusement dances in her eyes.

I chuckle, shaking my head. "Not a chance, Midnight."

My elation disappears the minute I see another text

from my father. I knew she wouldn't listen. I knew she'd come in after me. I knew whoever took her in the first place would see her and know we have her. Everything went mostly according to plan—except for the fight. Even my father's disappointment was predictable. But his text still creates a pit of fear in my stomach. Duke flashes before my eyes.

DON:

Manor, now. Bring the girl.

CHAPTER 15

KAI

As we pull into the compound, the weight in his silence and the stiffness in his muscles are clear, unspoken signals that the energy between us has completely shifted, and not in a good way. At least with Spider I could give myself a reason as to why what happened, happened. Kind of. But what the fuck is this? Maybe Han's right; maybe I do need to get out of here. I'm making an already messy situation even messier. Tor hasn't spoken a word the entire ride. He hasn't once acknowledged my existence. Just gripped the steering wheel with white-knuckle focus, his jaw muscles working furiously the entire time.

The look in his eyes in that parking garage was impossible to ignore. Gentle, sweet, and full of more of that pleading. Begging for someone to notice him, to see him, to understand him. As if screaming, 'I fucking care, so much, but I can't afford to'. His words never seem to match his eyes.

Fuck me, what am I even talking about? He's the Don's heir. And my life isn't a fucking fairytale. I have no idea

"

what just happened, but I am the one who can't afford to think about it. I must be fucking projecting. I'm fucking my way through the enemy's ranks and I still don't have what we need to finish what I started. I may as well hop on Blade to complete the circuit. I fight back the laugh; yeah, I'll do that when hell freezes over. The only thing I'd fuck Blade with is a knife. A little chuckle escapes me and I stifle it. I look over to Tor, to see if he'll ask what I'm laughing about. But still nothing. It's like I am not even here. Now that we're parked, though, I know I can expect a few words from him. He'll tell me to 'stay in the car' in three... two...

"Let's go, they're expecting us inside."

"What the fuck?" I whisper to myself. I grab my phone to shoot off a text to Han.

"Now, Kai." Tor's voice startles me. I get out of the car and walk as slowly as I can, typing as I go.

KAI:

At compound. Taking me inside.

HAN:

No. We're coming to get you.

KAI:

Stand down.

"There a problem?" Tor asks as he ushers me toward the castle doors.

"No, just checking in with friends. They haven't heard from me in a while, don't want them to worry," I reply.

"They should," he mutters under his breath. That's not all that comforting.

"What was that?"

"Nothing, this way." He gestures with his hand down a long, gold adorned hallway. Jesus, it's so fucking gaudy; it's somehow even worse than the monstrosity of a fountain outside. No wonder my father despised the guy. The excessive opulence screams 'I'm an asshole with a micro-penis.'

A chill runs up my spine as we step onto the plush Persian rug in the office of Signor Amato. No amount of studying him could prepare me for the vile taste in my mouth upon laying eyes on him. I'm still not certain it's him I'm after, but the hate coursing through my veins is pointing in that direction. I let my eyes flick around the room, identifying the men Amato keeps close, and I realize Blade is here, too. I probably should have listened to Han; but listening isn't something I'm capable of. Han's right; my stubbornness is going to get me killed one day. Hopefully, it's not today.

"So, you're the mystery girl at the center of my troubles." The Don's gaze runs up and down the length of me, causing bile to rise up in my throat. Fucking disgusting. I know his type. Had run ins with quite a few in my father's clan. He's the kind of guy you never want to be alone with in a room. The kind that feels entitled to a woman's body as if she was placed on this earth to cater to his every whim.

I don't respond. I'm pretty sure the question was rhetorical anyway. His demeanor, his gaze, his energy screams 'I take what I want regardless, everything belongs to me.' I fight back the urge to charge toward his desk and gouge his eyes out with my knife. *Get your disgusting stare off of me, you slimy piece of shit.*

"So tell me," he continues, a sneer snaking across his face, "why were you deemed worthy of kidnapping by the men that dared fuck with my business?"

'Deemed worthy of kidnapping.' Fucking asshole. As if it was because they thought I was cute. "I don't know. The first thing I saw after coming to was your injured son. I didn't have time to ask questions."

The look on his face tells me I likely failed hiding the disdain in my voice.

"I see. Who blemished your pretty face? Was that my boy?"

"No, Father. One of the men at the Lotus attacked her. The man I hit—" Tor is cut off by the Don's sharp, condescending tone.

"I'm not talking to you, son. I'm asking your little friend." He almost looks disappointed to learn it wasn't Tor who did this.

I can't stop the sarcasm from flying out of my mouth. "Likely the man who inspired the Titanic to sink with just the sound of his voice." Fuck. I feel his eyes slowly turn back to me and I force myself to not break eye contact. Fuck, fuck, fuck. He does not like sarcasm.

"Like I said, she's useless, knows nothing, and needs to be put down."

Thanks, Blade, I love you, too. Asshole.

"Tor, can you handle babysitting duty, or is that also beyond your meager capabilities?"

The way Tor deflates, his head slightly lowering, makes my heart swell, defensiveness swirling inside me. I don't like that shit at all.

"Yes, Father."

"Blade will take over from here. I'm putting him in charge. As of today, you report to him. Do you understand me?"

"Yes, Father."

"Blade and I have discussed his plan. It sounds promising. It will require your little house guest. Keep her in line until her presence is required."

I look from one man to another, confirming that they're just going to talk about me like I'm not in the room, or a person with autonomy and free will. *Cool, cool, cool.*

"You're dismissed. Try not to cause any more problems."

It is infinitely unfair that a man like my father is taken from me and this world before I'm even old enough to drive and yet a serpent like this is blessed with the ability to continue to exist. None of us deserve to live. This entire world is meant to be burned to the ground. We destroy everything good then cry about it when it's done, like it wasn't demolished by our own hands. But this guy, whether it was him or not, does not fucking deserve to live. There is no good left in him.

Tor grabs my elbow and leads me out of the room. Blade follows.

I take my place in the backseat and fire off another text to Han.

KAI:

All good, headed back to the wolves' den. Call off the dogs that I know you already put in motion.

HAN:

Fuck, ok. What's the plan?

KAI:

I'm not sure yet, but for now it seems worthwhile to stick around and find out. The Don is at the center of this. I can feel it. Will be in touch.

HAN:

Please for the love of god, don't do anything reckless.

TOO reckless, gotta keep those
expectations realistic.

KAI:

lol I'll be fine. Were you able to track down
the next drop?

HAN:

Not yet, been focused on digging into
Amato's files. Don't worry, we're on it. You
need to know, the ATF is digging too.
There's chatter about new players in town.
Amato and Satō aren't our only problem
now.

KAI:

We can handle it. Keep me posted.

I realize the car hasn't started. When I look up I see Tor staring off into space, motionless. Blade has shifted in the passenger seat to face him.

"Tor, I didn't know—"

"Shut the fuck up," Tor replies cutting him off. "I don't want to hear it. Let's just get home. I need a shower."

Blade deflates. I think this is the first time I've seen that fool display an emotion. His shoulders slump, his eyes lower in the most non-aggressive, submissive state I've ever seen him in. He steals a few glances at Tor every few minutes and looks almost... sad? I can't fucking tell, his expressions are obscured by the alternating shadows and blinding glare shining in from his window from the passing streetlights.

As I squint and struggle to make out what he's feeling in between the shifting glare, I take a deep breath to slow down my heart rate and I stop myself. I'm acting like a dumb cunt, my head is so incredibly far up my own ass. I remind myself that I'm not hanging out with friends. It's none of my business what these guys are fucking feeling. A couple of raw—yet still fleeting—intimate moments and I'm analyzing these fuckers' emotional states like a school-girl with a crush. They are a means to an end. I need to get my head in the goddamn game. I need to think. What is my next move?

This speck of trouble in paradise among these normally tight boys may actually work in my favor. I can work this to my advantage. As I think through potential next moves, the sadness coming off of Tor in his father's office, the look of inadequacy and failure in his eyes keeps replaying in my mind. The man that easily took down a half-dozen of the Yakuza, went verbally toe to toe with me—no small feat, if I say so myself— and then throat fucked me like a champion, that man was nowhere to be found. In his place is a little boy who just appears sad and heartbroken. Like all he wants to be is enough, but he somehow never is.

I steal a glance at Blade again and see that he looks equally as sad. Shit. I'm worrying about them again. What the fuck is wrong with me? I can't give a shit about this. I've stayed too long. These aren't my friends, but my mind is having trouble not blurring that line. Yes, they are three incredibly hot fucking men who any girl could lick from head-to-toe—fuck me man, even in this too-close car and smelling of rain, they are delicious. I need to clear my head and stay on task. I shake my head from side to side as if the physical motion has a chance of tossing all these thoughts out of my stupid brain where I cannot allow them to take up residence.

As we trudge into the mansion, Spider pops up.

"What happened?"

Shit, I don't have time for the awkwardness right now. Fuck, I do not have time for three sad men. Most of it my fault. Jesus fucking Christ. I'm pretty sure I'm the asshole here. I need some air.

"Fuck, who did this to you?" He reaches up to stroke the bruise on my cheek and I pull away. He awkwardly pulls back his hand. "I'm sorry, I didn't mean to touch… I mean, I just. Are you okay?"

"I'm fine. You're my captors, remember?" I raise one eyebrow and keep my voice cool. "Stop pretending like you give a shit. I'm never going to be the Beauty to your fucked up, lacking the best part of the whole deal, like seriously where the fuck are the gifts, you know which ones I mean, Beasts. Just hurry the fuck up and do whatever you need to so I can get out of here and get on with my life." I shoulder check past him, ignoring the pained reaction on his face.

"Stop," Tor yells after me.

I stop in my tracks and turn around. I take a deep breath. Fuck, this is going to hurt him. It doesn't matter. His feelings are not my problem. I suck in one more deep breath. "Should you really be giving orders? I thought that was Blade's territory now."

His brows pull together, first in hurt then in uncontrolled anger. He charges toward me and Spider steps in between us on his path.

"What is she talking about?" Spider places his hand on Tor's chest. "Tor, what is she talking about?"

The question causes Tor to freeze. He looks down at the floor before lifting his head to look Spider in the eye. "Blade's in charge now."

"What?" Spider looks between Tor, Blade, and me.

"I got your text about cracking the phone. Give whatever you found to Blade. Ask whatever you need to of Blade. He's in charge now. I'm going to bed." Tor looks up at me one more time and behind his livid expression, I see it. Pain.

Unfiltered, raw, deeply burning up everything from the inside to the point of consuming all of the remaining oxygen he had left to breath until he's suffocating, pain.

I feel tears begin to well in my eyes so I look away.

Tor storms off toward his room.

Spider turns to Blade, a questioning look on his face.

"I didn't... It wasn't—" While Blade struggles to find his words, I use the distraction to get to my prison cell. At least it has luxury, high thread count sheets. I start the shower and hop in.

Tor's dejected look keeps burning into my mind. I should have kept my fucking mouth shut. Fuck this. I'm leaving, now. I can't be here. I have no idea what they have planned. I don't know what the Don has in mind, and if Blade's the mastermind I can sure as fuck guarantee my safety is nowhere even near to being a consideration.

And I'm about to *cry* because I hurt two of them. I'm weak, and it's embarrassing. Han is right, I can't stay here. I reach out of the shower, grabbing my phone with soaking wet hands.

KAI:

You're right. Arrange an extraction. I'll text when I'm ready to be pulled.

HAN:

What happened?

KAI:

Nothing. I've gotten everything I can here. It's time to put it to good use.

HAN:

Awaiting your go.

I heart the message and place my phone back on the counter. No matter how hard I scrub my skin, I can't seem to get the look on Tor's face out of my mind. The sadness in Spider's.

Now I'm the one that can't breathe, the guilt is overwhelming. My chest feels so tight I place my hand on it to remind myself I'm still capable of breathing. I can't quite place the feeling because I have never felt it before, but I think what I'm experiencing right now is shame. I need to go apologize, and then bolt. I put on a silky royal blue slip brought to me by that boy's annoyingly cheerful lady friend. Still not pajamas, but it's good enough, I guess. I tie the belt of the matching silk robe around my waist before making my way to Tor's room.

I knock gently on the door. No response.

It's cracked slightly open.

I push it a little further and notice him sitting in a tight white shirt that clings to his muscular torso in all the best fucking ways and grey sweatpants. He is on the edge of his bed, head buried in his hands. He hasn't noticed me or looked up. I take a moment to observe him. My heart stutters and leaps into my throat as I realize he's... crying.

I can't... I should leave. I should turn around and leave right now. Yet I don't.

I sneak quietly into the room, bare feet padding across the carpet, and stand in front of him. I cup his hands with mine.

He startles and quickly knocks my hands away. "What the fuck are you doing here?" He clumsily wipes his eyes. "Get the fuck out of my room."

I pull him into me, burying his head in my chest, and stroke the back of his head, smoothing his hair.

His attempts to push me off are half-hearted at best. "Kai, I mean it, get the fuck out." It doesn't come out as a command this time. I'm not even sure he felt like he meant that one.

I place a kiss on the top of his head. I have no idea what the fuck I'm doing. I should listen to him. I should get the fuck out. I can't seem to make myself let go, though.

He remains stiff in my hold, gently pushing me away at the waist. Until he's not. He stops pushing and slowly runs his hands from my pelvic bone up my hips, curling around until he reaches my ass. He relaxes in my hold and pulls me in closer. Sliding up to my back, his arms are wrapped completely around me. He envelops me in one of the best hugs I've been on the receiving end of since I was a child. I run my hand through his hair down to the nape of his neck, and shift his face up to look up at me.

For a second, I see myself in him. We aren't so different. The clawing feeling in the depths of my soul that screams, 'I fought with everything I had and it wasn't enough.' My best—and his best—was and always will be inadequate. No matter how hard we tried, the reality is we failed. When it mattered most. We failed. We will never, ever be good enough.

I don't know what I'm doing, but I do it anyway. I lean down, and place the softest, gentlest, most tender kiss I can on his lips. Rivaling the way he kissed mine in that parking garage.

I try to capture everything I want to say in that kiss.

I'm sorry.

I understand.

I feel this, too. Everyday. It doesn't go away. It won't. It never will. You just learn to live with it. No, you don't, you let it eat every part of you until all you have left to give is anger, frustration, and an insatiable need to distract yourself in whatever way you can. You hope that if you can just do this one thing right, that maybe you'll feel a little better. If you can just achieve this, then maybe you can drown out the voice in your head that screams you can't do anything right.

The way he tastes my lips, the way he repeatedly pecks at them, and just slightly licks them with the tip of his tongue sends tingles down to the tips of my fingers.

It's as if he can hear me, and he's slowly replying back. As if he's saying, 'I know it will never go away. So please, I'm begging you, do the only thing that brings me any peace, even if just temporarily. Help me forget.'

He pulls away and looks at me, brushing a strand of hair behind my ear. I'm not sure what he's looking for from me? Permission? Does he still want me to leave?

"Do you want me?" I ask nervously.

"Yes, desperately," he whispers urgently. His voice low, soft, and undeniably sweeter than I have ever heard it. I lean back down to kiss him, sinking into the taste of him. He pulls me down, wrapping himself around me entirely, and he flips me on the bed onto my back. The weight of his body on mine is comforting. A delicious pressure I yearn for. He rubs his thigh in between my legs, spreading them further apart, and I'm all too eager to comply.

Our mouths crush together in a frenzy of tongue, saliva, and teeth. His hands firmly press against my body, searching frantically for their destination. I pull at his shirt in vain trying to scrape it off him while refusing to separate from his lips. Jesus, if I had those muscles, I'd want to show them off too, but the shirt doesn't need to be so tight that it's impossible to take off.

His fingers find their way under the slip, sliding into my panties. He uses his index and middle finger to spread my lower lips apart. I suck in a deep breath of air. Fuck, his hand feels so good. I decide the shirt can stay for now; I just roll it up so I can run my hands all over him. Up his chest, back down the side of his muscular torso. I feel a sting on my bottom lip where his teeth dig in.

He pulls away from me, his fingers still firmly pressed against my entrance. "You're so wet, baby." He smiles, and it is so fucking charming.

His eyes lock onto mine, smoldering with intent as his middle and ring fingers slide into me at an agonizingly slow pace. A shiver ripples through me, goosebumps rising, as he curls his fingers inside, massaging my most sensitive spot with precision. His touch is soft but unyielding, each stroke deliberate, sending waves of pleasure coursing through me.

He doesn't break eye contact, his gaze pinning me in place as he moves with a relentless rhythm, riling me up until my body teeters on the edge of release. Just when I'm about to shatter, he withdraws, leaving me trembling and empty.

A whimper escapes my lips, my body aching at the loss of him. I want to scream, to beg him, yell, 'please, more,' but the words remain stuck in my throat, lost in the haze of desire. I only manage to muster one more desperate whimper, betraying my need.

His lips curve into a wicked smile as he brings his fingers to his mouth, tasting me, savoring every drop while his eyes never leave mine. That sight alone releases a fresh rush of wetness between my thighs, my body imploring him to fill me.

"This is what I've been craving, but never knew it. The taste of you. I didn't know it was possible to crave something I've never had before. You taste so fucking good... I'll let you taste yourself on my dick later, but for now I'm going to go insane if I don't get to feel all of you."

He bends down to kiss me again and I can already taste myself on his lips. I claw at the elastic waistband of his sweatpants, sliding them past his ass. My hands clamp down on his butt cheeks, squeezing them with all my might. Once my hands can no longer reach his pants, I use my thighs, my calves, my feet, anything I can use to gain purchase to remove them the rest of the way. I can feel his hard on pressing against my entrance, and I wiggle futilely trying to bring him home.

He separates from me.

I swear to fucking god, this guy. But then, I realize he only angled away from me to help me remove his pants for good. I release a moan of relief and he fails to suppress a prideful chuckle in response. It's a beautiful sound, but it also kind of ignites an urge within me to slap him or spank him, or I don't know, but it definitely makes me want to take out my frustration on him in some way. "Don't worry baby, I got you." Ok, maybe not. I like that. *That sounds so good*, spilling from his lips as he smiles down at me with promise in his tone.

As his weight presses back down on me, I feel the tip of his dick nudging at my entrance. When I try to thrust up to take him in, he puts both his hands on my hips and pushes me down into the mattress.

"When are you going to learn, Midnight? I decide what happens and when."

I can feel the retort on the tip of my tongue but an image flashes across my mind: his head hung low, his father chastising him about the problems I caused. And I am silenced.

Instead, I look up at him and reply, "Yes, sir. Whatever you say, sir."

The look on his face makes me quake with desire. Every

agonizing second of allowing those words to depart from my lips was worth it, to feel the rush of desire between my legs.

He plunges into me with such force that we both slightly bounce off of the mattress. I'm so wet that he slides in easier than a freshly made key into a lock. "Fuck, baby."

"Fuck me, sir, please."

He groans his satisfaction at my subservience.

His pace is slow, measured, steady, as if he is relishing in my warmth, like he never wants this to end. I realize I never want it to end; this isn't about his comfort anymore. I *want* to be underneath him, his to command. I can't help it, he feels so fucking good.

I let out a strangled moan. I want more. He picks up his pace slightly. Thrusting into me in a perfectly steady rhythm. I can feel myself pushing up against the edge again. My legs, wrapped around his waist, begin to shake, my breath ragged. Every muscle in my body constricts.

He must be able to tell I'm close because he cups my face, kisses me, stares deeply into my eyes and says, "Fuck yes, baby, cum for me. Cum all over my fucking dick. Use me to make yourself feel good."

"Tor, oh my fucking god, Tor." I cum so fucking hard I have to hold onto his hips to halt his movements. I'm so sensitive that even the slightest shift feels overwhelming. He studies me and stills, realizing what I need from him. As soon as my breathing begins to steady, I smile up at him and he takes that as his cue.

"You like this dick, baby?" He pulls all the way out and slams all the way into me to the hilt. He pauses, as if waiting for me to answer. "You want more?"

He still waits. Oh, so that's not a rhetorical question.

"Yes... sir." My voice is hoarse and my interior clenches involuntarily. "Fill me, baby, I need you."

That does it. He picks up speed and fucks me into the mattress like a man on a mission. His hand snakes up, groping a tit through the flimsy slip I am still sort of wearing, then moving on, sliding around my throat, pushing me firmly into the bed.

The look of pure elation on his face as I feel warm ropes of his cum empty inside of me is devastatingly beautiful. I begin to shudder again. His chest swells with obvious pride as he realizes he is taking me over the edge with him again. He rolls off of me to the side and sits up, staring down between my legs. Watching the mixture of his cum and mine pour from me.

When he finally lays onto his back, I speak. "I thought you were going to let me taste my cum off of your dick."

The look on his face is priceless, equal parts shock and arousal.

I roll onto my knees, straddling his legs, and lick him clean. He twitches beneath my touch, straggling bits of salty cum dribbling onto my tongue. I crawl up the length of his body, licking my lips. I place a kiss on his lips and he drives his tongue into my mouth.

"Fuck, baby, that was..."

"I know," I reply. I move to get up off his bed and go to my own when he grabs my arm and pulls me back toward him.

"Where do you think you're going?"

"To bed."

"It's cute that you think I'm done with you. Get back over here, I'm just getting started."

CHAPTER 16

BLADE

The guest room door to where Kai is staying is wide open, the bed made. It's 5:00 AM, where the hell did that bitch get off to? The idea of her having unfettered access to everything here, roaming around as she pleases in the only calm space I have, builds tension in my shoulders. If these fuckers can't stomach killing her we should at least cut her loose and let the fucks we're chasing finish the job they started. A smile breaks out on my face as I realize it's actually my call, but my momentary joy dissipates when I remember the Don wants me to keep her here until he calls for her.

Fuck, I'm not looking forward to today. Signor shouldn't have put me in charge. I fucking hate people and now he wants me to tell them what to fucking do? People looking to me for answers... this whole situation is fucked. I'm a weapon, not a strategist.

I was just trying to get this shit squared away while Tor was on his little side quest with princess so his father wouldn't yell at him. I royally fucked that up. This was the worst possible outcome. I just wanted to get rid of this fucking girl so I could have my fucking space back.

This house is the only place where I have ever felt peace and that bitch is ruining it with every fucking breath she takes.

Fuck, Tor has always been a little bit of a dick to me, but it has never felt like he hated me. Until now. He really does hate me right now, and I'm not sure I can find it in me to blame him.

After walking through the whole fucking house, I opt for checking Spider's room; she has to be with him. He's probably cuddling with his fucking pet. Spider loves to have something to take care of. I barge in, smiling at the thought of giving her a taste of the ruined peace she's brought upon me. I'm robbed of vindication when I spot the empty bed. He's not in his bedroom and neither is she.

"Where the fuck is everyone?" I mutter to myself.

I storm in the direction of his computer cave. Ah, finally, at least *something* is where it's supposed to be.

"Hey, where's your pet?" I ask.

He looks up from the screen. "Probably asleep." He shrugs. "I decrypted the phone; there isn't much on here, just two texts from Han to someone named Sora."

"She's not asleep in her room or yours."

Spider pushes away from his desk, a storm brewing in his expression.

"What the fuck? Maybe we should have listened to you and chained her to the bed. She's gone?"

Spider pushes past me and stalks down the hall toward Tor's room. I follow, not sure why we need to enlist Tor's help on this. I'm in charge.

I push past Spider at the last second. If we're doing this, we're doing it my way. We bulldoze our way in. "Wake up, bro. She's gone," I bark at a sleeping Tor as I flick the overhead light on.

He stirs and turns from his side onto his back.

That's when I see her. Was he fucking *cuddling* with her?

Jesus fucking Christ. First Spider, now Tor. Is she fucking her way through her captors trying to earn her release? I snort; I guess she is. At least she's resourceful.

"Fuck man, not you, too." I roll my eyes and throw my hands up in the air in defeat.

She stirs and the blanket pulls down slightly, revealing her perky breasts. Fuck. I get that she's hot, but she's also a fucking snake, just like her tattoo. I turn to see the expression on Spider's face as Tor quickly pulls the blanket on her to cover her up. Spider looks like he's trying not to cry or like he wants to punch a wall or maybe both.

"What time is it even?" Tor sounds groggy but furious. "You know what, I don't care, this shit is your problem now, not mine. I don't need to know what time it is. Blade, get the fuck out and go do your job as daddy's new bitch boy."

It takes Spider a second to find his words. The hurt in his eyes is enough to reinvigorate my pressing desire to end her immediately. "I cracked the phone. Just a couple of messages between Han and someone named Sora."

Our mystery guest pops up on the bed, holding the sheet to her chest, her hair tousled. She fumbles around while we all stare at her. She finds Tor's shirt and pulls it over her head.

Tor's eyebrows furrow and he stares at her with a confused look on his face. My shoulders tense; why did she wake up like that? Was it Spider's words?

Spider turns his head away as if seeing her in Tor's clothes is too hard for him to bear.

"What did it say?" she asks.

The three of us snap our heads in her direction in unison. I see her chest rising and falling at a rapid pace. Is she breathing heavy because she got woken up suddenly by big angry men or does this have to do with what Spider just said?

I can see Tor's shoulder muscles tensing from here. At least he notices it too. Spider still looks like an abandoned puppy. For fuck's sake; I'm going to kill her now. Fuck this.

She averts her gaze but storms in our direction. She pushes past Spider and me and makes a beeline for her room. "Never mind, I'll leave you to it."

"Not so fast." I grab the back of Tor's shirt and yank her backwards until her back slams up against my chest. I grab her and flip her around to face me. I glare my hatred directly into her eyes. "Why did you ask? Do you know those names? Han? Sora? Who the fuck are they? Who the fuck are you?" My heart races as I await her answer. One quick flip and I could snap her fucking neck. Blood rushes to my head and I see red. I don't even realize my hand is wrapping around the back of her neck until she contorts under my hold to get away, struggling to breathe.

"Let go of me you, you twisted fuck. I have no clue. *They* kidnapped *me*, remember? I want to know who they are just as much as you do."

If looks could kill, I'd ignite on the spot under her infernal gaze. This bitch sure has murderous fucking eyes.

"Let her go," Spider and Tor demand simultaneously.

I let go of her but she remains rooted in place. "I don't know what kind of witchcraft that pussy of yours is enacting on my boys, but that shit and your beady doe eyes won't work on me. Who's Han? Who is Sora?"

"I don't fucking know." She storms off toward her room

again, and I start to follow her when I feel Spider's hand on my chest pushing me back into the door frame.

"She said she doesn't know. Why would she? They were shooting at her the same way they were shooting at us. And in case you forgot, she covered my ass while we were there, putting herself in danger to protect *me*."

"Yeah, she has a habit of doing that," Tor mumbles under his breath.

"Tor, what are you doing with her?" Spider asks, sadness seeping from the question.

"She's a good fuck," Tor replies nonchalantly.

Spider charges toward him ready to take a swing. Tor puts up his forearms to block the blow while shouting, "What the fuck, Spider? She's just a girl, what are you so bent out of shape about?" Yeah, these two are fucking goners. I guess I get why it's all on me now.

"Fuck this," I say. "You two are clearly pussy drunk. You don't find it strange that she's fucked her way through two-thirds of this house in less than a week? She uses her pussy like a sorceress uses spells, to magically enchant you dumb fucks into a stupor. She's up to something and you two are too busy getting your dicks wet to see it. If you won't help me find out what it is, I'll do it on my own."

Tor pauses his tussle with Spider to mockingly reply, "It's your job now anyway, *boss*."

I throw him my worst glare and then sulk all the way to my room. I fucking hate everything about everything right now.

Fuming, I don one of my god knows how many black tailored luxury Italian designer suits. My hands tremble with fury as I button, zip, tie, and buckle everything into place. I send a text to the team to meet me at a Little Tokyo location. One of Signor's men sent me a tip that this place may have a tie to this new crew.

I can hear Spider knocking around in the kitchen, relying on his rituals, and Tor in the shower as I march to the basement. I guess they're done fighting over that bitch for the moment. I relish the sound of my shoes on the stairs and the concrete floor before I place my fingerprint on a 1980's-looking mirror to reveal my personal weapons stash.

Loaded up with three guns and six knives, I storm out the front door. Maybe I'll have a chance to shoot something today. Get the bitch out of my head.

THE RESTAURANT'S interior is a mix of red lantern lights, the sharp scent of soy sauce, and sake. It's tucked quaintly into a corner of Little Tokyo. The place is packed, bustling with diners laughing, imbibing, and enjoying mouthwatering plates of sashimi.

The air stills when we walk in. I have five of Signor's men with me. We are all black-suited, pressed and polished, more appropriately dressed for a black-tie event than a lunch stop at Sakura Sushi.

Heads turn and conversations hush as we make our way through the dining room toward the kitchen in the back. Servers pause mid-step, their gazes lingering a moment too long. I see the recognition in one of the servers' eyes as he runs toward the back presumably to warn them we are coming.

Good, then I don't need to introduce myself.

I drink in the room with disinterest. If this is the new crew's headquarters, their operation doesn't seem all that impressive, but I know better than to underestimate them. Again. The faintest smirk tugs at the corner of my lips.

Dante turns to me. "Your smile is fucking creepy right now, man. Is there a private joke only you're in on right now?"

I stare at him menacingly until he stammers, "Sorry, boss, I mean... what are our orders?"

"To stay focused and follow my lead," I command.

We slide through the double metal doors into the kitchen, casually occupying the space like kings claiming our throne. I scan the room, my icy gaze sweeping across faces, until I see him.

Near the back, a man with a coiled, dangerous energy stands speaking to a group of men. A dragon tattoo creeps up his neck, partially hidden under his shirt collar, giving him away.

No fucking way. It can't be.

Akira Satō.

I recognize him immediately. The memory of him tousling my hair as he hands Ava a stuffed donkey flashes viscerally in my mind.

Akira Satō is a name that used to be whispered in the criminal underworld like a ghost story. I asked my mother about him after he left that day, years ago. She spoke of him with a mixture of fear and reverence. Akira had been her connection to the Yakuza, the last remaining thread that tethered her to her past life. All she told me was that he was a protector. She told me that if I was ever in trouble, he would be the one I should go to for help, but never let anyone know that I sought him. As if he was both safety and a threat wrapped into one.

Akira hasn't been seen in over a decade. Presumed dead, suspected of being killed alongside the former oyabun. As the oyabun's youngest brother, Akira wasn't his number two, but he was always with him.

My pulse quickens, though I make sure my face remains impassive.

Akira's dark eyes flick toward me, narrowing slightly in recognition.

A silent understanding passes between us. If he was a protector, then he was a terrible one. He failed my mother. And when I needed him, he was nowhere to be found.

He'll pay for that.

"Trouble," I murmur to the men, tilting my head toward Akira's position to convey the location to them. "Stay sharp."

Before I or my crew can react, Akira's men make their move. Swift, calculated, like sharks scenting blood. It starts with words, biting insults exchanged in Japanese and English, but quickly erupts into chaos.

Pans and utensils clatter to the floor, stainless steel overturns as fists and bodies collide. The kitchen is a cacophony of shouts, and shattering plates and glass. The room is filled with the thrum of violence.

I charge Akira, who is standing back, and get separated from my men. My path is blocked when I am cornered in the back hallway by ten of Akira's crew. The narrow space leaves little room for maneuvering, but I thrive in tight spots.

"You should've stayed away," one of the men sneers, brandishing a knife.

Akira ducks out the back door out of my reach.

My lip curls. "You're going to need more men."

They lunge.

The first man goes down with a single strike to the throat. I am liquid fire: precise, brutal, and unrelenting. I dodge a carbon steel frying pan swung at my head, driving my elbow into another man's jaw with a sickening crack.

A blade slices across my side, searing hot pain blooming as blood soaks my shirt. Another catches my shoulder. Well, fuck. Maybe they do have enough men.

And maybe I shouldn't have picked a fight in a room full of easily accessible knives, but I persist. What I have that these dumb fucks don't is that pain is my fuel. I *love* when it hurts. It's the only time I feel alive. I slam one man's head into the wall before using the momentum to drive a knife into another's thigh.

By the time five men are on the floor groaning or unconscious, my vision is blurred. Blood drips from my wounds, pooling at my feet. The remaining attackers circle me like vultures, eager for the kill.

Still, I am faster. I use the narrow space to my advantage, driving one man into the wall with a brutal kick and using his weight to disarm another. Blood coats my hands as I fight tooth and nail, reducing the remaining men to a battered heap.

Panting, I stumble out back, my steps uneven. I need to get the fuck out of here before I pass out. The stench of garbage in this back alley makes me nauseous. My suit is ruined, bloodstained and torn. My men spill out of the restaurant behind me as the driver screeches into the alley. I almost trip over the overflowing black trash bags obstructing the pavement. We practically fall into the SUV and drive off.

At least I got what I came here for. Now we know who we're dealing with.

The distant shouts of the remaining Yakuza sound in the background as the driver backs up and we drive off into Manhattan's streets. A crooked grin tugs at my lips despite the agony. My men trade tidbits of information around me as I focus on not passing out. Blood drips into my eyes and I swallow down bile as the car whips around.

Names are shared, identifying marks described, an inventory of injuries taken.

But I have the most important pieces of information of all: the yakuza are in a civil war and we're caught in the crossfire. The new crew is led by Akira. Fucking finally, we're getting somewhere. I pull out my phone.

BLADE:

Akira Satō was at the restaurant. The new crew is Yakuza, just not the Yakuza we're in business with.

DON:

Good work, son. We'll start running him and his associates down. I'll let you know when we'll need you to move in and make them pay for daring to fuck with what's mine.

BLADE:

Understood

WHEN I WALK into the house, it's quiet. Good. I don't have the energy to deal with Tor's shit right now, or Spider sulking over losing his girl, and I sure as shit don't have any patience for the fucking whore herself.

I drip blood everywhere I go, smearing it on doorknobs as I move around the house. I grab the first aid kit and collapse onto the leather sofa. The cold leather feels good against my heated skin and leather is easy to clean. Easier than rugs—Spider will have a conniption when he sees what my shoes are doing to the rug beneath my feet.

After taking off my suit jacket, tie, and button-up shirt, I take out some gauze to try and treat the oozing gashes on my side and shoulder. I look up when I hear a slight creak in the wooden floorboard.

Kai is standing there in a tight red dress, courtesy of Mia, no doubt, staring at the blood all over my torso.

Fuck, I don't have the energy for her right now.

"What the fuck? What happened to you?" she asks, as if she gives a shit. She's sucking on something—probably one of those sour belts Spider started stocking in our pantry for her. She mentions she likes something once and somehow there's immediately a never-ending supply of them at her disposal. She's probably relishing in the sight of me, ripped and battered suit, covered in blood, cooking grease, and smoke.

"Go away." I struggle to reach the gash on my shoulder.

"For the love of all things holy, you stubborn fuck, give that to me," she demands as she marches over to where I am seated, slowly licking the sour sugar off of her fingers.

Fuck. Why does that look so hot?

I slouch on the couch, my face tight with pain. The makeshift bandages of gauze loosely secured in place by blood around my torso do little to stop the slow seep of my life force. My shirt and suit jacket are both discarded, revealing taut muscles marred with fresh gashes and bruises. The room smells of antiseptic and iron, a reminder of the chaos I just escaped.

Kai stands in front of me, clutching the first aid kit she grabbed from the coffee table. Her expression flickers with reluctance.

"I'm fine," I say, "I can take care of it." I continue to struggle to reach the wound slashing from the top of my arm toward the back of my shoulder.

She ignores me, kneels down beside me and says in a flat voice, "Everyone else is out, so it's just you, me, and this first aid kit. Shut up and let me help you. And try not to bitch or die while I fix you up."

My lip curls into a sneer. "Don't worry. I'd never give you the satisfaction of outliving me. I still plan on killing you as soon as I get the green light from the Don."

Every muscle in her body tenses at the mention of the Don. I was there when they met; yeah, he was a dick, as usual, but that reaction doesn't quite fit their interaction.

She rolls her eyes and leans in, her hands steady as she peels away the soaked gauze.

I flinch, but don't pull away, my gaze boring into her with the intensity of a predator. I may be cornered but I can still snap her neck if necessary.

"Hold still," she mutters, dabbing at the deepest wound. "You're going to make this worse."

"Does it matter? You'll probably botch it up anyway," I drawl, my voice strained.

She apparently deems me unworthy of a response.

The sharp press of the antiseptic-laden gauze against my skin feels like her vindicated rebuttal. I hiss, a string of curses slipping through my clenched teeth.

"Fuck, princess, be careful," I say, my tone darker now, laced with something that feels closer to anger, or something else entirely.

Her hands slow. She refuses to meet my gaze. The tension between us crackles, heavy and suffocating. It must be because we're both dying to kill each other.

"You're welcome," she says drily.

She reaches for another bandage, her hand brushing against my thigh, and I see the chills creeping up her neck. She releases a deep breath and pauses before speaking,

"You're going to need the Doc to stitch this up; it's pretty deep."

My body stiffens, and I'm not sure if it's from the pain or her proximity. Fuck, she really is a witch. My breathing deepens, my chest rising and falling in time with hers. The small space between us feels charged with something unspoken. I try to create some distance between us. I tell myself it's the adrenaline drop, not her. I can always use a good fuck after a fight, but my dick is staying away from this cunt.

"You're hovering, you don't need to be this close" I say, my voice low, almost guttural.

"You're bleeding," she snaps back. "Should I try and bandage you up telekinetically?"

I don't answer, but my eyes drop briefly to her lips before I yank my gaze away. Grinding my teeth, I force myself to stare at the far wall as if it might save me from her sorceress pussy powers. My rock-hard cock is pressing visibly against my slacks, but she's busy tending to my wounds, so maybe she won't notice.

"So," she says as she pushes her hand further up my thigh, "it turns out you do like what you see, huh?" She traces the outline of my dick before grabbing it, much rougher than I suspected her dainty hands could be.

My eyes can't decide where to focus. My stare travels all over her in that red dress, suctioned against her curves. I glance down at her panties peeking out from where the fabric rolled up while she was working.

She unzips my pants and pulls me out.

"What the fuck do you think you're doing?" I ask through labored breath, but I don't stop her. Finally, my eyes find a place to focus as we lock gazes.

"Taking what I'm owed." She starts stroking, working me with a firm grip, keeping her eyes locked on my face.

My eyes dart back and forth between the bobbing head of my dick and her entrance. I wait with bated breath on her next move. My eyes trace down the smoothness of her legs, then lift up to her heaving chest before landing on her—fuck, they really are beautiful—eyes.

She attempts to hide her wild excitement by controlling her breathing, her tongue barely grazing across her lower lip. She's failing; her breath is erratic.

So is mine. She must see that my eyes are filled with desperation and need.

She straddles me, that fucking dress hiked all the way up to her hips now.

With my dick still firmly in her grip, her other hand steadying herself on my chest, she uses my dick to push her panties to the side. She rubs me along her clit and pussy.

Fuck, she's so wet. She feels so fucking amazing. No wonder Tor and Spider can't resist her. She's so warm and soft, a cross between velvet and silk. My gaze drops down to where we're connected, staring intently. She uses extremely languid strokes, back and forth. Fuck, how can she feel this good when I'm not even inside her yet? My entire dick is covered in her juices and I can't stop staring at it. My hands find her hips, fingers digging into her flesh.

I can't fucking take it anymore. I need to take her. I try to thrust upward, but she denies me entry, keeping me from getting what I want. My movements become more frantic, my hands gripping her harder, frustrated that she is denying me access to heaven and I need to fight my way in.

She's playing with fire. I'm pure animalistic need right now. Driven by testosterone alone.

Her hand finds my hair and she pulls my head back, forcing me to stare up at her.

The weight of her, the pure torture of feeling her, being this close to her, but not being inside her must reflect deeply in my eyes, because she is clearly enjoying this. She's getting high off of promising to engulf me in the bliss of heaven yet denying me entry at the gate.

Every muscle in my body wants to grab her tight and fill her with my dick. I fight once more to thrust up into her. If I weren't currently bleeding out on this couch, it's a fight I would win. The only thought running through my mind is that I need to take her. I can't fucking stand her, but each caress of her pussy along the length of my dick drives my instinct to stab into her. I want to fuck my rage into her so good that it permanently wipes that smug, self-satisfied little smirk off her face. I need to own her, make her mine, if only to put her in her place.

Holding my head by the back of my hair, she keeps my gaze pinned as a slow, mischievous smile spreads across her face.

She positions me at her entrance and sinks down onto me, torturingly slow. Her smile broadens into a gasp as she spreads around me, millimeter by millimeter.

A sense of euphoria washes over me and my breath is ripped from me, I cannot make a sound. It's as if my entire body has been in subzero temperatures and is now being plunged into warm water, dick first. As if I'm enveloped deeper and deeper into her soul. As if I'm wrapped in the warm embers of a fireplace that delivers warmth to a log cabin. The electric current between us completes a circuit I didn't know needed to be completed. I. Must. Take. Her.

I feel her muscles soften slightly beneath my grip as soon as I'm fully sheathed inside her. The beast within me, barely confined behind the flimsiest of cages, surges to the surface. I claw at her desperately. The tips of my fingers and nails find purchase into her soft voluptuous curves. I dig into her flesh, leaving bloody furrows on her body staking my claim, detailing my ownership of her.

She claws at me, drawing more blood, I'm sure, but I don't give a fuck.

I stab in to her repeatedly as her hot breath caresses my cheek following each breathless pant. I sink my teeth into her neck at the curve of her collar bone and bite down. Hard. She hisses but does nothing to stop me. Her blood tastes sweet. Our bodies are seemingly at war, each attempting to conquer the other into submission. After several, sharp, furious strokes, Kai stops fighting and gives in to me.

For the first time since I've met her, Kai seems undeniably soft, docile in my arms. I can't hold back. I pick up my pace, ignoring the searing pain from the wound in my side. The only sensation I can focus on is the intense grip of her pussy on my dick as she clenches for me. I feel her pulsing and can tell she's seconds away from release, so I keep my pace and movements steady.

"Fuck yes, princess, cum for me."

The instant she cums, screaming my name, I completely lose it. I shoot my cum deep inside her, burying my fingers into her thighs as every muscle in my body constricts and then releases almost instantaneously.

She drops her head down, resting on my neck. I can feel her moist lips and the tip of her tongue on my sweat covered skin. For a moment I feel nothing but victory, elation coursing through me faster than the adrenaline pumped in my veins at the restaurant.

Yet, as I catch my breath, I can't help but panic.

What have I done? I spent so much time giving the guys shit and I caved to her just as they did.

"Get off me." I throw her down next to me on the couch. Fuck. She's covered in my cum and blood and I love it. I'm disgusted with myself. Why is she the most beautiful thing I have ever seen? I stand. Whatever work was done to bandage me up is in ruins.

She looks up at me, eyes narrowed, staring at me in contempt.

"What? You thought that just cause I fucked you, I'd follow you around like a puppy dog the way Spider does, or try to cuddle you like Tor?" I snort. "I still want you dead. Thanks for the fuck, though. Helped take the edge off. Go clean yourself up. You're a fucking mess. Disgusting."

She slaps me across my face so fucking hard I fall back slightly and have to regain my balance. I could have stopped her, grabbed her arm before she made contact, but it felt right to let her have that. I storm away toward my room. That was fucking harsh, even for me. When I reach the hallway, I turn around to see if she's still there.

She's gone already.

I don't know where she went, but it's for the best. What am I going to do? Apologize? Comfort her? It can't be much longer until Signor gives me the green light to finally put her down.

And I don't give a fuck about her.

My chest tightens as I turn on the hot water in the shower. It is so constricted for a few minutes, it's hard to get in a deep breath. I punch the slate tiles, leaving one long, single crack and the feeling eases.

Fuck. What was I thinking? I never should have fucked her, but I can't shake the feeling of pride in knowing that

I've staked a claim on her. If only for a few moments, I was sheathed in something sacred. And I made that something sacred all mine.

CHAPTER 17

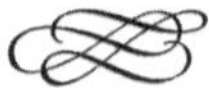

SPIDER

"What the fuck happened to you?" I ask Blade as he walks into my office shirtless, in nothing but grey sweatpants, covered in bandages.

"Nothing, I'm fine. Doc's already been by to stitch me up." He sits on the lounge chair that contains the wardrobe I rotate through when I'm working. "Hey, those texts you found? Between Han and this Sora character? Can you check if there is any association between Han or Sora to Akira Satō? Turns out that fucker is very much alive and in town."

I let out a whistle. "Akira Satō is alive?" I raise both eyebrows, but Blade just nods.

"Sure," I say, turning back to my computer. "I'll take a look. You just going to ignore my question? Is Akira the one who did that to you?"

"Nah, his men." Blade waves a hand dismissively. "Don't sweat it; you should see the other guy."

"I'm not sure I want to." I start digging into Akira Satō and after a few minutes, I come across a company name. "Sora Industries, huh. Looks like it's a shipping company, owner is Akira, left to him by Takeshi Satō. Wait... isn't that Akuma's brother, the former... hold on—"

"Yeah, this isn't making any fucking sense. Why would Takeshi's baby brother be fucking with Akuma's business? They're also brothers."

"Okay, Takeshi Satō, former oyabun. Died twelve years ago in Los Angeles. Murdered exiting a restaurant with his twelve-year-old daughter. Jesus."

Blade grunts; we might be cold-blooded, but we don't mess with kids.

I continue. "Killer never found. Police suspected the perp to be a member of a rival crime syndicate. Akira, his younger brother was also shot, suspected to have died as well, body never found. Huh, I guess now we know why. I can't find much about the daughter, looks like she disappears the same night after an attack on Takeshi's home." I dig for a few more minutes. "Her mom died when she was ten—wait, eleven? When is her birthday—okay, yeah, she was eleven but just barely. Mom died of ovarian cancer. Fuck, the poor girl. Loses both her parents within a year."

I look over at Blade. He lost everyone he loved in one year, too. His stare into nothingness tells me that's probably where his mind is at. I clear my throat; Blade reminiscing never leads to anything good.

"There isn't much else," I say when he looks back to me. "Looks like Takeshi's brother, Akuma, takes over the Yakuza and brokers the deal with your father a few months later. That's all I can find for right now."

"When does Akira resurface? My guess is he's the Sora in the texts you found. He's working with Han. We figure out their deal, and I think we'll finally land on some answers."

My mind is already filling in the blanks. Han was

spotted in Bhutan. Kai was spotted in Bhutan. She has to be involved, but I know if I say something right now, I'll be sealing her fate. I need to know more before I bring this up.

Wait.

"How old is..." I stop myself before finishing the question. Fuck. I look more carefully at the years, the birthdate, the dates of the disappearances.

It's her. It fucking has to be her. Why would her own uncle kidnap her? That doesn't make any sense. Akuma didn't seem to know anything about her; he didn't do it. Did she—? No, she was completely fucked up when we found her. In and out of consciousness. There is no way.

"How old is who?" Blade spits out.

Come up with something, Spider. My brain whirs for a split second before I blurt, "Akira."

"I don't fucking know," Blade says, looking at me like I'm crazy. "Why the hell does that matter?"

"It doesn't, you're right." My heart slams around in my chest, but I force my voice to be calm. Dismissive. As if it was a passing, errant thought. "Leave this with me. I need to run some diagnostics on my system. Something's been off the last few days. Once I'm done with that I'll see what else I can find. Where's Tor?"

"No idea, his ass has been avoiding me since Signor gave me the reins. Reins I don't even fucking want. I have to attend the party tomorrow night at the Amato compound with you fuckers this time. Fucking torture. Signor wants us to bring the girl, and I will delegate the task of letting her know to you. He says her presence is non-negotiable, so I don't care if you have to tie her up and drag her there on a leash. Get it done."

"Alright, I'll keep digging." I intend it as a dismissal, and Blade usually isn't one to linger. I watch him carefully as he stares at seemingly nothing yet again. "You sure you're good, man?"

"Yeah, I'm off to bed." He shakes his head and stands. "Let me know if you find anything else. This shit isn't adding up. Why the fuck would Akuma's brother sabotage his own family empire? We're fucking missing something. My mom knew Akira. She told me he was her protector. Told me if I was ever in trouble, he was who I should go to." Blade stares off into the distance, slowly shaking his head, before speaking again. "What the fuck is going on? Do your thing, Spider, figure out what the fuck that is. I want answers before the party tomorrow night."

Blade storms off and I turn back to my computer. Data, code, evidence. Cold, hard facts.

I let out a slow breath, willing my heart to slow its pace. There are a lot of women in their early twenties. It doesn't need to be her.

I start running the programs to check my computer, trying to figure out what the fuck has been dragging its performance. No one has access to my system; I'm on a closed network and the only way to access it is locally, in person, but it feels like someone is in my machine nonetheless.

A light knock on the door interrupts me, I don't even know how long it is later.

A freshly showered Kai in powder blue silk shorts and a laced trimmed silk camisole stands in my doorway. "Come in, sweetheart." I take a second to look at her carefully, trying to see the resemblance.

It has to be her. Kai Satō. If Kai is even her real name.

My eyes travel up from her bare legs to her tits before landing on her beautiful face. Fuck, I want to feel her against me so badly. She ran from me though, straight to

Tor. The idea of never caressing her skin again is unbearably painful and distracts me for a moment. I don't know how long I have been staring and it registers she hasn't said a word. When I finally look into her eyes, sadness is all that registers.

"Sweetheart, are you okay? What do you need?"

"You."

It takes a second to register. She can't mean... "Me?"

"Yeah, can you help me with something?"

"Oh, okay." I let out a huff of humor. That's what she meant, of course. I'm an idiot. "Of course. How can I help?"

"I want to leave, Spider. I want to go back to my life. Can you help me get out of here?"

"I... I want to. It's just..."

"It's okay, I understand." The way her chest deflates, the way her eyes drop to the floor, the way she's hanging her head in disappointment.

My heart drops down to the pit of my stomach. "Sweetheart, come here."

She looks up at me for a moment. As if contemplating if she wants to comply. After a beat she walks over to me. I stand and open my arms to wrap her into a hug. When I pull away, I walk her over to the lounge chair and direct her to sit.

I kneel in front of her on the floor and cup her face in my hands. I have to help her leave. If she is who I think she is, as soon as anyone finds out, she's as good as dead. I should let that happen. I should tell the guys. But as I look at her, all I see is a scared girl doing what she believes she needs to do. She must have a good reason for all of this. I'm sure of it.

"Fuck, sweetheart, I'll help you. Give me a little bit of time to figure out how to do it safely, okay?"

"What if they won't let me go?" Her voice is small.

"Don't worry about that. I'll handle them. Just give me a day or two, okay? Signor is demanding your presence at the party tomorrow at the compound. Can you get through that? We'll figure out how to get you home after the party. Deal?"

She looks up at me, that same look she had the first night I met her. Like she needs me. I realize I would do absolutely anything for her as long as she keeps looking at me like that.

She leans forward, hesitantly, the warmth of her filling the space around me. I should resist, but I'm having trouble remembering why. My eyes search hers, and hers flick from my lips to my eyes and back again. I take a sharp intake of breath and then she's pressing her lips against mine. She pulls back slightly, her breath mingling with mine and I can't take it. I pull her back in, prying her mouth open with my tongue.

"I want to taste you. Do you want that?" I pull her face away from mine with my hands, still holding her neck and jaw. She nods. "Say it. Tell me you want it. Tell me you want me."

"I want you, Spider."

Any semblance of control I was maintaining promptly leaves my body. I don't know what dangerous game she's playing, but she wants out and I'm going to help her. I grab her shorts and panties and pull them down, flinging them away. I trace my fingers along the stretch marks on her thighs as she squirms underneath my touch. I follow the path they lead to her ass and grab it firmly in my hands pulling her pussy toward me. "Fucking beautiful."

"Stretch marks." She laughs and closes her eyes.

"Look at me."

I wait for her to look down into my eyes. I trail my fingers along her thighs. "You're a work of art, Kai. Your body a canvas and these marks the strokes of paint contributing to a masterpiece."

She pulls at my shirt, pulling me up to kiss her again. She kisses me hard, her fingers threading through my hair and pulling just enough to send a thrill through my entire body.

I can't help but run my fingers along those stretch marks, marveling at their texture, smooth yet distinct, warm under my touch. They aren't imperfections. They are poetry etched into her skin, a quiet testament to her strength and the life she's lived. Beautiful in their honesty, they make her feel real, raw, and utterly irresistible. Just like her tattoo-covered scars. She's imperfectly perfect.

I kiss down her neck, listening to the sweet little groans she lets out. I push aside the straps of the camisole and drop kisses on each of her breasts. Swirl my tongue around each nipple, and she arches her back for me, pressing her body into mine. I kiss my way down her stomach, licking my way down the trail my fingers just explored. I can see the moisture beading on her pussy, calling out to me to devour her.

Watching her body respond to me fills me with warmth. She runs the fingers of her right hand through my hair while her left hand makes a path down her body to her clit. The more I kiss and lick around her pussy lips the more she pushes herself into me. I smile when she starts to rub herself with slow, steady circles. I want her to feel good. I dip my tongue into her warmth.

"You're such a sweet boy, Spider."

I love it when she says my name. I gently push away her hand that was drawing circles on her clit and take its place with my tongue. I suck her clit into my mouth before releasing it. Following with slow, deliberate strokes of my tongue.

"Goddamn, that feels good."

Fuck, I want more. I want her to praise me more. She locks her legs around my head, squeezing me tight. I increase the strokes of my tongue when she starts to buck her pussy onto my mouth, trying to ride my face.

Her movements still and she goes quiet. I look up at her to gauge what I'm doing wrong, but her eyes are locked on the door behind me. It's him, isn't it? It's always fucking him.

When I turn, I see Tor standing in the doorway wrapped in nothing but a towel. His hand is rubbing his erect cock, almost absently, as he stares at the two of us.

"Do you like what you see, Midnight?" Tor smirks.

"What the fuck is wrong with you?" I exclaim in annoyance.

"What the fuck is wrong with you? You're the one keeping the lady waiting," Tor replies arrogantly.

I look back at Kai, who looks down at me. "If you want this to be just yours, it can be," Kai whispers, as if she could see the conflict rushing through my mind.

"Tell me what you want, sweetheart. Whatever it is, you can have it. All you have to do is tell me what you want."

She looks in Tor's direction, then back at mine. I see the question in her eyes. Bloody hell, she wants us both. The instant it registers, I nod. I don't even need to think. Anything she wants.

"Are you sure?" she asks hesitantly.

"Yes, sweetheart, I'm sure," I reply.

As soon as the words leave my mouth, she extends her hand out to Tor.

He looks at me, then he looks at her, then he looks down at his hand rubbing his cock. I watch as he looks back to me, then finally to her.

It's the most awkward moment of my life, but I'll deal with any awkwardness required to give her precisely what she wants.

When his eyes trail back to me, I nod to him and he makes his way into the room.

He looks down at us, her pussy on display, my face hovering inches above her.

"Kai?" Tor asks, his voice husky. "Do you want this? Do you want us?"

She nods.

"Say it. Tell us, do you want this?" I ask as Tor simultaneously says, "Use your words for us, baby."

"Please," she whispers breathlessly.

"How do you want us?" Tor asks hesitantly.

"I don't know, I've never…" Kai responds, and for the first time I see blush covering her cheeks. Fuck, that's so adorable.

"Do you want me to fuck you while Spider eats your delicious pussy? He doesn't look like he's had his fill yet."

Her whole body tenses, her pupils blowing wide.

I look down at her pussy; my god, she's so fucking wet. She's dripping onto the lounge chair, making the most beautiful fucking mess.

"You're soaked, sweetheart. Is that what you want?"

"Please," she replies, barely audible.

I grab her hands and pull her up so she's standing. Tor sits on the lounge chair behind her, letting his towel fall to the floor. She stands in front of him with her back to him.

I see Tor's hands snake around her ass and hips, dipping down toward her pussy. "Fuck, baby. Fuck."

Her wetness glistens along her skin as he grabs her hips and positions her on his dick. Their collective gasp as she sinks down on him causes my already pulsing dick to beat like a drum. I watch as her eyes flutter shut and her tits bounce, Tor's dick sliding in and out of her.

As she moves on top of him, sliding up and down, I kneel back down in front of her and begin to lick her clit again in slow circles. The moan that escapes her lips is the most intoxicating sound I have ever heard. All her coyness immediately out the window, Kai starts bucking her pussy into my mouth while Tor keeps her positioned on his cock so that each buck causes him to fuck into her.

"Just like that, baby boy, suck that pussy."

Fuck, the way she's owning what she wants from me is so fucking hot.

"You love the way I taste?"

"Yes, sweetheart," I say breathlessly, "you taste like fucking honey."

"Keep doing that and I'll cum so good for you."

Tor and I look at each other. At this point, we don't know which one of us she's talking to but the silent agreement between us is clear. We don't fucking care. We just want her to cum.

I stick my hand in my pants and grab my dick, furiously timing my strokes to those of her and Tor and my mouth on her. Our three bodies move in unison and I cum hard as soon as she explodes in my mouth.

She screams our names so loud, I am pretty sure the neighbors heard her. I lift up to kiss her and hear Tor behind her, moaning her name as he cums. "Kai."

As soon as my lips leave hers, she grabs my hand—

seemingly not bothered that it's covered in my cum—and locks her fingers with mine. Tor grabs her jaw and pulls her face back to him, kissing her with intense fervor as he comes down. As soon as he's done, Kai looks at me, she looks at Tor, we look at each other, and she starts giggling. Fucking hell, that is the most incredible sound I have ever heard. I want to record it, replay it, taste it, and carry it everywhere with me.

"Oh my god," she says. "That was fucking amazing. Tell me that's not a one-time thing. Tell me that's something we can do again. Like later tonight, or tomorrow? Or like right now? I can do it again right now." She starts giggling again.

Tor and I can't help it, her enthusiasm is infectious. We both look at each other and start laughing.

"Yes, sweetheart. Maybe not right now, right now, but, yes." I grin at her.

"Of course, baby. We can do it in about fifteen minutes if you want," Tor says, smiling ear to ear. I don't think I've seen him smile like that in years.

"Come on, let's get you to the shower," I say as I pull her up and wrap Tor's towel around her.

"I guess I should take another one, too," Tor says. "Before you go—" Tor grabs her again and pulls her to him, his arm wrapped around her waist. He dips his head slightly and kisses her. My dick pulses at the sight. "Listen, Midnight, if you're serious about that, and you want to go again, head over to my room after your shower. None of us want to go to this fucking party tomorrow, so how about we fill tonight with enough memories to get us through tomorrow's shit show."

She looks back at me. I think she wants to go with him. "It's okay, sweetheart, I have work to do. Go with Tor, he can help get you cleaned up."

Tor raises an eyebrow at me. "Fuck the work, Spider. I have a big bed, and she has two sides. If she wants us both there then she gets us both there. You two go shower and then come to my room."

I turn to her. "You want me there, too?"

"Fuck, yeah. Yes. Oh my god, yes. Please come. If you want to?"

"Of course." Is she kidding? I'm about to risk my fucking life for her. Sharing her with Tor is nothing.

The smile that spreads across her face might be the first genuine one I've seen since we met her and I don't know if I have ever seen anything more magnificent in my life. She turns to Tor. "Sir?" she says hesitantly.

Sir? That's interesting. Tor must fucking love that shit.

"Can Spider please come join us?"

"I already said yes, but, baby, call me 'sir' and giggle for me like that again, and you can have whatever the fuck you want."

The way she giggles and blushes while darting her gaze between us, the way she bounces up, gives him a kiss on the cheek and grabs my hand to lead me toward the shower, it is all the convincing I need. I don't care what the fuck she is into. I don't care what she was trying to do. I am never letting anything happen to her. I'm going to get her out of here. It's going to kill me to see her go, but there is no way I am risking anyone ever hurting her.

But for tonight... "Come on, sweetheart, I want to dirty you up one more time before I clean you up."

CHAPTER 18

KAI

I peek around the corner to the kitchen. Fuck. I need coffee but that asshole is sitting on the island with a pencil and a notebook. Probably taking notes on all the different ways he'd like to kill me. I steel my nerves and take a deep breath. I'm not in the mood for his shit, so hopefully he ignores me.

I won't be that lucky. I grab a mug, and he startles and shuts the notebook.

Yup, definitely writing down the various methods he'll enact for my demise. I feel his eyes on me, studying my every move like a predator assessing its prey. I jump when his voice interrupts my pour.

"You're right," is all he says.

I finish pouring and wait for him to continue.

He doesn't.

So I cautiously turn around and yelp; he's stalked his way to right behind me, and I didn't hear or sense his approach. I lean back against the counter, trying to put as much space as possible between our bodies.

"Right about what?"

He stares at me for a beat too long. He gazes intensely into my eyes and continues, "I'm not wanted. Anyone that has ever given a shit about me, they're dead. All I have left are those two boys you're toying with in that room. I'm making you a promise right now, princess."

I drop my gaze.

"No," he commands as he grabs my chin and pulls me back to face him. "Look at me with those pretty doe eyes of yours while I'm talking to you."

"Just spit it the fuck out, Blade. Say what you need to say," I reply defiantly, my heart hammering in my chest.

"For some god forsaken reason, my boys are addicted to you. The only rational explanation being you have some sort of weird magical sorceress powers or whatever. Doesn't matter what it is, either way, fuck them over, and I will relish every second of agony I inflict upon you as I tear you apart."

"Appreciate the warning, but—" Before I can finish, he grabs me by the back of my neck, presses me up against the counter with the full weight of his body and kisses me. While Spider's kisses are sweet, and Tor's are soulfully all encompassing, Blade kisses like he is trying to consume me. As soon as I open my eyes, and before I can even register what is happening, I hear her voice.

Blade is nowhere to be found.

"Hi, gorgeous, you ready?" Mia asks.

I shake the memory of Blade's kiss out of my head as I say, "Yeah, just give me a second." I trudge back to my room and grab my Nephilim hoodie as I try to regain my composure. I've always loved the weight of this thing. It was the closest thing I'd experienced to a hug before I infiltrated my way in with these boys. Plus, the way the inset red material looks like blood seeping through the slashed-up outer layer reminds me of the scars that led to this entire operation in the first place.

I tell myself that I need to get my shit together as I stalk back to the kitchen where Mia waits for me. Last night was probably the most fun I've ever had in my life. Spider has been nothing but kind since I met him, and Tor, without the weight of responsibility on his shoulders, is a pretty fucking cool guy. Affectionate, kind. The only piece of shit in this house is Blade, because what in the actual fuck just happened? It makes this whole thing unnecessarily confusing.

The good thing is Han and the boys figured out a way to get hired at the party. Han has a plan to set up everything we need for the endgame while there. I won't even need Spider's help. My exit is fast approaching, and the timing couldn't be better. I woke up with a goofy ass grin on my face and metaphorically kicking my feet, sandwiched between Spider and Tor. And as for Blade... well, my heart rate still hasn't regulated back to a steady beat. I can't be out here giggling like a schoolgirl. We need to figure out who the fuck pulled the trigger on my father so I can end this once and for all. The fact that I'm even thinking about how I'll miss those two when I leave is a fucking problem. I might even miss Blade. Fuck. Ugh. No. This needs to end, now.

I look up and Mia is staring at me blankly with her hands raised.

"Well... are you ready to go?" she asks impatiently yet somehow still oozing elegance and grace. Fuck, her entire demeanor is so annoying. How can so much perfection exude from one living being? It's sickening.

"Oh, sorry, yeah, but is this really necessary?"

"I promise, you'll have the best time. Paulo and Natasha

create absolute magic. You're going to look even more like a goddess when they're done with you."

I want to smack the sickly-sweet smile off of her face. She's everything I'm not, but could have been if my father hadn't been stolen from me. A princess, completely taken care of, in every sense of the word. Carefree without any weight threatening to swallow her whole if she pauses for even a moment. You can just tell that her life is so fucking together. She probably manifests everything she wants in life and shit, and it probably fucking works.

I follow Mia out to her car, which of-fucking-course is super cute, a purple luxury SUV with an interior that smells like jasmine. I'm inundated by the floral scent and lost in thought regarding how different my life could have been. I wonder if I would have done things like perfume every spot I take up space in, doll myself up, use a fucking moisturizer. I scoff at the image of me standing in front of a mirror applying a face mask when her voice cuts through the fog.

"The boys give you a rundown of what to expect tonight?"

I stare at her as she drives, not sure what to say. I don't know what *they* think I should expect, but I know what I actually do expect. Han and the boys will be there. They'll set up what they need to in that house so we can maintain eyes on the Don and gain entry whenever we need to. Once they confirm they're set, I can finally bounce and get back to base with Uncle Akira and plan out the next phase. I must have been silent for too long because she continues—goddammit, even her air of disappointment comes across pleasant and sweet.

"Of course, they didn't. Do not veer too far away from the boys or me at any point at the party. The majority of the men there are not men you ever want to be caught alone in a room with. Blade's sister made that mistake and it ended in tragedy."

My gut swoops. "Blade's sister?"

"Yeah." Her voice takes on a somber tone. "Ava was raped at one of the Don's parties. Took her own life a week later. Their parents were killed a month after that, trying to nail down who did it."

Anyone that has ever given a shit about me, they're dead.

"I didn't know." I shift uncomfortably in my seat, my heart pounding harder than I want to admit. If I find out who violated her, I'm killing them, too. Fucking cowardly, cocksucking piece of shit, forcing himself on a woman against her will. Death is too kind an end. I'm torturing that motherfucker. I've never met Ava, but I'm ready to add her perpetrator to my kill list, too.

"He used to be a sweetheart, an artist who drew breath-taking work. But he was never the same after that."

I can't tell if the sweat forming on my skin is from the sun beating down on my face or a repellant reaction to the idea of Blade being sweet. "Fuck," is all I can manage to get out. My chest constricts as I try to picture a happy, loving Blade. He's me. Robbed of innocence and forged into a weapon. I hate him because he's the closest representation of me. Nausea swells inside me and I force myself to focus on the cars stuck in traffic alongside us. I see an adorable corgi poking its head out of the window, trying to find the wind that bumper-to-bumper traffic is currently preventing him from experiencing. Something inside me softens at the sight.

"Don't base your idea of the men at the compound off of your interactions with the boys." Mia keeps talking, as if I'm not spiraling in her passenger seat, "Spider is the kindest man I know, Tor is a lover boy beneath all that bravado, and Blade, well, I know he is rough around the edges, but he has a heart of gold buried deep beneath all the ice encapsulating it. Blade was an artist, through and through, and *fuck* was he talented. He looked up to his sister so much. He loved her something fierce and when she died, it was like a piece of his soul died with her. And when their parents died, it was like all the light that shined out of his big brown eyes went completely dark. No longer saw beauty in anything. The boy who always wanted to create became the boy intent to destroy. He's in there though. I know he is. I just hope he lets him out again."

I sit up straighter, wiping my sweaty hands on my jeans. I sigh through my nose. "Right, so the three hardened criminals are all little sweethearts on the inside. Next, you'll tell me the Don is a closet romantic."

I guess my little joke wasn't funny, cause Mia doesn't laugh. "The Don and his men have no redeeming qualities. They'll kill you for sport, and honestly, death is merciful compared to the atrocities those men are capable of. My father has never left me unattended anywhere near them. He's been the Don's accountant since before I was born. You'll get to meet him tonight. Daddy's amazing, you'll love him. If you lose track of the boys or me, stick with him okay? No one else there can be trusted. The rot bleeds down from the top."

I don't respond; that's not a sentence I expected out of Mia, '*the rot bleeds down from the top.*' I continue staring at her and I guess she feels the need to fill the silence as she pulls into the valet. "Kai, do you understand?"

"Yes," I reply before turning to look at the entrance to the salon she has dragged me to.

She shuts off the engine and turns to face me. "Kai?"

Fuck, I know she means well but I wish she would stop

fucking talking, I'm trying to think. Where did that corgi go? Maybe its smile will lighten the fucking mood.

"Yes, Mia?" I look into the windows of the salon that's bustling with warmth and good vibes. Paulo—at least, I'm guessing that is Paulo—is wearing a hot pink tank top and skinny jeans, standing at the door with two glasses of champagne in his hands. I'm going to be sick, I don't have it in me to stomach being poked and prodded at right now.

"Whatever you're planning, whatever you're into. Back out. It won't end well. He always wins." She runs her hands along the smooth leather of the center console. Her red nails stand out in sharp contrast to the black interior.

My eyes shoot up to meet hers, my eyebrows furrowed. My shoulders tense and I feel my chest constrict. "I don't know what you're talking—"

"Kai, I don't want to know anything. I am not going to ask any questions. I have no intention of speaking about it, but I urge you to please, let it go. Back out. It won't be worth it. He always wins. He will always be a step ahead of you."

I start to speak and she cuts me off again. "Let's go. They're waiting for us. Like I said, I am sure whatever you are trying to do, he deserves. Regardless, get out while you still can. You won't win. Please, Kai, you seem like a nice girl, please just let it go."

She exits the car and I stumble out of the car and follow her into the salon.

I'm assaulted on entry by vanilla, coconut, and lavender, intermingled with a pungent undertone of ammonia and bleach. Her words bounce around in my head on repeat. *He's always a step ahead.* Akira and I have this down pat. If he is the one who pulled the trigger, I'll annihilate him before he can take his next breath.

The next few hours pass with me in silence as Mia makes all the decisions. I just try not to stab Paulo and Natasha each time they jab at me like a prized pony. I kind of felt bad for the nail tech who had to research how to place a nail on a bare nail bed. The look of disgust on her face made me initially recoil. Five hours of pure torture later —sitting still was never my strong suit in training either, just ask the poor monks tasked with overseeing me—they finally step back from me and I can breathe again.

"You're a masterpiece, take a look," Paulo coos as he spins me to face a full-length mirror with gold framing.

I almost don't recognize myself.

"Oh my god, Kai," Mia breathes, "you look so damn beautiful. Paulo, did Kendra drop off the gowns I asked for?"

"She sure did, follow me." Paulo leads us to a small dressing area in the back. He pulls back a glamorous lavender velvet curtain to reveal a massive space decorated in various shades of pink. It looks like somewhere meant for trying on wedding gowns. Full length mirrors on three walls and a large round central platform to step onto to get a wall-to-wall view of every inch. Fuck. I hate mirrors and now not even a centimeter of me is hidden from plain sight. The lighting is bright, topped up by a gorgeous crystal chandelier that hangs directly above the platform. I try to hide my recoil, but the lights and mirrors capture it all.

Three lavender chaise lounges surround the platform on the only non-mirrored side. How many people were going to watch me try on clothes, the fuck?

I'm staring at myself in the mirrors, trying to keep my breathing under control, my eyes wide and panicky, when I notice that Mia has removed her clothes, stripped down to a pair of blue lace panties. Nipple piercings were not on my list of things I would have ever guessed she'd have. I drop my gaze hurriedly before the sense of being watched draws my eyes back up to her in the mirrors.

She pinches the barbells casually as if it is the most natural thing in the world for the pretty, clean cut, fairytale princess to have them and clears her throat. I look up at her to see her smiling at me.

"Sorry, I..." I stammer awkwardly, shifting my gaze away from her.

"They're the one thing I did for myself," she says with a hint of rebellion in her tone. "I don't have a very long leash, but this, this I can have. A little secret no one can see and no one can take from me."

"They're sexy as hell," I reply without really thinking, my cheeks flush with embarrassment.

"Thanks. I think so, too. Here, let me help you with that." She grabs a red gown and helps me step into it. Cool, cool, cool, so she's just going to help me get dressed on full display, topless. Where the fuck am I supposed to look? She's in every goddamn mirror.

She spins me around to close the zipper and I can't believe what I am seeing in the mirror in front of me. The red is a bold, vibrant crimson that oozes elegance and drama. The rich, silky fabric caresses my skin and catches the light with every movement, giving it a luxurious sheen. The off-the-shoulder neckline sweeps gracefully across my collarbone, revealing my Neptune tattoo and baring my shoulders. Fitted through the intricate corset bodice, the gown hugs my curves before flowing down into a floor-length skirt. A daring thigh-high slit runs up the left side, adding a sultry edge and revealing my upper thigh tattoo. The slit not only enhances the gown's allure but also gives it a modern, confident flair. I have no words. Mia pulls my hair to the side, rests her chin on my shoulder, grabs my arms and peeks over my shoulder, looking at me through the mirror. I feel a rush of tingles along my skin when I feel her nipple piercings against my back. I steady myself with a deep breath.

"You look stunning, Kai. The boys are absolutely going to flip."

"I think this is going to draw too much attention to me, don't you think?" I shift awkwardly from foot to foot. Fuck, my hands are shaking and I keep looking to the floor. Literally anywhere but at the walls of mirrors. I can't go out like this. Everyone is going to be staring at me. I'm much more comfortable in the shadows.

"I know, and it's perfect. Let's go, the boys just texted, they are waiting in the limo outside."

"They're what? Wait, why? I don't want to go out like this." The wardrobe Mia brought me is bad enough. I start fidgeting with the dress, instinctually trying to take it off.

Mia places her hands on mine as I slide into the black heels with five-inch gold spikes. "They are going to lose their shit when they see you, relax. Oh, and don't forget this." She hands me an intricate mask.

I look up at her, perplexed.

"They really didn't tell you anything did they? Not even Spider? Boys, I swear. It's a masquerade party, Kai. Come on, I am dying to show you off."

I fidget in the mirror, trying to find a posture that feels natural in this dress, these heels, this hairstyle, while Mia slips into her glam like it's a second skin.

Mia's dress is a long royal blue silky slip that slides over her head in one fell swoop. She grabs two adhesive patches and sticks them in place underneath the dress on her boobs, then slides on a pair of patent leather black kitten toe heels. She fluffs her hair and her cleavage, grabs a patent leather clutch and then turns to me. She smiles widely as she grabs my hand and pulls me toward the door.

"Shouldn't I ride with you?" I ask.

"No, the Don specifically requested you arrive with the boys in the limo. Don't worry, I'll see you there."

The sun is setting into beautiful oranges and pinks and for a moment I'm struck by how pretty the sky looks. That is until Blade, Tor, and Spider emerge from the back of the limo. Holy fuck, each man looks more mouthwatering than the next. Each in a crisply tailored suit, each slightly different from the others. Lots of black fabric hugging muscular thighs and broad shoulders, and Blade's shirt is unbuttoned enough that I can see the very top of the divot between his pectoral muscles and a glimpse of his tattoos.

My mind is blank. Completely blank, but my heart is racing. And my eyes keep darting from man to man.

"What the fuck is taking so long?" Blade spits out. "We've been waiting out here for..." The words dissipate into the air as soon as his eyes land on me. He makes no effort to hide the way he is drinking me in. When he reaches my eyes, he stares like a serial killer measuring up his next victim. There he is. I am not even sure he has blinked. "Fuck," is all he manages to get out before he adjusts his pants, then clears his throat and turns to get back into the limo.

Tor walks up to Mia and kisses her on both cheeks.

"Thank you, Mia, you both look breathtaking." He turns to me, pulls me in for a hug, and sniffs my neck before whispering, "I am going to rip this dress off of you before the night is over. I'm going to run my tongue across every goddamn surface of your skin. I'm going to fuck you so hard, you'll go back to being a mute after you're done screaming my name." He pauses, kisses me with a hunger I try my best to match, pulls away and looks me dead in the eyes and asks quietly, "Tell me, Kai, how wet are your panties for me right now?"

I look down, a bit embarrassed, then look back up at him before whispering, "I'm not wearing any." I feel his sharp intake of breath against my face.

Wetness pools uncomfortably between my legs, as he whispers, "Oh fuck," under his breath. I almost let out a whimper when Tor steps back.

Spider steps up to give me a hug after having greeted Mia. His right hand slides down to my lower back, while his left slides onto my right hip. "You look beautiful, sweetheart, but I can't wait to turn you into a mess again later."

Mia lets out a giggle as she yanks open the driver's side door of her car. "See you later, boys. Bye, Kai, enjoy the ride."

Spider plants a sensual kiss on my lips and then helps me into the limo following Tor. When I step in, the slit opens and I catch Blade staring intently in between my legs as I sit. He scoots away, awkwardly shuffling along the long bench seat that runs along the side of the limo, moving further in and turning away from our direction.

Sandwiched between Tor and Spider, I wiggle slightly into the smooth leather surface. Fuck, I hope I don't end up with a wet spot on the back of this dress. I really should have worn underwear, but Mia insisted that visible panty lines would be a travesty. I'm not sure if my discomfort is due to Blade's eyes shooting daggers in my direction, the moist sensation between my legs, or the stiffness of the bench seat.

The driver lets us know we'll arrive in about forty-five minutes, then pulls up the privacy screen and we feel the limo push into gear and take off into traffic. The hum of the engine pulses through me as I try to regain my composure. Fuck, it's hot in here. Purple LED lights running along the floor of the limo give the interior a sensual feel. Goosebumps erupt on my skin as Tor brushes my hair aside from my neck and leans in to kiss me. Spider's hand travels up my exposed thigh.

"Oh fuck this," Tor whispers as Spider's hand reaches the apex of my thighs. "I can't wait, baby, can I taste you?"

"Spread your legs for me, sweetheart," Spider says while Tor keeps kissing me.

I spread my legs slightly and gasp as Spider pushes them further apart, as far as the slinky dress will allow. He slowly runs his hands up and down the inside of my thighs.

Every muscle in my body tenses in anticipation of contact. Two of his fingers penetrate me and I let out the loudest moan before I bite my lip to shut myself up.

Fuck, I hope the privacy screen is soundproof. My heart is racing so rapidly, I assume even Blade can hear it from the far end of the vehicle. As the thought crosses my mind, I look up at him, catching his eyes immediately. He is staring at me intently with a hunger I've not seen in him before. I notice his left shoulder is moving and slowly let my eyes follow it down to his hand rubbing his length through his pants.

My eyes dart up at his face again and I can't look away. I've never seen that expression on him before. It's akin to reverence. While my focus has been locked on Blade, I hadn't noticed that Tor has moved to the floor of the limo and is now kneeling in front of me.

Using both of his hands, he pushes my legs even further apart and runs his hands up the back of my thighs, pulling up my dress. "Lift up for me," he commands as he pulls my dress completely up and settles me back down on the cold leather seat. "Don't want to ruin your dress before the party," he smirks.

I watch him as he watches Spider's fingers push in and out of me. The car hits a bump on the road and Tor and Spider both steady me with their hands. While they jostle around slightly, I barely even move.

The three of us all turn in Blade's direction when we hear a zipper. I scan the faces of Tor and Spider and they both have the biggest, most adorable smiles I've ever seen plastered across their faces. Tor leans back, ensuring I am on full display, a feast for Blade's eyes. My eyes are transfixed on his hand as he runs it up and down his length. He stops briefly at his leaky tip, gathers the liquid, and spreads it down to the base.

Tor turns back to me. "Do you want him? Because he sure as fuck wants you."

A shaky "yes" escapes me.

"Then you'll have him, baby, but first, I'm hungry."

Tor dives straight into my pussy headfirst, licking up and down the seam, working around Spider's fingers, their teamwork already a well-oiled machine. A wave of tingles courses through every inch of my body. Cognitive function, deceased. The only thought running through my mind is *fuck, more, please give me more.*

Tor teases me with his tongue as he says in between licks, "You're so greedy, baby. My tongue and Spider's fingers aren't enough for you, you need Blade's cock, too?"

"She is so needy, isn't she?" Spider coos as he pumps in and out of me at an excruciatingly slow pace.

I hear the squeak of leather as Blade shifts in his seat. My eyes remain locked on his as my orgasm builds to a crescendo within me. Right as I am about to cum, both Spider and Tor stop.

"Uh uh, not yet, baby." Tor gently blows on my pussy as I let out a sound so needy I'm embarrassed for myself.

"Tell Blade how much you want him." Spider's voice is a demanding tone I hadn't yet heard. "Now."

I turn to look at him, my chest heaving as I try to catch my breath. My body shifts to the left away from Spider as the limo makes a turn. He places his free arm around me and pulls me back to him.

"No, sweetheart, don't look at me, look at him, and tell him how badly you want him."

I turn to Tor where he still kneels on the floor of the undulating limo, his dick now on full display as he strokes it while looking at me. He rises and sits back down on the bench beside me. I startle when he picks me up, and positions me on his lap with my back to his chest. No matter how intent I am to regulate my breathing, it remains erratic. His exposed cock rubs up against my entrance as I focus on trying to inhale and exhale. I try to position myself so he'll slide in, but he grabs my hips, halting my movement. "No, baby, don't look to me to save you either. Spider's been very clear on what you need to do right now to get what you want."

The memory of Blade tossing me to the side after our last encounter flashes across my mind. I believe Blade sees in my eyes that I'm reliving that moment.

He breaks and says, "You win, princess, you win." His voice is soft, softer than I have ever heard it.

I remember the feel of his lips on mine in the kitchen this morning.

"If you want me, I'm yours. All you have to do is say it." He shifts his body forward, waiting, yet I can't seem to find my voice. After a beat he leans back again, his chest deflates as if bracing for rejection.

I don't know what comes over me or who I even am when I sit up tall, as tall as I can with Tor's cock rubbing up against my entrance. The certainty in my voice doesn't just shock the boys, it shocks me. I can feel the blood coursing through my veins as I demand, "I need you to fuck me, but first, taste me, make me cum, and I'll spread this pussy open just for you."

Tor sucks in a deep breath, Spider chuckles, and Blade? Blade is looking at me in a way he never has before. Like he wants to protect me, please me, take care of me. The hardness I've grown accustomed to in his gaze is replaced by something I can't name. Blade gets down on the floor of the limo and crawls over to me on the bench at the back of the vehicle. He's fucking *crawling*, like a starving wolf. I half expect him to howl when he arrives. He places his hands on my knees, and pauses to look up at me.

"You have to stay. Promise me you'll stay." The softness in his voice, the pleading. I didn't think he was capable of such things. He stares at me patiently, his eyebrows slightly raised, waiting for my response like it's the oxygen he needs to breathe.

"I..."

"Princess, say you'll stay. I need to know you'll always be here. I need to know that I can keep you. That you'll let me keep you safe."

Mia's words from earlier flash in my mind. He lost his whole fucking family in one fell swoop. I knew they were dead, but learning how. Fuck.

"I can promise you, with certainty, that I will stay safe, I always do." I can't promise him I'll stay; I'll be gone in a few hours. I suck in a breath. For the first time since I put myself in Tor's path in that warehouse, I think… maybe I don't have to leave.

Blade accepts my offering, though, and he pushes my thighs tightly down onto Tor's lap, spreading me open again and locking me in place. He doesn't stand on ceremony, just licks me once then sucks my clit into his mouth. He's relentless and the pressure building is overwhelming. I want to moan, but no sounds seem to escape me, just heavy, uncontrolled breaths. My thighs begin to shake uncontrollably, and right as I am about to cum, he pulls away.

The whimper that escapes me is so loud there is no way the driver didn't hear it. Fuck these guys, what the hell. I hear all three of them chuckle softly as they take in my deflated posture and clear frustration.

I need them to let me cum, like *now*. My breaths are rapid and I can't stop saying, "Please. Please. Please."

"You sound so pretty when you beg, princess," Blade says as he lifts up on his knees and attempts to stab into me repeatedly without success. Spider continues to alternate between blowing his hot breath down my neck and kissing it, while his hands massage my tits with the perfect amount of pressure.

Tor's hand dips back down, playing with my clit. I look up to see him and Blade exchange a glance. Blade nods slightly and hisses out a breath. When I look down, Tor is spreading my wetness on Blade's dick. Blade trembles above me as Tor grabs his cock and gives it a couple strokes before guiding him to my entrance. The sight of Tor's hand on Blade's cock is so fucking hot I think I've fully stopped breathing.

Fuck me, fuck is this actually happening? I want to look around to take in my surroundings. To make sure I am still awake, that this is real. But no matter how much I try, I cannot look away from where Blade is letting Tor stroke him and panting in response. As Blade slides in, I can feel Tor's dick pulsing against my entrance, Blade's cock rubbing against him each time he pumps in and out of me.

"I want both of you," I moan, desperate to not just see them rubbing up against each other but to *feel* it.

All three of them are staring at me and speak over each other.

"Sweetheart, they're both big boys, I'm not sure…"

"Fuck, baby, you can have whatever you want."

"Princess, are you sure you can take it?"

"I want you both, stop worrying about me. Use me like your own personal fuckdoll. I want to feel all of you. Right fucking now. Like now, now. No more teasing. And Spider, I want you to cum in my mouth."

The chorus of, "oh fucks," and, "oh shits," and faltering breaths and moans that come out of the three of them fills me with a sensation I struggle to describe. It's like being drunk on ultimate power. Like there is nothing in this world I can't have. Like these three powerful men that the world cowers before are all mine. They belong to me. I command them.

I whimper as Blade pulls out of me, and the three of them laugh.

"Relax, baby, we just need to reposition you a bit. We're going to give you exactly what you need," Tor coos in my ear, one hand still working my right nipple.

Tor slides to the floor of the limo, taking me down with him. My back is plastered to his chest and he's holding me up by my hips so I am slightly hovering over him. Blade backs up slowly on his knees to give Tor room to move us around. Tor lays back at a forty-five-degree angle against the bench and slowly lowers me onto his dick.

Just as I'm starting to adjust to the fullness of him, I feel Blade's tip on my pussy. The stretch at first feels like too much, and I tense in response to the intrusion.

Spider bends in my direction from the bench, gently brushing my hair off of my drenched face. Five hours of hair and makeup ruined in less than fifteen minutes. The boys notice my wincing and pause their movements.

"You okay, sweetheart? If it gets to be too much, just say the word and we'll stop."

"No."

"No, you're not okay?" Spider replies, concern etched on his face.

"I am."

"No, you won't tell us?" he pushes.

"No, don't stop, ever."

The boys chuckle. Tor's cock mimics a vibrator as his laughter causes him to pulse rapidly inside me.

Blade grabs my chin and pulls my face in his direction. "Look at me," he demands as he presses against my entrance, more insistently this time. "Relax for me, princess." Small whimpers of pleasure drop from my lips as he enters. "Yeah, just like that, atta girl. Trust me, it'll feel so much better if you relax." I breathe deeply, trying to tell my entire body to relax, to succumb.

Tor halts all of his movements completely as Blade pushes in further and further. I squeak when the sensation becomes slightly shattering and Blade stops. He tightens his grip on my chin and pulls my eyes to his.

I can't tell what he's asking of me, or what he's looking for. His eyes almost look fearful.

Before I get a chance to look deeper to confirm, I feel his

lips crash against mine. His tongue demanding entry. I am again taken aback by the differences in their kisses. Spider's kisses feel like warmth and love, and Tor's kisses feel like passion and pleading, but Blade's feels like an all-consuming fire that burns through my entire soul. While each kiss lays claim in its own way, Blade's is an imprint that demands permanence.

I soften completely in his arms. By the time his lips release me, I'm gasping for air. When I look back up at him, I realize he and Tor are both fully sheathed and finding a rhythm inside me. I look to my right and see that Tor's hand is braced on Blade's shoulder, and Blade's hand is holding the back of Tor's neck. I wonder if they realize how unbelievably intimate they are with each other in this moment.

I look up to see Spider is noticing the same thing. He leans over and whispers in my ear, "Is it okay if you taste me another time, sweetheart? I want them to have this."

So he sees what I do, too. I nod quietly and watch as Spider sinks down next to Tor and leans back on the bench. We're jostled a bit as we feel the limo come slowly to a halt. Have we arrived or is this just a red light? I forget the question when I see Spider begin to stroke his dick to the same rhythm as Blade's and Tor's strokes. As if the stretch of Blade and Tor isn't enough stimulation, Spider reaches down with his free hand and starts running slow circles on my clit again.

Within seconds, I'm not just moaning, I'm screaming their names at the top of my lungs. Cycling between them like I'm begging them to bring me back to life.

When I open my eyes, I look around to see the three of them staring at me in awe. I quickly shut my eyes again as fast as I can. Fuck, I never want them to stop looking at me like that. Like they care about me, like they want me, like I matter to them.

I open my eyes again and see them smiling at me. My thoughts are immediately erased by the overload of how handsome they look and the havoc their touches are wreaking on my body. I can barely survive any further movement. Each stroke, each languid circle, each thrust so overstimulating that I cannot breathe. Not a single word is uttered. Just moans, breaths, grunts, and whimpers, until Tor breaks the silence. "Fuck, baby, I'm cumming." Ropes of Tor's warm cum flood my insides. Tor stops thrusting, but continues to work my nipples as each thrust from Blade pushes Tor's cum deeper and deeper into me.

Seconds later, I hear Blade whisper to me with that reverence I haven't yet comprehended, "Where do you want it, princess?"

"In my mouth. Let me taste you."

His whole body shudders and he pulls out rapidly.

I take him into my mouth and his cum seeps into me instantly.

I twirl my tongue around his dick and swallow as he exclaims, "Fuck, princess, fuck, fuck, fuck. Just like that."

Spider lets out a labored breath and I flick my eyes over to see him cumming into tissues he must have grabbed from the limo bar. When, I have no idea.

For a moment no one moves. Spider slumps his head back on the bench. Tor hasn't moved in a minute; I should probably get off of him, but I can't because Blade is holding onto the back of my neck, stroking my hair. He slowly pulls out and sits back down on the floor, I finish swallowing and gasp. No one says a word, no one moves. For a moment, it's so quiet I am not sure any of us are breathing.

Tor breaks the silence. "Fuck, baby. You took us so well," he says as he finally seems to regain some post-nut clarity.

Spider passes around tissues to the boys. Once he's done, he returns his full attention back on me. "You did so amazing, sweetheart," he says as he brushes away the wet strands of hair clinging to my sweat-covered neck.

I pull back in shock as Blade dips down and begins to clean me and the remnants of Tor up with his mouth. Goosebumps erupt over every available surface of me.

After a few moments, he takes the tissues from Spider that he was holding in his hand and fully cleans me up himself with soft, gentle caresses. Then plants a kiss on me before whispering, "Okay, fine, I admit it, your pussy is fucking magical."

All the boys let out a laugh, and fuck it, I do, too.

"Dick," I retort as I turn away from him.

His laughter stops abruptly and he turns to me. "Kai. Look at me."

I look up.

"You really are a good fucking girl. In the worst possible way." He grabs the back of my neck with such a tight force that I am sure the marks of his fingers are imprinting into my skin. What now, is this dick going to threaten to kill me again? Not even the euphoria of the orgasm of a lifetime can cool this guy's inner beast? "Don't forget what you promised me. You stay."

Oh. I... Okay. That's not what I expected. I stare into his eyes. He means it. Fuck. I didn't promise I'd stay; I promised I'd be safe. So I lean forward and kiss him gently, hoping he doesn't notice the guilt in my eyes.

Tor and Blade lift me up and place me on the bench. I adjust my dress, not bothering to look to see if it has stains on it. Nothing to be done for it, and I have zero regrets.

Spider kisses my right cheek as Tor kiss the left, then says, "Nah, fuck that." He tilts my face toward him and kisses me hard. My heart rate was just starting to steady and now it's picking all the way back up. There was always a risk these boys were going to kill me, but this was not how I thought they'd accomplish it.

Spider laughs and replies, "Yeah, me too," before kissing me too.

Blade's voice cuts through the bliss of the moment.

"I have no idea how long we've been here, but we need to move, now. Don's texted twice. Mask up, let's go."

CHAPTER 19

TOR

I walk on auto pilot past the guards into yet another of my dad's opulent parties. Twinkle lights cover every available surface and hang in the air as if we are walking into a fairy tale, but really it's just a fucking nightmare. Red and gold decorations give the space a royal feel. Makes sense; the asshole always walks around like he's the fucking king. Takes whatever he wants like one, too.

My arm around Kai's waist is more of an anchor than affection. Fuck. What happened in that limo? Every fucking second of it was amazing, but what does it say about me? Maybe I am the little bitch my dad has accused me of being all these years. I grabbed Blade's dick; I fucking stroked it. I try convincing myself that was just a heat of the moment thing, that it doesn't mean anything. It was just a one-time occurrence. But when he grabbed the back of my neck, I... My stomach filled with butterflies. And when he ate my cum from Kai's pussy, I started to get hard all over again. It must have been Kai; her pussy was so warm, so tight. That has to be it. Blade even called it: Pussy drunk.

We make our way into the main room. I am doing my

best to avoid making eye contact to prevent tedious small talk when I look over at Blade standing in the corner hiding from the crowd by the back garden exit. As usual, he is lurking in the shadows, looking like he always does: Pissed. His eyebrows are furrowed, his stance one of high alert, as if he is a matador and he expects the bull to charge at him any minute. There is no trace of the smile that was on his face in the limo; it has been replaced by his signature scowl.

Fuck, and now that I am looking at him, I can't stop replaying the way he quivered at my touch when I stroked him. I can't stop replaying how good it felt to rub up against him. A chill runs up the length of my spine and I am pretty sure my dick is pulsing. Fuck. And with Kai in between us, it was overstimulating in the best possible way. Blade looks up at me, and... what the fuck? Is he smiling?

I quickly look away, tightening my grip on Kai's waist as I lead her toward the grand staircase. I don't know how to describe it. It felt *right*. It was like something just slotted into place. Something I didn't even know was missing.

It's not that deep. I am probably just reading into the situation. It was simply the intimacy of the act itself, the sexiness of Kai, the taboo of the whole thing. Why am I not panicking? I'm not freaked out. Why am I not freaked out? Did he feel anything? If I'm being honest with myself, I fucking liked it and that scares the shit out of me.

I keep a tight hold on Kai as we move through the crowd of guests, smiling tightly at people I hate knowing. These parties are the absolute worst. The guest list unveils the hypocrisy of the world we live in. "Upstanding" members of high society rubbing elbows with murderers, drug peddlers, traffickers, arms dealers, and thieves. Moral character means nothing when there is a bank account someone can utilize for their own gain in some way.

Everyone knows exactly who my father is and what he stands for, what he's capable of, what he's done, yet they show up filling their faces with Michelin-starred hors d'oeuvres, guzzling thousand-dollar bottles of champagne and wine, telling terrible fucking jokes as if the money paying for this isn't drenched in crimson blood like the color of Kai's dress.

The tuna tartare on crostini, topped with a ponzu sauce and a thinly sliced jalapeño does look fucking delicious though. Fuck it. I grab two from the tray and lean down to Kai. She goes to take it from me and I hold it out for her, waiting for her to open her mouth.

Kai opens her mouth and lightly shows me her tongue.

A flashback to the parking garage fries my senses.

She clears her throat and I place the little toast in her mouth. I watch her lips close around it, her eyes flutter closed as she gives in to the sensation of enjoyment. I love the little sound she makes when she swallows it down. I place the other one in my mouth.

I can honestly say my father never skimps on food. This shit is so good.

"Has everything in this house always been so…" Kai trails off, gesturing like she's searching for the words.

"Too polished, too loud, too goddamn perfect?" I respond quietly. I sigh sharply through my nose. "From the Murano glass chandeliers—" I gesture to where they drip like icicles above, "—to the marble floor that somehow remains completely spotless, despite the gallons of blood that have been washed off it more times than I can count."

Kai looks down, and I swear I can see the shift in her demeanor. Good. I want her to see him the way I do.

Ever since he handed the reigns over to Blade and made it clear I will never be anything other than a disappointment, the desire to play my role has completely dissipated. And tonight? Tonight, attempting the act feels more farcical than ever.

The masquerade ball is his favorite charade. Most people cannot face who he is, who they really are, and how fake it all is. So, one night a year, he gives them all a chance to obscure their image and come pay their fealty to him. The masquerade allows the guests to stomach their own behavior.

I stop with Kai at the mid-level of the grand staircase, watching from the mezzanine as the guests swirl around the room like a pit of snakes in silk. Masks glitter under the chandelier light, eyes peer through bejeweled holes, and laughter rolls through the hall like smoke. Thick, artificial, and suffocating. Every man here is terrified of my father, though about half are pretending not to be. And every woman is just another pawn moved on the board without their consent, or worse still, an eager player.

Across the ballroom, my father holds court like the damn king he thinks he is. Masked, of course, like anonymity could ever possibly apply to him. Everyone knows who he is, the way people shrink when he passes is a dead giveaway. He laughs, that practiced, charming laugh, and drapes an arm over some politician's shoulders like they're old friends. Maybe they are. Everyone's his friend when they owe him a favor.

My stomach turns at the performance, the artifice. The show of elegance and class. As if lace masks and Vivaldi's *Four Seasons* somehow cleanses the blood off my family name. As if any of this could ever be anything other than gold-plated rot festering at its core.

A waiter passes, offering more hors d'oeuvres on a silver tray. This time it's arancini with a perfectly fried crust. As amazing as it looks, I can't seem to find my appetite any longer. Father's eyes lock on mine, then immediately drop down to my arm around Kai's waist. As soon as I see the familiar look of disappointment, I drop my hand like Kai's on fire.

Spider materializes to my left and hands both me and Kai drinks.

I take a sip. Whiskey. Neat. It burns a little going down, but not enough to cleanse the disgust rising in my throat.

Bruno and Dante—the two pricks who were in the room when I was dressed down—walk up to us. Bruno's got a smug look on his face I want to slap off. He must be loving the fact that dad dethroned me in favor of Blade. Dante is chattering as they approach. "Yeah, but Boston's a mess. Internal fighting, instability. I wouldn't be surprised if we decide to move in. Now's the time."

Bruno raises his eyebrows as he turns to look at Spider. "Isn't that where you're from, Spider? Any insight into what is going on up there?"

"No idea." Spider looks away, clearly pretending to be disinterested. I know him well enough to see the tension in his jaw, but Bruno and Dante both seem not to notice. The chatter turns to mindless ogling of political mistresses standing on the floor beneath our vantage on the mezzanine.

What could be going on with the Boston boys? We have no business there. They've been stable for years. Ever since —Kai's angelic voice cuts through my rapid cycling thoughts.

"Where can I find the restroom?" She looks up at me, waiting for an answer, but I can't seem to formulate words.

All I can muster is a pathetic smile while I stare at her. Fuck, she's so goddamn beautiful. I find myself picturing what my life would be like if I could just grab her hand right now. She's looking up at me with an emotion I don't think I've ever seen on a woman's face before: respect. Adoration. The most beautifully disarming smile.

She isn't fazed by me dropping my arm and turns her body toward me. A flood of warmth engulfs me as she brushes her hand up against my side. I want to walk her out of this party, get on a plane, and move to some remote as fuck Caribbean island. No more disappointing stares from my father. No more gut punches each time I remember that whatever I do, that who I *am*, will never be good enough. It could just be us. We would fuck endlessly, everywhere, on the beach, in the shower, in every corner of the house, maybe even on the bed occasionally.

I would sit by the ocean and read all day, Spider would cook and play on his computer; the guy would actually get a chance to game. Blade would play with weapons all day, maybe hunt us some food. I pause my thoughts. That can't be what Blade wants. Maybe he'd start to sketch again. I remember how beautiful his art was when we first met as kids. How it pulled me in. He hasn't drawn anything since they died. I think he'd like a chance to be that guy again.

Spider in the kitchen cooking, Blade in the corner drawing, me reading in an oversized chair while Kai...

What would Kai be doing?

Wait, what does Kai like? What does she do? How do we not fucking know that yet?

Spider's voice cuts through the fog. "I'll take you," he responds to Kai.

Fuck, she asked for the bathroom. I shake myself

mentally, focus on making my expression feel normal. "Kai, I'm—"

She looks up at me, and interrupts. "Tor, he's wrong. He couldn't be more wrong. You're more of a man than he'll ever be and he resents you for it. Fuck him." She leans close, her lips dangerously close to my ear. "We'll make the appearance he wants and then we'll go back to the house so I can swallow you whole. I will never be able to get enough of you." Her hand grazes along my package as she walks away and follows Spider.

My eyes follow the shape of her as she and Spider disappear into the crowd. I shake myself mentally yet again and turn to see my father, Mia's father, and Mia standing in front of me. I force myself not to startle and smooth down my jacket front. My elbow lightly bumps into someone— Blade. Blade was in the corner, but now he's standing right next to me. His stealth will never stop being unnerving.

My father's voice cuts through my thoughts like a butter knife. "Tor, doesn't Mia look beautiful? Mia, you've grown into such a fine young woman." The way he looks at her fills me with disgust. He's always been slimy around women, but I've never seen that 'I will conquer you and throw you away' gaze directed at Mia before. Mia steps back slightly and smiles. Her father moves toward her, and stands up a little bit taller, as if he's ready to challenge mine to a fight.

Down, boy. He'll kill you on the spot.

"Why don't you ask her to dance?" Mia's father chimes in. Smart man, trying to get his daughter as far away from my father as he can, as fast as he can.

I scan the room for Kai, though she's only been gone a few seconds. "I...I..."

"Why are you stuttering, boy?" My father sneers, his tone oozing with disdain.

I compose myself. I don't need Kai to save me. I've survived this long in my father's life without her. "Mia, may I have this dance?"

"It would be my pleasure, Tor."

I take Mia's hand and as I am about to lead her to the dance floor, my father grabs my shoulder. "One dance, then meet us in the pool house. We have business."

My blood runs cold as I take the steps necessary to put distance between us and him. Father doesn't tend to business during parties. Too much risk involved, particularly given the guest list includes the Manhattan district attorney, the state attorney general, and multiple Department of Justice bigwigs. It's one thing for them to get paid to look away. It's a complete other to risk them witnessing what they shouldn't.

Mia wraps her arms around my neck and we begin to sway slowly on the dance floor. "Stop doting on her in front of him, Tor, and convince her to stop whatever madness she's got planned. I like her. I don't want her to die."

"What she has planned?"

Mia snorts before saying patronizingly, "Oh, boy. I swear. Yes, Tor, yes, whatever she has planned. She's after something. And whatever that something is, it has to do with the Don. Tell her to stop. You know better than anyone else what is in store for her if she doesn't."

I'm grateful for the dim lighting that obscures the shock on my face. My eyes focus on the gold gilt reflecting the red hues of the Murano chandeliers. The dark red velvet curtains they've hung in place of the usual gold paisley print resembles the blood rushing to my face as fury overtakes me. No, Mia's wrong. I felt her. I saw what I mean to her in her eyes. The way she looks at me. Fuck.

"What does she have planned?" My mind starts to replay all of our interactions, trying to see when she could have been using us, using me. Has it been this whole fucking time? My heart is pounding so hard, the pulse has made its way into my head. The room starts to blur. I can't see straight. I can't think straight.

"That I can't tell you, but whatever it is, I can guarantee it's going to get her killed. If you care about her at all, get her to stop."

"I'm sorry, Mia, I have to go." I let go of her and turn away.

Mia reaches after me; I'm sure she's just trying to help but I can't think about that or the look of disappointment on her face when I shove her away.

My blood continues to boil, my pulse roaring in my ears as I thread through the crowd. Masked faces with garish lipstick laughing. Champagne flutes sparkling. Beads, jewels, false fingernails clicking. It's all too much.

I walk outside into the backyard, ignoring the sycophantic greetings as I go. The perfectly manicured garden abrades against my inner turmoil. Does Kai even want me —us—or has she been fucking using us to get something from my father. Like everybody else in this godforsaken house. I have to get the fuck out of here.

The first time I've ever felt that someone sees me, the real me, and still reaches for me and wants me... it's a complete fucking lie. My brain starts trying to piece together the puzzle, starting with the night we met. I convince myself that she's the one behind this whole fucking mess, the reason I got shot.

Rage bubbles just beneath the surface, threatening to

explode. I imagine this is how Blade feels all the time. Fuck. It's making it impossible to think. Father doesn't need to kill her, Blade won't get the chance either. I fucking will.

Footsteps approach on the pavers. I turn to see Spider and Kai walking up behind me as I approach the pool house. I wait for them. Take her in. Head to toe. The traitorous fucking cunt is smiling at me. I want to slap that simpering smile off her face. She probably thinks I'm an incompetent idiot, just like my fucking father.

Grabbing her arm and pulling her away from Spider, I snarl at her, "What the fuck are you after?"

Spider tries to step between us, but I shove him away so hard he hits the brick wall.

And there it fucking is, I see it, right there in her fucking eyes. Guilt. I push her up against the brick wall of the archway to the pool area. "What the fuck are you after? Tell me, Kai, now."

"I... I..." Her parallels to my stuttering earlier pushes me over the edge. I pull her forward by her dress and shove her back into the wall again, hard, but I drop my hands from her the minute she lets out a sharp cry of pain.

Spider is between us in a blur. "What the fuck, Tor?"

I start, "This bitch—" but stop dead when she pulls away the hand that was rubbing the back of her head and it's covered in blood.

"Fuck!" I fucking hurt her. Fuck me, why do I fucking care? She's a goddamn liar. I want to scream, punch the wall, run. I have no idea what I need to do but the rage in my veins mixing with my constricting chest paralyzes me in place. My eyes are transfixed on the blood on her hands. I did that. My hand instinctively lands on my gut where a bullet passed through me. Did she do this? I can't seem to find the words, a frustrated hissing sound is all I manage to get out as I pace frantically back and forth.

Spider rushes to her, but before he reaches her Blade appears out of the shadows.

"Let's go. The Don wants to see us all in the pool house now." He looks at Kai's hand. His eyebrows raise, his expression softens. "Whose blood is that?"

He gently but decisively starts inspecting her. When he sees the blood in her hair he grabs both her arms. His voice lowers to a dangerous thrum, plucking at something deep inside me. "Who did this to you?"

She doesn't respond, just looks between him and me with her stoic expression from the first night with us.

"Kai, who? Tell me, now."

"You said the Don was waiting, she's alright," I hear Spider say as I spit onto the ground and turn toward the pool house. I keep my eyes focused on the travertine pavers set in the perfectly manicured lawn that winds in a curved pattern from the house to the pool. I don't even notice I am counting them with every step. 25, 26, 27, 28.

"Give me your hand," Spider says. "I need you to act like you're fine until I can get you out of here, okay?"

For fuck's sake, I need answers and this asshole is still playing hero to this lying, scheming cunt.

The atmosphere takes a complete turn when we march into the pool house. Steam rises from the water in the indoor pool and jacuzzi. My father is surrounded by his four most trusted men. Their tuxedos resemble a uniform of sorts and their Venetian masks look a whole lot more menacing under the muted light emitting from the sconces surrounding the pool.

Three more men in suits and masks walk in behind us and take up their position to the left of my father's men.

The current oyabun and his two most trusted guards.

I look over at Kai, who is staring at the oyabun with a murderous look in her eyes. Does she know him? She's in what can only be described as a fighting stance. Blade and Spider notice, too. Blade surprises me when he brushes his hand down her side covertly to get her attention. Her eyes flick to him and he shakes his head.

Does everyone know something I don't? What the fuck is going on?

The oyabun doesn't seem to recognize her. So why the fuck is she the embodiment of wrath, nostrils flaring and anger oozing from every pore? A Japanese man in his fifties with a dragon tattoo on his neck is on his knees in front of us. I've never seen this man before.

Blade's muscles tense when he sees him, though. They've clearly had this man for a while; his face beaten to the point that it is almost unrecognizable as a face.

I look more closely at Kai, and that's when I see it. The concern etched across her face. A helplessness I haven't ever seen in her gaze. Her face is cycling through so many different expressions. Her body is stiffer than a board, her fists clenched at her sides. She looks like she is gearing for a fight. She knows him. She knows the man on the ground.

"You thought you could move into my territory?" My father's voice draws my attention away from Kai and back to him. "Fuck with my business? And we wouldn't find you?"

The man stays silent. My pulse quickens. I don't know what to do. I'm not even fully sure what is happening right now. Does Kai work for him? Does my father know she's connected to this man?

"No one fucks with what's mine. Do you know why I've been Don for as long as I have?"

The silence in the room is deafening. I notice Spider holding Kai's hand. She is squeezing it so tightly her knuckles are chalk white.

"I don't just cut off the head of the snake, I slice through its entire body."

I see every muscle in Kai's body tense even further. She would shatter if I were to touch her. She's about to step forward, but Spider stops her.

When I look back to the man on his knees, I see the recognition in his eyes, the pleading, the slight shaking of his head. He's telling Kai to stand down.

What the fuck is going on?

I look back at her and see brightness building in her eyes, tears that she refuses to let fall. Does she think her mask obscures it? It's obvious she's about to break.

I turn back just in time to see my father's knife slice through this man's throat. Bile rises in my throat, but I do not turn away. The blade drags down the man's sternum, scraping bone and slicing flesh. He doesn't even bother to remove the knife, he simply releases the handle and lets gravity take care of the rest. The man's body falls forward. The silence in the room amplifying the echo of the grotesquely visceral sound as he hits the stone floor. He twitches in a pool of blood my father steps over.

He shakes the oyabun's hand. "I trust you'll assist us in cleaning up the rest of this mess. Share intel on anyone else who was working with him?" There's a question in the tone, but everyone in the room knows there is not actually a question being asked.

The man bows at my father. "Of course. Thank you for helping me settle an old score. It's unfortunate that it caused a minor rift in our endeavors, but now that it's handled, business should go right back to usual."

As the oyabun and his men take their exit, Kai's expression shifts and her body pulsates with what I think is rage. My father and his men remain. Kai. And us.

"Blade, clean it up," my father commands before turning to Kai. "Do you recognize this man?"

The stoic expression on her face is one I haven't yet seen. It's not the one I witnessed when I found her. Not the one she carried the whole next day, but it looks familiar all the same. No, this, this look, is completely different from what I've seen on her. Her face is a stone statue with no expression. Devoid of all emotion.

Then it clicks. Where I've seen that expression before. The stillness. The fury pulsing deep beneath the surface. It is the same look Blade has when he is out for blood.

She nods.

"How do you recognize him, Kai?"

Her eyes are transfixed on the man lying dead beneath a sea of designer Italian loafers. The scent of copper is so strong it overtakes the potent odor of chlorine. The squelch of blood squirting out of this man as Blade picks him up unceremoniously and throws the body over his back travels through my entire being.

I flinch and shoot my gaze back toward Kai. Her stare is fixated on the lifeless body being carried out by Blade. After a beat that continues for uncomfortably too long, she turns to the Don.

"Kidnapper," she grits out.

"I see." My father's condescending tone assaults my ears.

I don't know when it happened, or how I got here, but I have somehow moved closer to Kai. My body now a barrier between her and my father. My chest constricts as I try to make sense of what we all just witnessed.

"Stay close by, Kai," he says coolly. "I have some more questions for you, but for now, my guests are waiting. Enjoy the party." As soon as my father finishes his sentence and walks past us, my muscles relax. I didn't know they had tensed to begin with.

My father and his men leisurely walk back toward the main house as if they didn't just participate in a gruesome slaughter at their own party.

Kai's hand is now limp in Spider's. Her eyes travel back to the pool of blood on the floor. The only sound emanating from the room is the hum of the motors maintaining the jacuzzi and the pool. The buzz is somehow louder than my thoughts.

I open my mouth. To say what, I don't know. But Spider shakes his head at me. Fuck that. I have no idea what this weird fucking show was all about but I need to know what the fuck she's after. My father may think this is done, but I know it isn't. Spider lets go of Kai's hand, grabs a towel from the rack and goes to place it on the back of Kai's head.

She doesn't move. Back to being the still mute we met on that first night.

Blade returns drenched head to toe in blood. "I'm out, I'm covered in that fucker's blood. Guess he wasn't much of a protector after all."

Kai snaps, bolts toward Blade in a blur. She grabs his knife from his sheath and puts it up against his throat.

No one sneaks up on Blade. No one disarms him. No one touches that knife. He had to have let her get that close.

One of the first things I notice, though, is that Blade's hard. What is wrong with me? Blade's hands are clutching the hi-top round table she has him pinned up against. She looks down and notices that he's hard and the rage on her face intensifies. There is no warmth or playfulness in her eyes. He bites his lower lip and runs his tongue along it. He's staring at her and I see it, the moment he recognizes that she's not flirting, she's about to kill him.

"Go ahead, princess, I usually get to have all the fun. That Yakuza fuck was the man who failed my mom, and the Don robbed me of the ecstasy of killing him." She pierces the skin in the hollow at the base of his throat, then stops.

My breath catches as I watch them watching each other. They stare at each other, breaths shallow and intense. She turns around, her dress swishes, and without a word, she walks out of the pool house. Her movements aren't rushed, they're deliberate, like a conditioned fighter choosing every step with precision. The click of her heels fades further and further away.

The three of us stand in silence for a beat. Spider, bloody towel in hand. Blade still leaning against the table, his hand holding onto the shallow wound on his throat. And me, still standing petrified in the middle of the room, trying to make sense of what the fuck is going on. We need to go after her. My father's house is a prison; she won't get far.

"She was using us," I manage to get out.

"For what?" Blade's eyes flick to mine.

"I think she is trying to figure out who killed her father," Spider chimes in.

I ask, "How long have you known that?" as Blade asks, "Who the fuck is her father?"

Spider is quiet for a long time, twisting that damn towel in his hands, blood squeezing out of it and over his skin.

"The former oyabun."

CHAPTER 20

SPIDER

Three weeks. She's been gone for three weeks.

The Don has been ferociously hunting down everyone involved with Akira, activating bloodhound Blade in the quest. We haven't been able to find anything since the night of the gala. Everything went dark. A fight broke out with some kitchen staff and in the chaos she vanished. She and everyone targeting us disappeared like ghosts.

It's been utterly quiet since she's been gone. Almost as if she was never even here.

Tor has been restless and focused on nothing else other than finding her. When he isn't searching for her, he's drunk and unruly. Each time he gets blasted, he reminds me of his father, something I never thought I would see.

We went to search her apartment and found the phone I bought her with the tracking chip I embedded. I'm not even sure that was actually her apartment. It certainly didn't feel like her. I had to remind myself that I don't really know how her apartment would feel.

I found the rootkit she planted onto my computer. Confirming that I was right—that I knew something was in there, slowing my systems down—is cold comfort. I don't know when she placed it there. My best guess is that she did it when she gave me head that first night. I thought she wanted me, but I guess she just needed a reason to get under my desk. A pang erupts in my stomach as I think of that moment.

Was any of it real? It had to be. I found the files they downloaded, but it's all encrypted. They are files I don't even have the decryption key to, which is strange. I thought I had access to everything the Don ever had access to. I've been racking my brain trying to figure out who encrypted them because it sure as shit wasn't me. I've been running a program of my own design for three weeks and I'm still waiting for it to crack the code. Tor has turned over every rock in this city. He drinks, gets high, chases a lead, and when it inevitably leads to disappointment yet again, he drinks, and gets high, on repeat.

The normally pristine desk I keep is a fucking mess. Fast food bags, empty energy drink cans, wrappers, trash, there is no surface of the desk that isn't covered in garbage other than the keyboard and the mousepad—even those are dusted with crumbs and grease. While the view elicits a burning sensation underneath my skin, I can't seem to force myself to spare the time to clean it. I've been glued to this chair every possible waking moment praying for something, *anything* to prove she was real. That I didn't imagine everything. That I didn't imagine her.

I jump as my chat window pings.

Seaside Motel, Route 1.

What are the fucking odds? They fucking found her. I push up off my swivel chair only to run smack into Tor. He and Blade are standing at attention behind me.

"We heard the ping," Blade says, his voice strained.

Blade resembles a wolf ready to pounce on my word and Tor is barely able to keep himself standing. Fuck, he's drunk again.

"Is it her?" Tor asks, his voice harsh, desperate.

"I don't know yet. I reached out to my father's old contacts in the Irish mob, sent them her picture and they think that they found her."

"Let's go." Tor is already turning away.

"Yes. Let's go," Blade chimes in, the edge in his voice haunting.

"Look, we don't..." I start. Before I can barely get a word out, Tor interrupts me.

"Shut the fuck up, Spider, and let's go." Tor's tone leaves zero room for argument. At least some things haven't changed.

By the time we reach Boston, it's almost midnight. While we drove, I filled them in on what the Don has found so far, how I'm working on the decryption key so we can access the files she and Han took. While I know Blade was paying attention, I don't think Tor took in a single word. We stopped at Lady's Burger to get a quick bite to eat. No matter how hard Blade and I tried, we couldn't get Tor to get out of the car to join us.

"This isn't a road trip, it's a fucking hunting trip," was all he'd mutter in response.

I think back through all the years I have known Tor and I can't think of a single memory where he behaved this way. Heartless and enraged in a way that would make his father proud. I feel like I'm going to vomit. This is the same kid I held for hours when his father ordered Duke be killed in front of him because he loved him with everything he had. The same guy who—despite his abrasive words—always cared so fucking deeply that it tore him apart from the inside out.

And now, I don't even recognize him. I'm not sure he cares about anything other than finding Kai, and I can't even bring myself to think of what will happen when he gets his hands on her. We bring him a burger that I know he isn't going to touch, so we enjoy the aroma of grease and fries for the rest of the trip.

"How do we want to play this?" I ask as we pull up to the valet station at the Grand Schmunt Hotel. The valet starts to walk up to the door but freezes five feet away once he sees Blade's and Tor's expressions.

"Would you two fucking chill?" I say as the trembling young man waits for us to exit the vehicle. "That's all we need, a witness that has our mugs engrained in his memory."

"I told you to drive straight to her." Tor's agitation is only escalating the tension in the air.

I stare at the red brick facade of the building. I watch as a group of businessmen smoke on the sidewalk, laughing and gesturing vigorously. It is a continuously horrifying thought that the world just keeps on spinning for most people. They smoke and joke and go to work, but for the three of us, time stopped the moment she left us.

I sigh. Close my eyes and shake my head. I startle at the sound of Blade's voice.

"Look, you two head up to the room." Blade clears his throat. "Get cleaned up. It's been a long fucking drive. I'll drive over to the Seaside Motel and confirm it's her."

When did Blade become the rational one? Nothing has been the same since she's been gone.

"I'm coming with you," Tor insists.

"Tor, if she's there, I'll tie her up and bring her to you myself. Okay? You're still an inebriated fucking mess. Let me handle this. Go sober up." Blade speaking like the only adult in the room is proof that we no longer exist in reality.

"Fuck you, golden boy," Tor bites back.

Blade's shoulders rise and fall as he sighs heavily in frustration.

"My father gives you a bit of power and now you walk around all high and fucking mighty," Tor continues condescendingly.

"Spider, you got him?" Blade and Tor haven't spoken really since the night she disappeared. Whenever they share space, Tor bombards Blade constantly with an anger that Blade just stoically accepts.

Nothing makes sense anymore.

"Fuck you both, I'm not a fucking inept kid, stop fucking treating me like one," Tor says, ironically, like a fucking rebellious teenager. He then storms out of the car and into the hotel, barging past the doorman holding open the glass door trimmed in forest green wood.

"You sure are fucking acting like one," I mutter under my breath once he is out of ear shot. I hand Blade the keys. "I'll take care of him. Blade, don't fucking kill her."

"I'm not making any promises. The cunt stole my favorite knife."

CHAPTER 21

BLADE

*A*s I pull up across from the motel, my face twists in disgust. The neon sign has all but two letters blown out. The pool, filthy and green, has more dead leaves visible than water, and trash is littered across every available surface. As I walk closer, I notice the paint on the doors is faded and chipped. I sidestep a needle and a used condom.

Jesus Christ, what is she doing here? Every instinct is screaming to take her away from this place, to get her to safety. My princess doesn't belong in a rat-infested shit hole like this. Or does she? She's not my princess anymore. Hell, maybe she never was.

From my vantage point in the lot out front, I catch a glimpse of her silhouette through the curtains. Memories of the feel of my mouth on her silky skin flicker. A chill runs through me as I imagine her body pressed against mine. Memories of her curves pliant beneath my unforgiving hold invade my consciousness. My fury boils over as I shamefully admit, if only to myself, that I still want the traitorous bitch with embarrassing desperation.

I need to text Tor and Spider to let them know it's her, but I think I'll pay our little liar a visit first. It'll be much more fun to text them a photo of her tied up when I'm done.

I quietly make my way up the steps toward her room, footfalls barely louder than the fluorescents buzzing over-head. I can't wait to see the look on her fucking face when she sees me. I yearn to smell her fear, I tell myself, but I know I just want to smell her, period. I'm tempted to drive my fist into the stucco wall, but I know it'd do nothing to calm me.

Get your shit together, asshole. She fucking lied, she fucking stole from us, she fucking ran. She thought she could run from us? From me? There is nowhere on this Earth she could go that would be out of my reach, much less across a few state lines.

I warm in anticipation of the terror I'll see in her eyes when I walk into her room. I take the rest of the stairs and pause outside her door. The only things separating me from her are a water-warped putrid green door and a flimsy lock. Even from outside, I can hear the shower running. This is going even better than planned. Look both ways... coast is clear. I brace the heel of one palm against the lock and bring the other down sharply, making quick work of it, and creep in toward the bathroom door that sits ajar.

There she is.

For a moment I stand there, breathing in the steam, staring at her through the glass panel, leaving her oblivious to my presence a little longer. Briefly, I imagine what it would feel like to run my tongue across the water droplets on her slick skin. I shake the thought and make my way in.

Remember why you're here.

My eye is drawn to the shelf in the shower. The blade

she stole from me is resting atop it, open, within her reach. I step in fully clothed and rapidly wrap my arm around her from behind. Our hands meet on the shaft of the blade as we both snatch at it. Tightening my grip, I force both our hands in position with the blade's tip against her neck.

My voice comes out sinister as I say, "Did you miss me, princess? Cause I fucking missed you."

The way her breath hitches in response rushes all the blood to my cock, making it press uncomfortably against my now soaking wet jeans. She rubs her ass against my dick. A sharp exhale escapes me before I force myself to regain composure. This fucking bitch.

"Nothing to say for yourself? No pathetic excuses? No half-truths? Am I not even worth the effort to lie to anymore?"

She tries to pull away from me, driving my knife into her neck, breaking the skin.

I force her palm open and let the knife clatter to the floor, kicking it out of reach. I don't want her dead. Not yet. I drop my hand to her stomach, pressing her back up against my chest. On its own volition, my other hand, currently gripping her waist, slides up the front of her body, through the center of her breasts, tightening around her throat. A droplet of blood stains the water as it runs through my fingers and I'm transfixed to the sight as it travels down her chest.

She's so lovely when she bleeds for me.

I want to lick it up.

As she struggles to break free, her ass grinds further against my straining cock.

Fuck it. Will Tor and Spider kick the shit out of me for what I'm about to do? Yes. Do I give a fuck? Absolutely not. I have to have her right now or I'll lose my fucking mind.

I spin her around to face me, the defiance in her eyes a drastic change from the sweet little doe eyed look my princess directed my way while in my arms just a little under a month ago. I can't fucking look at her but I need to taste her. My lips slam against hers, demanding the entry she refuses for only a beat before giving in.

She tastes like her favorite sour belt candies, smoke, and turmoil.

As our tongues war for dominance, I bite her lower lip gently until she relinquishes control. God, I fucking missed the way she tastes. She wraps her arms around my neck and jumps up, her legs wrapping around my hips like a vice. The momentum pushes me against the tiled wall and all I can think about is that I need to remove the barriers between me and her skin. With one hand secured around her waist, I drop my other between us to open the button of my jeans. The wet material makes it nearly impossible to release the button. Pulling as hard as I fucking can, I hear the clink as it pops off and drops to the floor. I lower the zipper, and pull my pants and boxers down, letting my dick spring forward, jutting in her direction.

She adjusts her position, squirming in my arms, lining herself up.

Without hesitation, I immediately stab into her as if her pussy is a homing beacon. Fuck, she's so wet.

Her face is buried in my neck, and—

"Don't fucking bite me, or I'll bite back."

She says nothing, simply licks the mark she left, soothing the sting and sending a chill clear down my spine to the tips of my toes. Fuck, she feels so warm, and so tight, I never want to not be inside her. A shiver rolls through both of us in unison, and the rage bubbling just underneath the surface consumes me. How dare the lying cunt feel this good? I'm not going to last at all.

"Fuck, I fucking hate you. You really thought you could fuck us over and get away with it?" I grit out.

She stills in my arms, so still I'm not even sure she's breathing. My hands are gripping into the plump thickness of her ass, my cock digging deep inside her, as I halt all my movements as well. The water droplets raining down on us are the only sound in the room. For a moment time ceases to exist, and then I feel her shudder, spasm, inhale, and start to move again, slamming her body against me fervently. My gaze locks on to where we're connected, where I'm taking out all my aggression and stabbing into her, then draws back up to her face. Why won't she fucking say something? Fucking anything! Why won't she look at me?

I flip us around until she's plastered up against the shower wall, driving her head a little more forcefully into the tile than I intended.

She winces, but steels herself with a defiant look as if daring me to do my worst.

The newfound leverage improves my ability to control every movement of her body. I drive into her with quick, brutal thrusts, trying to exorcize my anger. I need her to feel the storm she unleashed. I want her to burn. I want all the hateful feelings I can't contain to utterly consume her. I can't quite place my finger on what else I want to pump into her, but I know whatever it is, I need it out of me. My hand gravitates to her jaw to try and lift her face up toward me, but I'm distracted. I can't stop staring at the rivulets of blood mixed with water, slowly traveling down her neck over her perfect tits like a river of red.

She's so fucking hot.

I lower my head and suck her nipple into my mouth.

The sharp intake of air into her lungs spurs me on to suck harder. Her fingernails claw at me, scrabbling and scratching, urging me on.

I release her tit with a pop and when I finally look up, she's biting her lip and a look of anguish is plastered across her face, as if it is taking all of her concentration to suppress her needy sounds.

Well, this shit will not do. "Drop the princess act, bitch. You don't get to ride this dick and deny me your screams. I'm going to fuck the prettiest noises out of you."

She bites down on her lower lip harder, drawing blood.

I lick it off before trying to force her face back up again. Her refusal to look at me is driving me insane. I can tell she's close. Two or three more well placed strokes and she'll howl like a whore in church. What the fuck am I doing? She doesn't deserve to cum. I pull out faster than I slid in, release my arms from around her and she drops to the floor like a newborn foal. I make sure my feet are placed well enough underneath her to break the fall and then immediately pull back so that there is no contact between our bodies.

Fucking... what the fuck am I doing?

"You're a little liar!" I yell as I swipe water droplets from my brow.

She doesn't speak, just stares up at me with those doe-like eyes I cannot look away from.

"You know you fucked up, right?" I'm shouting, but I'm pretty sure this shit hole motel has seen its fair share of men shouting at women. "Is that why you're fucking silent? Did you enjoy it? Breaking us all? Do you even give a fuck? This isn't the fucking mission." My voice threatens to break and I force myself to take another step away from her.

"What the fuck am I doing? I'm just here to take you back so we can extract whatever intel we can from you and dispose of you, like I fucking said we should have done back when we found you in that fucking warehouse. The mission doesn't involve greedily fucking you, or desperately staring at you, or pathetically chasing the look of elation on your face when you cum for me."

My gaze finally draws back down to her.

Yet she remains distant, as if she isn't in the room with me at all. She still hasn't said a word, and she still hasn't fucking looked at me. Fucking bullshit.

"Look at me."

She remains as still as a statue, the only signs of life the rapid expansion and contraction of her chest, as she pants in what I'm sure is the same frustration I feel. "LOOK AT ME, BITCH!" I yell, startling her enough to flinch and finally peer up into my eyes.

At first, I think she's going to talk. Good.

"I want to know why." The water keeps beating at her, dripping off my nose where I stand just outside the shower. "Why did you bulldoze into our lives uninvited and make us want you, fucking *need* you to breathe, just to take it all away? What was so fucking important? We've all been asking the same questions on repeat since you slipped out of our grasp. What is it? What was so fucking important that you needed to destroy everything in your wake to get it?"

She doesn't speak, instead, she maintains her obstinate silence. At first glance, with the now cold water pouring over her face it's hard to see, but her glassy eyes give her away. Her stare burrowing deep into me, reminiscent of the doe-eyed look I'm accustomed to, her tears mix with the water running down her face.

This is what I wanted to see, her pain, so why am I frozen in place now that I'm looking down at it? Will knowing the why of things make it any easier to seal her fate?

I realize I've been holding my breath and raggedly drag one in. My chest feels as if lava has replaced the flow of oxygen. The only other time I felt like this was when Tor was laid out on the surgical table, the one she fucking put him on. So why does each breath feel like inhaling fiberglass? Where is the vindication I was sure I'd feel?

I don't know what she sees in my eyes, but her gaze falls to the floor and her upper body begins to shake violently. Ultimately, after almost a month of silence, sobs are the first sound she gifts me.

Something I can't quite place breaks in me as I hear them tear from her throat. I don't know when or how it happened, but the next thing I know I'm on the floor beside her, pulling her onto my lap wrapping one arm tightly around her. My other hand pulls her hair out of her face and strokes it behind her head.

She buries her face so deep into my chest I'm afraid she'll suffocate.

I don't know how long we stay there like this, the cold water raining down on us, her naked body on my lap. My pants remain half down, my softening cock hanging down between my legs like a slithering snake, my shirt plastered against my torso.

Her sobs grow louder as I rub her back.

I whisper into her ear. "Fuck... Kai... Deep breaths, alright? It's okay. You're okay. We're okay, princess. I'm sorry. I've got you. You're okay."

She's fucking not.

I'm fucking not. I am the one that needs to kill her soon,

but I can't stop the words from escaping my mouth. Anything to soothe her. Eventually the sobs stop and when I look back down at her bewitching face, she's fast asleep.

My princess fell asleep in the arms of her hunter.

I'm pissed at her for letting her guard down, yet a strange surge of relief courses through me at the knowledge that she feels safe enough with me to do so.

I pick her up gently, careful not to jostle her awake, and grab a towel from the rack. I wrap it around her and lay her on the bed.

She doesn't stir, and she looks so peaceful aside from the puffiness around her eyes.

What fucking hypnotism just happened here?

I strip my wet clothes and hang them on the tattered desk chair to dry. I climb in behind her and for a little while I lay next to her, pulling her back to my chest, engulfing her in my arms. I stare at the profile of her pretty face, wishing that we either never met, or that she gets away.

Her hands grip my forearms so tight, pressing me into her, as if she's afraid that if she lets go I'll disappear. Like she forgot where we are, who we are, and what I have to do.

After a few hours, I unwrap my arms from around her, and get dressed. Still damp. Wonderful. She sleeps and I pace the room for what feels like an eternity, then, I grab her phone, place the chip that Spider gave me in it, and finally leave through the door. I shut it behind me and rest my body against it. Exhaling, I take a second to regroup.

Fuck. What the fuck am I doing?

Frustrated and more than a little confused, I trudge back to the car.

I settle into the driver's seat and unlock my phone to read messages from Tor and Spider.

TOR:

Is it her?

SPIDER:

Don't hurt her. Don't kill her.

Blade, don't you dare fucking hurt her.

TOR:

Yeah, don't, I want to be there when you
do. Just grab her and bring her back here
as fast as you can.

Fuck. I can't lie to them.

BLADE:

I need a drink. First round's on me.

CHAPTER 22

TOR

I step into the elevator in silence with Spider. The polished glass interior is a stark contrast to the black hole consuming me from the inside. Blade insisted we meet him downstairs for a drink. I would rather torture Kai on the designer linens in the suite, but I guess we can grab a drink first.

The bar is completely dead. It's the middle of the night, well past last call. I'm not sure the place is even open. I don't see any staff milling about. I don't see any patrons. It's dark. Good, light would be blinding right now. When I look to the back I see Blade. Alone. My vision turns red.

"Where the fuck is she?" I demand.

Spider sits down next to Blade. "Was it another dead end?"

"No, she was there," Blade states quietly. He pours each of us a drink into tumblers from a bottle of Scotch I assume he swiped from behind the bar. The backlit stone bar looks like lava, or maybe a Himalayan salt lamp. The bar top reminds me of a farmhouse, rustic wood in a rectangle encircling the bar itself. The glass lights hanging from the teak ceiling are covered in clean glasses.

I can't focus on Blade's words as he recounts what happened in the motel room. Steam feels like it is trying to escape from my ears. I catch a few words here and there, and when he says, "I kissed her," my hand darts out almost as if it is no longer under my control and wraps around Blade's throat. Blade takes in a steady breath, looks down, and then back up at me with fucking pity in his eyes.

Blade doesn't move or try to release himself from my hold. I want to fucking kill him. Spider stands too quickly, his head softly hitting against the hanging glass lights. He reaches his hand up to rub his head but remains focused and at attention. "Tor, fucking stop man, not here." He grabs my hand and forces me to release Blade.

The receptionist from the lobby is staring at me in judgment. "What the fuck are you looking at?" They look away and grab the phone, I assume to call security.

"We sent you there to bring her back, so we could..." Why can't I say the words? "Not so you could fuck her. How the fuck are you the golden boy?" How dare he?

"Are you listening to me?" Blade asks, his eyes pleading for me to understand... what exactly, I don't know.

"No, I'm not fucking listening to you, I'll go get her myself." I forcefully toss Blade to the side. He stumbles and regains his balance by grabbing my shoulder. I roll it to shove him off.

"Stop, Tor. Fuck me, just stop will you? She's not there anymore, man. I put Spider's tracker in her phone. She left about twenty minutes ago." Blade lets go of me and holds his hands up in a surrendering gesture. That gesture, more than anything else, pulls me up short. Blade doesn't surrender.

Glaring at him, I fish my phone out of my pocket and open the app Spider installed in all of our phones. Her little dot moves at rapid speed in what looks like the direction of New York.

"What the fuck, Blade. Jesus fucking Christ, what the actual fuck? You just let her go? She ditched the last tracker, remember?"

"She doesn't know about this one." Blade steps forward and looks down at my phone. He tenses his shoulders in frustration and then runs his hands through his hair, slightly pulling it as if he wants to tear it out. "Tor, you're not hearing me, she broke down. Completely. She was sobbing in my arms for what felt like an eternity until she exhausted herself and fell asleep. She *cried herself to sleep.* Something is really wrong."

"Yeah, she got caught. She knew you were about to kill her. And instead of being the wolf you're meant to be, she turned you into a little fucking cub with her manipulative tears. She played you, just like she played us. Like a fucking fiddle. And you let her. Fuck it. I'll kill her myself." I turn away and this time Spider grabs my shoulder while Blade positions himself between me and the exit. "Your funeral, bro. I'm willing to kill you, too."

"Tor, calm down, listen to him," Spider says. "The more I look into this, the more it seems like she's trying to avenge the death of her father. And... I think your father killed him. I think this all has to do with the death of your mother, too. And somehow it ties to Blade's family. I just can't put my finger on how that is, yet."

I death stare at Spider's hand on my shoulder and the smart man takes the hint. "Are you fucking kidding me? How much could you possibly know about it? How much have you been fucking hiding from us this whole time?" My voice climbs in both pitch and volume. "Is anyone here not a fucking liar? Fuck." I look up and Spider's eyes have softened. I want to punch the concern off his righteous martyred face. But then the words hit. They register slowly through the fog. I shift my body to face Spider and begin to pace erratically across the slate tile floor between him and Blade.

They both wait. Watching me.

"You're saying my father killed her dad and my mom," I say when my heart rate has calmed enough for my voice to be reasonable. "And what, are you going to accuse him of killing Blade's sister and parents too? For fuck's sake, Spider, get a grip, my father is a piece of shit, but he'd never kill his own wife."

"You really think he—"

"Not because he cared about her. But because it would make him look bad. His image is everything to him. He would never send the message that he can't protect his own. Her death wasn't to his benefit."

"Tor, I found messages between your mom and another man. I think she was..." Spider starts.

I stop pacing immediately and get in his face, poking my finger into his chest. "Enough. Now my mom was cheating, too? She didn't have a dishonest bone in her body. You'll make up fucking anything to save your precious *sweetheart.*"

"No, but she did have lonely ones," Spider replies.

It takes me a second to understand what he means, and when I get it, I shove him, hard and he falls back against the counter, knocking over a barstool on his way down. Blade helps him up and I take the opportunity to get away from these fucks. It wasn't bad enough she was lying to us the whole time. Now I've lost these assholes, too. What did

Blade call it? Her magical sorceress pussy. Fuck that bitch. She dies. Now.

When I reach the bar's entrance, I turn back to look at them. "I'm leaving. I'm driving back to New York. This time I'll find her and I'll kill her myself with my own two fucking hands. Thanks for at least putting the tracker in, hopefully that'll make it easier for me." I storm off, pushing past the security guards that have finally arrived.

As I drive, I am flooded with images of Kai. On her knees for me in the parking garage. Holding me while I cried in my bed. In my shirt. In the limo with me and—I let out a desperate sigh—with me and Blade. It was all a lie.

My mom... lies, it's all fucking lies. That's all women ever fucking do. They lie, and manipulate, and use. No wonder my father always told me never to care about them. He learned this before I did. Women are meant to be fucked and discarded. They should be controlled. A good woman is one who obeys. They're cruel and heartless when left to their own devices. She was never on her knees for me, she was only ever on her knees for her selfish fucking self.

My father's been right all along. Weakness is permission to be destroyed. Well, bitch, I'm not weak anymore. She's the reason there was a bullet that needed to be removed from my gut in the first place. She used my weakness against me.

It'll be the last fucking time I ever let that happen. I guess I should be thanking her. She helped cure me of my empathy. And I have the perfect way to repay her. I'm going to fucking kill her, and any weakness I have left in me will die with her.

CHAPTER 23

KAI

The minute I open my eyes, I bolt out of bed. I'm still in the shitty motel, a damp bath towel wrapped around my naked body. Where the fuck is he? I catch my reflection in the mirror and see the marks on my skin. My eyes are so swollen I can barely see out of them.

This spot's been burned.

I throw my shit in the go bag and get dressed as fast as I can. I throw on jeans, a black tank top, my leather jacket. A shiny metal object on the nightstand catches my eye.

He left his blade. He left. Wait, he left… me… his blade. And me. Alive. He left me alive. I can't stick around here and wait to find out why. It was probably a temporary mercy. I dial Han. He answers after one ring.

I run my hands along the back of the weathered chair. It's still damp. His clothes had hung here. So I didn't imagine it. He was lying next to me, naked, holding me.

"Sora, where the fuck have you been?"

"It's time. Gather everyone, take up your positions outside Satō's at 7:00 PM tonight."

"What happened? Are you okay?"

"No, I'm really fucking not. Nothing to worry about, though, can you get it done?"

"Yeah, we'll be ready for you."

It's a fucking beautiful day, the sunlight warming my skin. I instantly flash back to last night. Blade's arms around me, pulling me in, that hazy memory traveling through me with more warmth than the sun. I hop on my black and green sport bike and hit the open road. The hum of the engine vibrates through my entire being.

Tears stream down my face as I drive, the helmet fogging up as they fall. Jesus fucking Christ, I'm going to crash at this rate. I cannot afford to be emotional right now. It doesn't matter why he didn't try to kill me. It doesn't matter why he carried me to bed and held me. It doesn't matter why I let him. I've already wasted almost a month rotting in that motel room trying to regroup. I tighten my grip on the handlebars to ground myself back in this moment.

The plan is set, no more hesitation. It's time to execute. Literally.

Han decrypted everything he found from Spider's network and showed me the video of the Don and Satō plotting my father's death. Pure fury had coursed through my veins as I watched it. My chest tightens as I think about it. I was so close. I was literally right there. In a room with the fucking walking corpse that ruined my life. I let him kill Akira in front of me. Han was there, the men were there. Yeah, we were outnumbered, but I did nothing.

Again. Fuck, I'm fucking useless. I rev the bike and speed up on the highway. When it matters I always fucking fold like a goddamn wet blanket. I did fucking nothing. Just like I did nothing the night of my father's death. Frozen in place like a deer caught in headlights. Pathetic. There is no redemption for me now. There is no life left to live. Just death to distribute.

It all ends tonight. Including me. I focus on the breeze blowing against my skin as I race down the highway. This has always been the only place I've ever felt free. I fucking missed this bike. I start viewing everything as my last. My last ride. The last time the wind will kiss my skin. Last night was the last time I will ever be held. Fuck, and it's going to be by Blade. That has to be some sort of cruel joke. The universe has a sense of humor, that's for fucking sure.

I pull up around the corner to my uncle's brownstone.

It's 6:45 PM. I dial Han. "You in position? Is my SUV in the designated spot, loaded up with what I requested?" My tone is brief, no bullshit, no more research, no more digging for information. It's time to act.

"Sora, yes, everything and everyone is all set and ready to go. We don't need to rush through this. It's been three weeks, let's meet, go over the plan one more time, this is too impulsive. It's not like you. We've been meticulous thus far—"

"Han, there is no me left to be like. I just stood there. Again. Like that same scared young little girl. I let them kill Akira right in front of me and I did fuck all to stop it. That is who I am, and who I am is a useless waste of space with nothing but incompetent vengeance at my core. I'm not worth the oxygen I breathe. It's time for me to kill them all. I am ready to rest now."

I hear Han's sigh of frustration. Or maybe it's concern. I don't know, and I don't fucking care at this point. He needs to stop giving a shit. Everything that loves me breaks, or worse, dies.

"Sora, fuck this, I'm pulling the plug. We can't do this.

You're head's not on straight. What are you even saying? Let's fall back, we'll meet at the safe house and regroup."

"I'm going in, with or without you." The street is quiet. Perfect. I look at the steps of the brownstone. The same ones I used to play on as a kid. While they are the same reddish-brown sandstone and look exactly how I remember, they look like somewhere I have never been. Han's pleading voice pulls me back to the present.

"Fuck. Sora, please."

"Bye, Han," I let out, mechanically, robotically. I no longer sound human, even to myself.

"Okay. Okay, wait. We'll be in position. Your luxury Italian SUV is fully stocked and parked where you asked. Ren dropped it off earlier today. Everything you specified is in there. Please be—"

I hang up before he can finish the sentence. Han is the only person alive left who cares about me. I can't listen to him now. I need to end this or I'll likely freeze and have to watch him get buried next.

I ride around the city, tending to some final touches. Once everything is done, I ride to where my SUV is supposed to be waiting for me. And there it is. I love you, Han. You're the best friend a girl could ever ask for, and I have never deserved you. I park my bike alongside it, hop off, and walk to the back of my car. I open the trunk. I really do fucking love him.

My father's katanas, his guns, his blades. They're all here. But those are for later. I grab the small black velvet bag and the assortment of teas from Bhutan. I check inside.

Perfect. Time to pay my uncle a visit.

The silence is eerie as I walk up the steps to the brownstone of my uncle's home, my childhood home. Blood rushes through my veins and I can hear it travel through me. The spike of adrenaline quickens my heartbeat. I don't need to live long, just through tonight.

Moonlight reflects off the cold stone walls of the mansion nestled on the edge of the city. The house, once filled with so much warmth, now seems imposing. Like a decorated tomb filled with echoes of my past and the weight of its secrets. The air feels thick, heavy with anticipation. This is a place I had once been happy. It is also a place where I had learned the cruelty of the world first-hand. Where I was branded by the ghosts of my past.

My footsteps are measured, deliberate as I ascend the stone steps, the cool air licking at my skin. While I am in a rush to get this done, there is no rush in my movements, no urgency. This is my moment. One I have waited over a decade for. The calm before my category five storm.

I'd been gone for so long, cloaked in the shadows of distant lands, forging myself with the help of Akira and Han into the weapon I am now. Bhutan. A place of serenity, an optical illusion. My father loved the temple there. Well, he said mom loved it. When she died, he had donated a small fortune to the monks there for them to use charitably. He only asked for one thing in return: a safety net for me, in case anything ever happened to him. My father was the ultimate protector. His shield extended beyond the grave.

Akira taught me everything I know about how to become a ruthless leader of the Yakuza. The thing I miss most about the boys—who are likely plotting my death—is hearing the name Kai. Sora doesn't exist anymore. Everyone calls me Sora, everyone always has, but daddy? Daddy called me Kai, because the iridescent flakes in my eyes reminded him of the sea. It was nice to hear it again for a few weeks.

I recall the grueling existence I endured in Bhutan. I

sharpened myself, learning, training, preparing for the moment when I would return to settle the score with the one who took my soul from me. My uncle Akuma, the man who shaped me, twisted me, and abandoned me, and played a role in murdering my father, Takeshi—his older brother—and my other uncle, Akira—their younger brother—for his own power-hungry pursuits.

I ring the doorbell. There is no hesitation, no fear in the gesture. I have nothing left to lose now. My last true remaining family member is dead. The only men that ever partially cracked my heart open are hunting me, as they should. I deserve whatever wrath they have planned for me. I have nothing left but Han, he is the only person alive who still gives a shit about me, and well, he's better off without me. All that remains now is the inevitable reckoning.

The door swings open, revealing a butler. My butler, I realize. Fuck me, he's still alive? His tired eyes quickly flicker with recognition.

Fucking finally, someone recognizes me.

"Miss Sora," he says, his voice a mixture of surprise and veneration. He steps aside, allowing me entry. I see tears welling up in his eyes. Not now, old man. The girl you're looking for is dead.

"Is Uncle Satō home?" I ask, my tone sweet, feigned warmth dripping from my words.

"Yes, Miss Sora. He's in his study. We thought... You're..."

"Good," I reply with a nod, my lips curling into a smile that doesn't quite reach my eyes. "I'll surprise him, if you don't mind. Please bring us some hot water, I'd like to have some tea."

"Of course." The butler steps back, clearly flustered, unsure of the right protocol in this situation. The poor man just saw a ghost. He probably has no idea how to announce one, so I'll save him the trouble. I move past him with a graceful fluidity that surprises even me considering my current state. The heels of my riding boots clomp on the hickory solid hardwood floor as I walk toward the study.

Every step a beat in the symphony of my revenge.

My uncle's study, the one he stole from my father, is just as I remembered it. A large, imposing room filled with rich, dark cherry wood furniture, a wall of bookshelves, and a fireplace that crackles quietly in the corner. He didn't even bother to redecorate dad's space, just slithered into it like the conniving snake that he is.

I expected to feel more when I see him sitting behind his large executive desk, facing the window. I expected my heartbeat to spike, but instead I am engulfed in a sense of peace.

His posture is rigid, as always, but the years have not been kind to him. I guess betrayal ages a man. He looks older now, tired, the weight of his power seeming to have worn on him. Now that I see him up close and in profile, as opposed to the obstructed view at the karaoke bar or the masked view in the Amato pool house, he appears almost frail. His dark hair is peppered with gray, but his eyes still gleam with that familiar, calculating glint.

At the sound of my entrance, he turns sharply, his face momentarily betraying the shock before settling back into his controlled, distant mask.

"Sora?" Oh, so now everyone recognizes me. I guess that's good, it'll get this over with quicker if I don't need to make introductions. His voice is rough, as though he hasn't spoken in days. "What are you doing here? I thought you were dead."

"Uncle," I greet, my voice laced with falsified sweetness. I step into his study, my sharpened presence a stark contrast to the weathered, antiqued edges of the room. "It's been so long, hasn't it? I wasn't dead. Uncle Akira, Han, and I went to Bhutan after daddy died. We lived a quiet, peaceful life out there. It got lonely though. No family, no distractions. Just tranquility and peace." I step closer, surety flowing through my veins. "I missed you and decided it was time to come home. I thought of you often, of how we used to play teatime when I was a kid while dad was busy with work. I thought I'd drop by, see how you've been. I brought you a gift, for old time's sake."

His eyes narrow slightly, suspicion flickering in his gaze. "Bhutan?" he repeats, his voice tight. "And you've just decided to visit now? After all this time?"

I smile. "You always loved my surprises, didn't you?" I move in closer, standing over the chair across from him. "I brought you this." I pull the teapot out of the black velvet bag and place it on his desk. I pull out the two little matching cups. "It's from a renowned craftsman in Bhutan. I had it made especially for you. Will you tell me how you've been? I've missed our talks. You know, like when I was little... when you'd tell me stories over tea with Uncle Akira." The name almost gets stuck in my throat. But I smile and push past it.

"Speaking of Uncle Akira..." Fuck, it doesn't seem to get any easier to say. "Have you heard from him recently? I haven't been able to reach him these last few weeks."

He stares at me for a minute, studying my expression before he replies. "No, I haven't. It's been quite some time since we've spoken."

"It's okay, I'm sure he's just busy, I'll try him again later. This visit is about you. You know, I've always admired you.

Look at what you've built since daddy died. Something so... formidable. How did you do it? Achieve all of this?"

Uncle Satō's face softens. "You were always a curious child," he says, his voice a little more affectionate. "You've always had a thirst for knowledge."

"And I've learned so much," I reply, my words soft, while I hide the internal flicker of something darker. "You'd be proud of me, Uncle."

He watches me, and then, in a gesture that feels almost familial, he waves his hand. "Sit. Let's use this fancy teapot you've brought to share a drink while you fill me in on your adventures."

"That would be lovely," I reply, a smile playing on my lips.

The butler walks in with the hot water and places it on a trivet on Uncle Satō's desk.

"Perfect timing, thank you, Daisuke."

The teapot is small, intricately designed, a gift I had made especially for him in Bhutan. I wasn't lying about that.

I place the tea into the pot and pour in the hot water. The rich scent of jasmine fills the room. We wait in tense silence for the tea to brew, just a minute or so. Long enough for certainty to settle into my bones. I carefully pick up the teapot and fill Uncle Satō's cup. I place it on his desk in front of him. When I pick the teapot back up, I place my thumb on top and wrap the rest of my fingers around the handle.

I take my cup, inspecting it for a moment before bringing it to my lips and blowing on it. "Thank you, Uncle," I say softly, my voice dripping with feigned gratitude. "It reminds me of when I was younger... when you would make me tea. Do you remember?"

"I remember," he replies, his expression softening further. "It's good to see you have maintained your same nature. You were precocious and so eager to please as a child, it's good to see that some things haven't changed."

"You used to let me serve you and Akira my special tea, remember?" I take another sip, letting it linger on my tongue, feeling the warmth spread through me. For a moment, I wonder if he could see through my carefully constructed façade, if he could sense the trap closing in around him.

I watch him carefully, noting the way his gaze lingers on me. Once I take my third sip, he picks up his cup and brings it to his lips.

At least he's careful, but still so quick to dismiss I see. After all, I am merely a woman. He is too consumed with his own power to ever see what lays beneath the surface right in front of him. A woman could never be a threat to him. A woman should have never been designated as the heir to the Yakuza. That's what he told the men he ordered to kill me. I instinctively touch the scar on my gut.

I set my cup down gently. "Uncle, I've thought a lot about what you've built... the organization you've run all these years since daddy passed away. I can't say I haven't admired it, in a way. You were a great man, once." My voice softens, as if I am speaking of someone lost to time, someone from long ago. "But somewhere along the way, things changed. And I was left behind."

His smile fades slightly, replaced by a look of uncertainty, but he says nothing. He'd never been good with emotions, never comfortable with vulnerability. Men can't feel, he would say. Feelings are a weakness and they will get you killed. At least he got that part right.

I lean forward slightly, my gaze unwavering. "I came

back to show you how much I've grown, Uncle. I came back to thank you."

"Thank me?" His voice is low, confused. He throws me a puzzled look, his eyebrows raised. "For what?"

"For everything," I whisper. "For making me who I am."

Before he can respond, I continue. The room seems to grow colder, the air thicker. "Do you remember the stories you used to tell me?" I ask, my voice now like ice. "How power is built on the destruction of others? How the weak deserve to have everything taken from them? How you told me that the ends justified any means? All that ever matters, Sora, is the result. Never make excuses, deliver. Never ask permission, take. Power is not earned, it belongs to those who seize it."

My uncle's face twists with recognition and just a hint of fear. I guess no one is immune to primal emotions. His hand instinctively reaches for the cup of tea he just finished.

A satisfied smile breaks out on my face. He knows.

"No..." he begins, but it is too late.

"You see," I continue, my voice steady and cold, "I've been learning from the best." I get up from my chair and take a step toward him, my eyes lock on his, never once blinking.

"But you... drank it, too... you're fine," he says as he claws at his throat that inarguably is depriving him of oxygen as it constricts.

"It's an assassin's pot. Funny how you were there at one of my tea parties when Uncle Akira told me that I should invest in one. Do you remember? You agreed with him, 'deception is cleaner, Sora. No need to get your hands dirty.' What was it you always used to say... ah yes, Sun Tzu, 'supreme excellence consists in breaking the enemy's resistance without fighting.' See, I told you I learned a lot from you."

Fuck, whoever said revenge isn't satisfying clearly doesn't know what they are talking about. This feels so fucking good. The look of shock on his face. Shock that he has been bested by a woman. You know, because we are chaotic and ruled by our emotions and can never execute and command. Fuck me, that look of shock is fucking priceless.

"It's not too slow, but it is a painful death." I square my shoulders. "The poison coursing through your veins does take time, but not too much. And when it's done... when it settles into your blood and begins to shut down your organs, I want you to remember who did this to you. I know what you did. I know you and the Don are the reason why my father is dead. Why Tor's mother is dead. Why I was almost dead. Why uncle Akira is dead."

My uncle's face drains of color, his breath becomes shallow as the poison starts to take its toll. His eyes widen in panic as he clutches his chest, struggling to breathe. Fuck yes. Die, you fucking piece of shit. I wish it hurt more. As the reality that he is about to die settles in, an uncomfortable wave of nothingness washes over me. I snatch at the euphoria, trying to claw it back. Oh. This is what they mean.

He claws at his neck and knocks a sakura paperweight off of the desk. Mom bought that for dad when I was ten. Dick. Going out destroying as much of what I love as he can.

I thought this would be more satisfying. It's anticlimactic. I watch him with a cool detachment, almost as if I am not present in the room anymore. I want that feeling of satisfaction back but I can't seem to reclaim it. It's almost as if I am not witnessing the death of the man who set the chain of events in motion that destroyed and derailed my entire life.

"I've done more than just learn, Uncle. I've been dismantling your empire. Bit by bit. Your network, your alliances... all of it, that has been Akira and me. Every move you made, I've watched. Every weakness you thought you had hidden, I've exposed."

I pause, savoring the sound of his labored breaths. "And do you know why I did it?" I ask softly, stepping around the desk, closer to him. "Because everything you have isn't yours. It never was. You stole it all, and I'm taking it all back. The worst thing that you said could ever happen to the Yakuza. That it be led by an unhinged woman? Well, that moment is here."

His eyes bulge as he gasps for air, his body convulsing uncontrollably as foam builds in his mouth.

"And thank you, Uncle," I whisper, my lips curling into a twisted smile. "Thank you for creating me. A monster with no weakness. No fear. I couldn't have done this without you."

With a final, gasping breath, my uncle slumps forward, his body going limp. The pen holder and telephone are knocked over as he collapses, breaking the silence in the room with a loud bang.

Daisuke runs in, and stands shocked at the doorway, his hand braced against the thick wooden frame. "Miss Sora, I..."

"Call the cleaners, Daisuke, I'll need them on standby. Send out the call. I want everyone here, now."

"Yes, Miss Sora, right away." He scrambles to exit the room.

I stand there for a moment, observing the dead body.

My posture unchanged, my heart cold and unmoving. After a moment, I step back and bow my head slightly. I will never mourn him. I will never regret what I have done. But I don't want the Yakuza. I don't want to own anything. I just want to kill the Don and rest, so we do what must be done.

I have become everything he had made me. It is time to finish this so I can finally let the woman he created become undone.

I call Han. "It's time to move. Set it all in motion, and gather all the men. He's dead."

"Yes, onna-oyabun."

SPIDER

This is the last place I want to be. I adjust the collar of my suit. I'm not sure what is worse, that I have to be here or that I have to play dress up whenever I'm in the presence of the Don. As if dressing like a businessman changes the fact that we work for the scum of the earth. I can't believe I didn't see it all this time. Or maybe I did and just didn't want to believe that the man who clothed and sheltered me when I had nothing is just as bad, if not worse than the one who sired me and left my mom and I to fend for ourselves.

As I park my car in front of the gaudy door I've grown to hate, I find I'm not even remotely looking forward to telling the Don it was us. We were the ones who let a tiger into our den of wolves. Not a tiger. A dragon coiled around bodies. Made of fury and pure fire, ready to burn everything to the ground. I don't know all of what she found that made her leave us. But I know it has something to do with the death of her father and the attempt on her life when she was just a little girl. I also know I'm close to figuring it out. I check the status of the decryption one last time before heading in to see if it's been cracked. It has to break eventually.

I walk into the Don's office, who lays in wait like a predator. I immediately look down. I hate this fucking rug. The blinds are drawn, and the room is dark other than a small green desk lamp. The air seems to crackle with the weight of unuttered words and barely restrained violence. Men move like shadows around the long, wooden desk where Don Amato sits, his heavy hands resting on the polished surface as if anchoring the storm that brews in his chest. They know something is coming. I can feel it, too.

I step close to his desk, my gait easy, but my muscles coil beneath my tailored suit. The low murmur of voices dies the moment I cross some unspoken threshold. My eyes scan the room, noting every gun, every hand lingering too close to a concealed weapon. I never let my guard drop. Not for anyone, and not especially with what I know now.

"You're late," Don Amato growls without looking up.

"I had to be sure," I reply. My voice is steady, my best attempt to keep myself from betraying the unease that twists my stomach into knots. "We found the girl."

The Don tilts his head to the side, his dark eyes narrowing into slits.

I nod. "It's her. She's been pulling the strings all along. The disruptions, the attacks on our shipments, the dismantling of the alliance between us and the Yakuza and Satō... it all traces back to her."

I watch Don Amato's tightening fists, tension rolling through his desk. A glass of whiskey trembles slightly before settling again. His men shift uncomfortably, eyes darting to one another, wary of the storm brewing in the boss's eyes.

"You mean to tell me," Amato says, his voice low and

venomous, "that the girl you decided to save, to bring into my empire, despite Blade—the only one among you three with half a fucking brain cell—telling you to put her down, is the one who's been undermining my business all along? That it wasn't Akira, but her who is the head of the fucking snake?"

I incline my head, not bothering to repeat myself. That question is definitely rhetorical. Unnecessary words might get me killed here.

The Don's knuckles whiten. He rises slowly, pushing back his chair with an ominous scraping groan. "You let this happen under your nose? You've been tracking her for three weeks, and this is the best you can give me? You did this. You brought this rot into my Eden." Ironic, for him to think we're in Eden. This is hell.

I hold my ground; weakness is also death in this room, but the tension in the air pulls tighter, like a wire about to snap. "We followed every lead, Don. She covered her tracks well. And besides... she's not just some girl."

Amato steps around his desk, coming to stand just inches from me. "What does that mean?"

I meet the Don's gaze without flinching. "It means she had reasons. I'd bet my life that you'd have done the same in her place. She's Takeshi Satō's daughter."

A silence stretches between us, taut and unyielding. I'm pretty sure I just signed my death warrant; silence would have been the better play. Why the fuck did I just say that?

The Don's lip curls in disgust, but he says nothing. Instead, he jabs a finger at my chest.

"Bring her to me. Alive. You understand? I don't care what her reasons are."

I take a step back, nodding once. "Yes, sir."

I slowly back out of the room, my pace calm but deliberate. Even as the door looms so close to me, I resist the urge to hurry. I never turn my back to anyone, and I am not about to start now. Especially not in Amato's house after I just royally fucked up. Seriously why the fuck did I say that?

The heavy front doors of the house shut behind me with a resonating thud. As soon as I step into the cool night air, my phone vibrates in my pocket. I pull it out, glancing at the screen. My code finally cracked the encryption.

My pulse quickens as I lean into the passenger seat of my blacked-out sedan. I grab my laptop, already booted up, and open the files. A steady stream of data comes to life before my eyes.

This was what she was looking for. This was what she found. This was why she left us.

And I was finally going to see it for myself. The screen flickers before grainy footage emerges. I lean against the car, holding the laptop in my left hand, my right hand tapping the trackpad to flip through the files.

My jaw clenches at the scene playing out before me. The Don, unmistakable even in the dim light of the footage, his hands gripping the wrists of Blade's sister. The raw agony on her face as she struggles to get away from him. The moment she stops fighting, I click away. He took from her what no one should ever unwillingly be forced to concede; I'm not taking anything else from her. I saw enough to know what happened, no one ever needs to see the rest.

My grip on the laptop tightens and I hear the hinges crack. I see messages from Blade's mother. She had begged Satō's brother, Kai's father, for help, telling him she suspected Amato was behind the events that led to her daughter's suicide. He turned her away. "I'm sorry, Izumi. Excommunicated is excommunicated. You knew that when you married your Italian husband. I want to help you, but I can't. My hands are tied."

The next frame is pictures of Izumi and her husband's murder at the hands of the Don. Blade's parents, bound and kneeling. Amato's men circling them like vultures. A single gunshot to each head. Two bodies collapsed.

I lean closer, barely breathing. The stream of images, files, messages, and videos continue, grainy but clear enough to capture every haunting detail. Kai's father, too. Specifically, the Don's murder of Kai's father. He had me unwittingly protecting this information for years. If I had known, I would have leaked it myself.

But it wasn't over. I don't know how much more my stomach can take. A series of messages follow. Text chains between Satō and Amato, their language clinical and cold. Plans for the murders. Discussions of alliances and betrayals. Satō's promise to kill Amato's wife in exchange for the life of his own brother, the Yakuza boss who had refused the alliance.

The oyabun's words to the Don, "You are not an honorable man." Holy fuck. He rejected the alliance because of what he learned from Izumi and in the end, they were both killed for it.

The Don is right about one thing. Honor will get you killed in this life.

A video of Satō going on and on about how women can't lead or rule.

My heart pounds its way out of my chest. I freeze, as if my entire body is made of lead. My eyes stay glued to the screen, in shock and yet somehow still, somewhere in the back of my mind, I realize the grave mistake I have made.

It has been less than a few minutes, but that is a few minutes too long.

My back is to the compound. Exposed. Vulnerable.

The first shot punches into my shoulder, knocking me forward. My laptop clatters to the custom paving stones, shattering and splintering.

I grunt, hiding on the passenger side of my car as pain flares through my back.

Another shot follows, grazing my ribs. I gasp, adrenaline coursing through me as I stagger forward, running toward the tree line to get away. The third shot sends me crashing to my knees. I am not making it out of this. I grab my phone and start sending files to Blade. All but the one of his sister.

My last conscious thought: Blade, please protect her.

CHAPTER 25

KAI

My uncle's body slumped unceremoniously over the desk is the perfect set dressing for what comes next. The emptiness of earlier has evaporated and in its place is pure steel resolve. I remember my father's words.

'You take care of your men, you look out for them, look after them like family, but never make the mistake of treating them like family. You do not count on them, have contingencies on contingencies, but you make sure they can count on you. To follow you they must respect you and to respect you they must never be able to predict your next move. Never let your guard down, never let them get close, and when necessary, make sure you show them exactly who they are dealing with should they fail to prove their loyalty to your clan.'

Well here it is, boys. Here is who you are dealing with. Ken and the other Yakuza heads file in and draw their guns as they enter the room. Han and my men stand in a semi-circle behind me. They draw their guns. Fucking men. I can't think over the sound of their incessant shouting.

"Enough. Put your fucking guns down."

Ken steps forward, pointing his gun directly at my face from across the desk. "Start talking, now. The punishment for killing the oyabun is death."

"Exactly, and I've just carried it out. Be happy I haven't decided to kill you, too, for the part you played twelve years ago." I run my hand along the scar on my lower belly. "Right now, I'm honoring the fact that you were just following orders. Shut up and back away before I change my mind." I turn on the monitor on my uncle's desk—no, on *my* desk—and turn it around. I press play on the video.

Grainy footage shows my uncle meeting with the Don, in this very study, the night of my father's death.

My traitorous uncle's voice grates at my skin as he facilitates fratricide using the hand of another. "He'll be at the dinner for the next two hours. He's with his daughter. Take care of the oyabun. We'll take care of the girl later."

"And my wife?" the Don replies nonchalantly as if killing your wife holds the same significance to him as his lunch order.

"I'll take care of her tonight. Text me the location," my uncle replies coolly. Every time I hear his voice my blood seems to freeze in my veins.

"It can't get back to anyone in my crew that either of our organizations were involved. If it does, we can't shake on the deal as planned." The Don focusing on business with callous disregard for humanity causes me to swallow hard to avoid regurgitating my tea, the only thing I've consumed in the last twenty-four hours. It's all in a day's work: kill your rival, have him kill your wife, shake on a deal. What did I expect? I saw how he treats Tor, his own fucking flesh and blood, why the fuck would the woman who gave him his heir be entitled to any better from him?

"It's mutually assured destruction, Amato. That's the only way this works. We handle this ourselves, we close the deal, and we both become very rich men." Once my uncle finishes speaking, the Don gets up, shakes my uncle's hand and leaves the room. My uncle pulls his gun from his top desk drawer and exits after him.

Fucking piece of shit. I should have picked a more painful poison. My entire body convulses at the sound of his words. I want him to get up so I can kill the fucker all over again.

I pull out Blade's knife and repeatedly stab my uncle's lifeless body.

For a moment I'm so focused on wanting to destroy him that I forget I have an audience. I look up, with blood drenched hands, to see the room staring at me with horrified, sickened expressions. My men take a step back and my uncle's men—fuck, wait, no, they are also my men—shift uncomfortably in place. I look down to see small droplets of blood on my jeans and t-shirt. Thankfully he was already dead so it's not too insane of a mess, though the desk is covered in his spit and blood. Fucking gross.

The muffled whispers in the room, while muted, have the same effect on my eardrums of standing by a subwoofer at a heavy metal concert.

Pretending as if I didn't just mutilate a corpse, I play the next video. I can't bear to watch it. My daddy's beautiful face fills the screen, in this same office, talking to Akira.

"If anything happens to me, you make sure that Sora takes the reins. Do you understand?"

"Why aren't you telling Akuma?"

"Because he is the one I am worried about. Promise me, Akira. Promise me that if anything happens to me you will die protecting her. I name her as my successor."

I shut the video off. I can't stand to see either of them for a second longer. My heart is bleeding so profusely it's made its way down to my gut. My chest constricts but there is nothing in there for it to squeeze.

"Any questions?"

The room erupts in those muffled fucking whispers again. I watch as the recognition I kept longing for strikes home in their eyes. They all know who I am now. Good. Fucking finally. After a beat, and likely because I look like a fucking psychopath with Blade's bloody knife still in hand, they all reply in unison, "No, onna-oyabun."

The sound of that in unison stops me cold. Fucking weird.

"Aright then, first order of business. Tonight, we kill the Don. Gather everyone. And I mean everyone. We attack the compound."

The unison, "Yes, onna-oyabun," still takes me by surprise.

I expected them to put up a fight. I expected resistance. Instead what I got was an army of men, marching out into the streets, carrying out my orders. *Thank you, Daddy. I will end this for you tonight.*

"The plan and your orders have been sent to your phones," I command. "We end this now. If you have any questions, Han will be happy to answer them."

I walk outside to where my bike and SUV are parked, the wind chill tells me a storm is brewing. Apropos. Leaves are flying around in every direction and the lack of any bird sounds must mean it's going to be a big one.

I slide my father's katanas in place on my back, buckle up my gun holster and place my dagger garter belt around my thigh. I go to put down Blade's knife, but decide to pull one of my daggers out and replace it with his in the garter holster on my thigh. It's the only piece of them I have left. I will carry it with me to the end.

Will my reign be the shortest in history? Probably, but it will likely go down as the most epic. I smile, fitting I think. Daddy always said I could never do anything half measured, it just wasn't in my makeup.

I shut the trunk and jump when I see him there.

Tor emerges from the shadows and towers over me.

"How did you find me?" I try to catch my breath.

He doesn't say a word.

"Fucking Blade. Where is it, where's Spider's tracker?" I ask, stepping toward him.

He doesn't move back, instead he crowds my space, body stiff, his face colder than I have ever seen it. "You don't need to worry about that right now. Tell me why."

"Why what?"

"Why did you pretend to care about me? You could have gotten everything you needed without making me feel like I mattered for the first time in my fucking life. You made me feel like I was enough for you. Like I meant something, and then you fucking left. Why?" His voice cracks a bit at the end. Fuck.

When I don't respond, he shoves me against the car. I'm pinned between him and the back of my SUV. The night air feels cool against my skin, yet my body is burning as if I am engulfed in fire.

"You never needed me. You used us. You used me. Why?" His dejected tone breaks something within me I didn't know I had left to break.

"Ask me to stay," I whisper softly.

"What?" He looks at me, eyes flicking all over my face, searching. Shocked. Like that was the last thing he expected me to utter.

"Ask me to stay. I am going to kill your father. I can't stop that, but if you ask me to stay, I will, as soon as it's done." My words come out more pleading than my pride can truly process in this moment.

"I don't fucking want you." He looks at me like I've grown a second head. "I don't want you to stay. Kai, are you delusional? You're not going to kill my father. If I don't kill you, an army of his men will do so before you ever even reach him."

I hear the words, but why does his tone sound like he's worried about me.

I hear the men filing out of the house. I'm running out of time. The sound of thunder in the distance startles me. Fuck, it's time to go, but I can't make myself leave.

"Highly likely." I try to laugh off the morbidity of my impending doom, then stop abruptly when I see the look of anguish on his face. I look up at him the same way I did that night when he was sitting on the edge of his bed after his father ripped into him and robbed him of his command.

It hits me: I am fucking in love with him. I'm in love with all of them.

Fuck. Fuck. Fuck.

I close my eyes and take in a deep breath. Fuck it. I don't care anymore. It's not too late to call it off; it would just take Han sending one mass text.

"Tell me you want me and I'll stop." I can't believe I am fucking saying this. Out loud. My words tumble out, rushing against my better judgment. "I'll walk away. Right now. With you, with Spider, with Blade. Tell me you want me and I will turn around and call it all off."

Should I tell him I love him? Yes, I decide, that's what I should do. I open my mouth to speak the words, but he cuts me off.

"I don't trust you. I will never trust you. I don't think I ever meant anything to you." The pain in his trembling voice guts my insides to shreds. "You were using me the whole time. I don't want you. And there is no point in killing you, if the compound is where you're headed. You'll be dead soon enough. Just fucking go, let them kill you, you're not even worth the mess of your blood on my hands."

I reach for him, but he steps back outside of my grasp. The air between us engulfs me, suffocates me.

I did this. I need to own it. "You're right, I just wanted to know who killed my dad. You were a means to an end. I never needed you. I just needed information. I never expected anything from you."

He looks up at me in anger, nostrils flaring.

I continue. "I never expected to fall for you, but here we are."

His expression softens and he takes a step back toward me.

My confession flows, unstoppable now that I've started. "I didn't expect to want you. But I do. I never expected to love you, but you know what, I fucking do."

The look on his face is a mixture of confusion, awe, hope, despair.

"In another life..." I take a steadying breath, trying to hold back tears. "I would have given you everything. If you ever fell, I would have gotten on my knees to hold you up. In another life, I would have never left you. But I don't want to wait for another life. I've wasted enough of this one. Your father and my uncle Akuma have taken enough from me in this one. We are here, right now, in this life, and I am telling you, as plainly as I can, you are everything to me. You, Blade, and Spider. The three of you have become *everything* to me. I love you so much that I am willing to walk away from the war I have been fighting my whole life. Since my father was gunned down in front me when I was only a child. Since I was attacked and almost killed in my own home that same night. That man your father killed in the pool house…"

I can't hold back the tears anymore. They slide slowly down my face, but I keep going, steady and sure that I am doing the right thing. "That was the only family I had left. He was my uncle Akira and he's the reason I made it out alive all those years ago."

I see tears building in his eyes. He didn't know. He didn't know any of this.

"He's the one who has been helping me find out who took my dad from me, almost took my life from me, so that I can kill them and finally rest. Your father has taken everything from me. And I am telling you right now, I am not willing to let him also take you, or Blade, or Spider." The tears spill from my eyes in an uncontrollable stream. I don't swipe them away. "In this life, I can't change what's done. But if you tell me to, I will walk away with you. We'll fly to a beach, anywhere you choose. We will live our lives away from all of this. Tell me you want me and I am yours. Tell me you love me and I will never leave you again."

He stares at me for the space of three full heart beats. "I want nothing to do with you." He takes another step back. Lightning lights the sky. The cruel, emotionless expression it illuminates on his face forces me to gasp.

I don't know why I keep talking. "Okay, Tor. Okay. But just so you know, I didn't need to be there as long as I was. I stayed because I wanted to." I see it plainly on his face: he doesn't believe me. He probably never will. "Yeah, I told myself it was to learn more, but we got everything we needed well before anything ever happened between you and me. I stayed for you, for Spider, for Blade. I would have kept staying."

Am I trying to change his mind? Or mine?

Honestly what the fuck, I can't stop talking. "Do not use what happened between us to reinforce that bullshit story your father has been drilling into your head since you were a boy. You were never not enough. You are one of the most amazing men I have ever met. I was never your enemy. I never would have tried to intentionally hurt you. I would have protected you at the expense of myself. I still would, if you asked me to."

I must be trying to make myself feel better because the words won't stop flowing from my mouth. I'm not even sure he is listening. Fucking guilt is a motherfucker. "You wanted control, and I watched you try to take it, over and over again. But the truth is, you never had to fight for it. It was always yours. I was always yours. Not because I was weak, not because you forced it, but because I chose you. The only way to control me is for me to willingly submit. And all *you* have to do is ask."

Oh, I am trying to convince him. I guess my heart hasn't caught up to my mind yet. Embarrassment sluices through me, the sting of rejection causing me to flush hot in the worst way. "Just like in the parking garage. I know why you won't believe me. I know I lied to you about who I was, but we both know that isn't what you're upset about. Maybe because no one else ever meant it when they said it to you. Maybe because you don't want to believe it's true even though you can feel that it is. But I do mean it. I fucking love you, Tor."

I don't think he notices that he takes a step toward me again.

I press the advantage. "You don't need to earn it, or prove you deserve it. You don't need to hide any part of who you are. It's just fucking you, I love you. And I will keep loving you, because my love is mine to give. I'm begging you, please ask me to stay. Tell me you love me too and we walk. Right now."

Jesus Christ.

The lightning crackles through the sky and lights up his face. His eyes tell me he doesn't believe a word I said. His expression is back to cruel indifference.

He doesn't say a word. He simply turns around and walks away.

I yell after him, "I won't be here when you wake up tomorrow."

He stops in his tracks but doesn't turn around.

"But I need you to remember something. You don't need to be anyone else, or try to be better. Fuck every expectation that has ever been placed on you. Just be you. The best version of you that you can be. I believe in the man I saw, the one you are at your core. That is the man I fell in love with."

He turns around to look at me, tears welling in his eyes and for one moment I feel like there is a possibility. Like there is hope. So I keep talking.

"If you think pushing me away will protect you from pain, you're wrong. I know you think I'd leave again, that I'd give up, that I'd prove you right, that you're unlovable like your dad has told you your whole life, but you're wrong. I don't know who I am without a thirst for the blood of the man who took my life from me. That has been my singular focus for over a decade, but I am telling you, say the word, and I will figure out how to be something different at your side."

My heart drops into my stomach before the words ever leave his mouth. "I feel nothing for you. I don't love you. I never did. And I never will."

He turns and walks away without looking back.

I thought all the pieces in me were already broken, but it turns out there was still a small shard left to shatter. Tonight is the first night I ever told a boy I love him. And tonight that same boy told me he doesn't love me. So this is what heartbreak feels like. I knew it was coming; I grieved them on the floor of that shower.

Tonight, at least, it ends.

Tonight, the Don dies.

Tonight, I die. I lock up the SUV and climb onto my bike, geared up and ready for battle. I take a deep breath, trying to quell the tears that won't stop falling. I rev the engine.

The sky begins to cry along with me.

CHAPTER 26

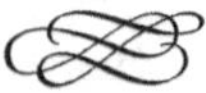

BLADE

I sit on the foot of my bed, in my dimly lit room, elbows on my knees, the glow of my phone screen the only source of light. Fuck, we should have all gone together. Something doesn't fucking feel right. The notification blinks on my phone as I feel the slight vibration. I open it, relief flooding through me at seeing Spider's name. It's instantly chased away by rage. Indescribable, insatiable blood lust and rage.

The attachments unfold like a curse.

At the bottom of the message, a simple line of text:

She's Takeshi's daughter. Find her. Help her. Keep her safe.

My hands tremble as I get up to grab my laptop and properly see what Spider sent.

I swallow hard as the files download, my fingertips trembling against the trackpad. My jaw clenches, my insides churning as I'm bombarded with more than I can take. I sit back on the edge of the bed.

Videos.

Emails.

Text chains.

My parents, and a fuckton of evidence that says it was the Don who raped my sister.

The Don. The man who took me in, raised me, named me his heir over his own fucking blood born son. No. Fuck no. No that's not fucking possible.

Why would he... just to...? I can't form coherent thoughts.

I click through most of it, skimming to glean what's necessary and then clicking away to avoid having to confront the worst, most gut-wrenching details. I do watch surveillance footage of Akira meeting with Don Amato in his office, though. While to the untrained eye his stance would look strong, the weight distribution onto his right leg tells me he is severely injured and hiding it. "I am his kari-oya, or how would you say it? Godfather. Blade belongs with me. That is where his parents wanted him," Akira says as he puffs out his chest, gearing for a fight.

"I have thus far not killed you out of respect for your brother," the Don snarls, "but if you say another word, I will. Leave now. He is not your concern."

Akira steps forward. "I'm not leaving without the boy." He pulls his gun from its holster.

The Don shoots before Akira gets off a single shot; where the gun came from, I can't see. He's too fast on the draw, even as I rewatch the moment.

Shouts of men in the distance can be heard, presumably they are on their way to kill Akira. I can see blood flowing down his arm and back as he runs out of the house. I check the time stamp. The day after the previous oyabun died.

I sit there for a minute thinking about what my life would have been like had I been raised by Akira instead of the Don. Alongside Kai. I stood in that goddamn pool house and let the Don kill him. I disposed of his body like it was trash. Did Kai know this?

Another message pops up, this one marked 'emergency.'

I click a link in the message and a live video feed streams through. Surveillance footage from the front gate of the Amato compound. It's hard to see everything that is going on. While I can make out the brick walkway, the angle has an obstructed view. The side of the mansion is blocking me from seeing what is happening around the corner fully, and the shadows from the tree line makes it all even harder to make out. There's a shape of a man under those shadows, shoes that might be familiar, if the footage was a little clearer.

I know, though. Only one person could have set this up, and only one person would have trusted me to know. Spider.

Don Amato emerges from the front doors, hands in his pockets as he surveys Spider's crumpled body on the side of the house. There is so much fucking blood.

Amato flicks ash from his cigar, making a dismissive motion with his hand. I know that motion. He's telling his men to dispose of the body. Then he points elsewhere. I squint at the screen, nearly putting my nose against it, as if I can actually get close enough to see. But I think it's a laptop on the driveway, near the edge of the fountain. I finally notice the nose of Spider's car, just barely visible in the frame.

As his men drag Spider's body away out of view, the Don turns without another glance, retreating into the darkened doorway.

I sit there for I don't know how long, staring at the computer screen, at the image of the driveway, in shock. My chest is constricted so tight that I can't breathe. I start gasping for air. Fuck, why can't I breathe?

No. No. No. This isn't happening.

Rain lashes against the windowpane like a thousand needles trying to pierce the glass, but inside this room, the weight of silence presses heavier than the storm outside. This storm is just getting started.

My shock is replaced by pure adrenaline in my veins. I get up and walk to the living room, outside to the driveway, unlock the trunk of the SUV, and open my duffel bag. I take stock of what weapons are inside. This isn't enough.

I reenter the house and stand in the doorway, drenched and dripping, my eyes steady and sharp when I see him there. I lock onto Tor, who sits slumped into the couch, feet propped on the coffee table, cigarette dangling loosely from his lips, bottle of whiskey in hand. He's also soaking wet. He's staring blankly at the flickering television, but neither of us seems to care what is playing.

Tor doesn't look up right away when I clear my throat, but I am sure he can feel my presence suffocating the room like a hand tightening around his throat. Sit the fuck back down, I yell internally to my cock as it stirs at the thought. We haven't been alone in a room together since that night. The last time I was this close to him, we had the buffer of Kai between us, and it wasn't to exchange words. But even now, the ghost of that intimacy barely lingers, it has been swallowed by everything that has come after.

"What do you want, Blade?" Tor exhales smoke toward the ceiling, pretending not to care how my knuckles whiten around the strap of my duffel bag.

I don't answer right away. I step forward, placing the bag gently on the floor. My movements are careful, measured, but the dangerous energy rolling off me in waves is anything but calm.

"Spider's dead." My voice cuts through the room, unfeeling and cold.

Tor finally turns his head, brows knitting together. I think this is the first time he's looked at me, really looked at me, since Kai disappeared. "What?"

"Your fucking father killed him." I step closer, my boots leaving wet prints on the hardwood floor. "Shot him in the back."

Tor drops his feet from the coffee table and sits up straight, the cigarette slipping from his fingers and hitting the floor with a faint sizzle. "No. That doesn't make sense. Spider... he wouldn't have—"

"He found something he wasn't supposed to." I cut him off, my voice gaining weight with every word. "He was trying to protect the girl. The one we thought was messing with us, the one we thought was pulling the strings. But it wasn't like that. Not really."

Tor's jaw clenches, his muscles tightening like coiled steel. "You're saying she's innocent now? After everything? What, she cries in your arms one fucking night and now it's suddenly *not* 'let's put down the stray.' Since when were you in the market to rescue?"

I shake my head slowly. "No. She's not innocent. But Spider was right, she had a reason. A really fucking good one."

Tor's lips curl into a humorless grin. "And let me guess, you believe him." He stands abruptly. I tower over him, yet I feel like the smaller man as he lowers his voice to a dangerous tone. "You're telling me that after everything we've done, after the people we've lost, you're siding with her? I heard her reasons, too. She's lying. Can you believe that dumb bitch said she *loves* us?"

"You spoke to her? When?" I feel like I've been doused in cold water. I couldn't have heard that right. Yet my heartrate seems held on to those words, quickly becoming erratic. I can't think about that right now. I need to act now; there will be time to process later. "You know what, it doesn't fucking matter that you went to see her. I'm going to kill your father."

He doesn't even flinch or react in anyway.

I ignore the way my heartrate accelerates at the thought that he got to see her again and I didn't. She loves us? She loves me? No. She can't possibly. My gaze remains steady, though my fingers twitch at my side. "Did you fucking hear me? Spider is dead. Your father killed him. I'm telling you Spider died trying to help her. I'm telling you I'm going to kill your father. He rape—"

"You're a liar." Tor's eyes flicker with something I can't quite place as he cuts me off. "You are all fucking liars," Tor spits out the words like venom. "Twisting things to suit your stories. All you ever want to do is kill things. And he fucking loves you for it. And now you're going to kill him? Fuck off, Blade. You're not killing my father over some stupid bitch that fooled us all because we were dumb enough to be addicted to her pussy."

I step back, but not because of Tor's words. Because I'm done explaining. Tor won't listen, not now. Maybe not ever.

"You think whatever you want," I say, my voice dropping to a deep growl. "But I'm done talking."

Tor shakes his head in disgust and storms past me, slamming the front door so hard the walls rattle. I don't move for a long moment, listening to the echo of Tor's stomping footsteps fade into the rain. I don't know where he's going and it doesn't matter. None of it matters anymore.

When I finally do move, it is to descend the creaking staircase to the basement, to the weapons cache to fill up this duffel bag. The cold air hits me like a slap to the face, but it is grounding, sharpening the blade of rage that has been festering inside me since the moment Spider's files hit my inbox.

Racks of guns line the concrete walls. Knives, explosives, and crates of ammunition stacked in neat rows like a shrine to the violence I normally thrive on. I move methodically, my hands working faster than my mind can keep up with. I load magazines, strap knives to my belt, and tuck a pistol into the back of my jeans, all the while picturing Amato's face.

The face of the man who raised me. The face of the man who molded me into his own personal weapon.

The same face of the man who ripped my family away from me. I thought for years that he helped turn me into a predator, while all along, I've simply been his prey. That he's been playing with.

My sister's eyes, lifeless and cold, flash in my mind. I'm the one who found her. I don't ever tell people that part. My parents' blood on the walls of our home. I found them, too. I don't tell people that part either. Funny how nobody ever asks.

For years I had buried it, convinced myself I had found belonging under Amato's wing. But now, every memory I have is tainted with the truth Spider unearthed. The man I thought I owed everything to was the one who took it all away in the first place.

My breath grows shallower as I shut the stash doors with a violent swing. I storm up the steps, past the kitchen, out the front door without bothering to lock it behind me. I'm not coming back. Spider isn't coming back, and honestly, fuck Tor. The rain is pouring, but I'm already soaking wet so who fucking cares.

I slide into the driver's seat of my car and slam the door shut. The squish when my ass hits the leather seats is fucking uncomfortable. The roar of the engine fills the hollow space inside my chest, but not even that sound can drown out the pulse of rage building to a crescendo within me.

Spider told me to find Kai. To keep her safe. My princess can take care of herself. Hell she conquered us without even trying, I can't even imagine what's she's capable of when she's spent her whole life planning for it.

Tonight, I can't think about her.

Tonight, all I want is blood.

My tires scream against the wet pavement as I peel out of the driveway, my grip on the wheel tight enough to crack bone. The city blurs by in streaks of light and shadow. My only focus is getting to the compound. The sky depicting what I don't have the words to express. The storm that has been building inside me for over a decade is finally about to break.

CHAPTER 27

TOR

The rain has been falling for hours, a relentless sheet of water that blurs the edges of the compound's high, rusted gates. I never noticed the tinge of rust on the edges of the iron. I wonder how long it's been there, who else hasn't noticed.

The air is thick, heavy with moisture and the sense of something looming in the distance. I stride through the muddy grounds of the estate, the land that surrounds the mansion, boots sinking slightly with every step, my mind clouded by questions that I am tired of pondering. The storm echoing the chaos that is about to ensue.

She told me that she loves me. She's lying right? She has to be lying.

No one loves me. Not even me. I'm unlovable.

She used me. She's on her way to finish what she started. She doesn't love me. She's just fucking with my head. Again.

Spider's dead. Fucking dead.

And Blade's lost it completely. 'I'm going to kill your father.' I laugh. Okay, fucker. Good luck with that.

I am trying to stop the girl who woke up my heart only to crush it beneath her feet and my best friend from killing my father. The only one of us that ever managed to bring reason into the equation is dead. There is no world where tonight ends well.

My heart pounds with a mixture of dread and resolve.

I received word that Kai's crew is moving against my father's compound, they should be here any minute. I should have delivered the warning myself, but my mind is fucked and I'm fairly certain I'm running on autopilot. Plus, I'm fucking drunk. I sway as I continue. Every step closer to the compound feels like stepping further into a web of betrayal. My dad's a prick, sure, but he would never kill Spider. Blade is wrong. He is under that whore's spell just like fucking Spider is—was—and it is going to get him killed too. The shock prevents Spider's death from registering. He can't be dead. There's no way.

It's too much. Tonight has been too much. Fuck, everything has been too much since I barged into that fucking warehouse office, bleeding from my gut. I should have stayed home that night. A new wave of rage overtakes me as I remember that Kai, that fucking cunt, is the reason I was shot in the first place.

I approach the heavy iron gate and nod to the guards who stand watch, their faces tense but unreadable. I parked outside the compound because I have no idea what is in store here tonight.

The guards nod in recognition as I pass.

My blood is as much a part of this place as the stone walls that house it. Still, I can't shake the feeling that everything is on the verge of unraveling.

The storm seems to intensify as I enter the compound proper, the heavy, steady downpour soaking through my jacket and darkening my clothes. I cross the driveway, the fountain on the verge of overflowing with rainwater, and make my way to the main hall, my thoughts swirling, images of Spider's body haunting me more than I'd care to admit. Images of Kai's face when I told her I don't love her. Images of Blade's disappointment when I told him I don't believe him.

Blade's accusation rings in my ears, my mind filling in the details I didn't let him say. My father killed Spider. He raped Blade's sister, killed his parents. Do I confront my father? No, the accusations are too ridiculous to entertain.

Yet the wind is screaming that everything is about to come to a head. My gut is screaming at me to listen, but I can't fucking think.

Why do Blade's accusations sound eerily similar to Kai's?

I stop in the living room and see my father standing near the fire, his back to me, seemingly lost in thought. The house is bustling with men arming themselves for war.

"Father," I say, my voice low but steady. "Did you kill Spider?" No point in beating around the bush. Everything is already fucked, so I might as well just rip off the fucking band-aid.

The silence in the room is loud, the crackling of the fire the only sound that fills the space. My father stiffens and turns to look me in the eye. I see the muscles in his shoulders tighten, a blink of something. Anger? Guilt? The firelight dances on his features, making his expression difficult to read. Fuck, he looks like the devil himself.

I stand my ground, the weight of the question anchoring me to the spot, dripping on the priceless marble floors.

"Tor." My father's voice comes in with a sharp edge,

more controlled than I had anticipated. "How dare you ask me that?"

My stomach tightens, my fingers flexing into fists. "I need to know, Father. I need to know the truth."

The old man's face hardens, his expression growing colder by the second. "You think I would kill Spider? The man who fought beside me for years? The man I trusted with my life? The man I raised as one of my own sons?"

I meet my father's gaze, unwavering. Maybe he's telling the truth? "Then who did? Blade says it was you."

My father's eyes flick to the left before meeting mine again. He steps forward, anger radiating from him. "Don't listen to Blade's lies. He's in love with that wretched girl. The whore's manipulating him son, twisting everything."

"But—" I start, but he cuts me off.

"No, Tor, your precious Kai killed Spider. It was that whore, and you know it otherwise you wouldn't be here. You'd be chasing her down like foolish Spider and Blade. You're my son, Tor. I raised you better than that, and that's why you'll be the last one standing."

For the first time in all my years, my father spoke poorly of Blade and highly of me. The number of times I wished for this moment are countless. But as the words flow from my father's mouth, I feel empty. Hollow.

There is no soul left within me to crave his approval. My breath catches in my throat. "Kai? Why would she…"

"Because she's always been self-serving," my father spits out, stepping toward me. "She's never cared about anyone but herself. She thought she could take down the Amato name by cutting off our supply line. She thought she could bring down the Yakuza and destroy our alliance. And your obsession with her pussy almost helped her succeed. She infiltrated you, seduced you, used you, and then started attacking the empire that will one day belong to you."

"I..." I start.

"Who do you think could really kill Spider? The man who raised him alongside you, or the woman who fed you lies from the moment you laid eyes on her? Spider was just a casualty in her little game. Collateral damage."

My feet are stuck in the ground as if my boots are filled with lead. Unable to move. The accusation strikes deep. It makes sense. Nothing he's saying sounds like a lie.

She did lie to us. She did use us. She did manipulate us. But kill Spider? Could Kai have really done that? Was the woman who just told me she'd walk away if we came with her, the woman who just told me she loves me, capable of such cold, calculated treachery? Did she already know Spider was dead?

Wait, she had said if we *all* came with her. She said she loves *all* of us.

I shake myself mentally. No, that was just her trying to throw me off her scent. Of course, she's capable of this.

My father's right. It's the only thing that makes sense.

I want to say something, but before I can, the sound of gunfire cracks outside.

"Get ready, Tor," my father barks, his voice filled with cold command. "That bitch's assault on our empire ends tonight."

Our empire?

My father never shares power.

He never compliments me. He never disparages Blade. This is all—

Before the thought can take hold, the heavy-set front doors of the compound are blown off in an explosion. I flinch, heat searing my skin, debris raining down around me. I stumble away, unable to see clearly for the smoke, not sure where I am headed but survival instincts simply telling me to *move.*

My ears are ringing as I try to see through the haze. A bullet whizzes past and hits a bottle of something. Glass explodes, shooting shards and liquid in every direction.

I recover my senses to some degree and get my bearings. I am in the foyer somehow, facing the doors that were just blown to hell.

The storm outside seems to mirror the violence that has erupted within the compound. Gunfire, shouting, the shrill wail of alarms. The battle has begun.

Kai, ever composed, leads several men through the front of the compound like a commander marching her troops to battle. Her eyes are cold and calculating. "Kill them all," she orders. "But remember, Amato is mine."

My pulse quickens. This is it. This is the moment I was anticipating when I arrived. The one where everything falls apart. I can't focus on anything. Not the confusion in my chest, the disorienting feeling of betrayal and uncertainty, nothing. All I can do is stare at her and her army I didn't even know she had, laying waste to everything I have ever known.

A hand touches my shoulder and I turn, obeying without thinking.

I follow my father and his men into the heart of the compound. My father is in full commander mode, a true Don, barking orders and pushing his men forward.

Within moments, the battle reaches us, and I'm thrust into the chaos of combat. The hallways of the compound transform into a maze of fire and destruction. The air fills with the stench of smoke, sweat, and blood. While my body remains present, my mind is anywhere but here.

As if called upon by instinct, my weapon is in my hand, my body moving like a reflex as I fire. My muscles are tense with the adrenaline that courses through me.

My father fights at my side, deadly and precise. It dawns on me that I have never actually seen him fight before. This is the closest his reign has ever been to extinction.

Kai's presence is like a shadow moving through the chaos, her body a lethal blur as she strikes down anyone who dares cross her path. She hasn't seen me yet. And for a moment I am enraptured by her once again. The sheer force of will, the precision, the complete and utter fearlessness with which she navigates the chaos is bewitching.

She has always been bewitching. I guess that is the problem.

If everything hadn't played out as it did, if she wasn't here to kill us, this would have been the precise moment I realize I actually am in love with her. She really never needed me at all. She really could take care of herself. Letting us take care of her was something she chose to do. For a moment I picture what it would be like if I let her take care of me. A gunshot flying past my ear interrupts the thought, the man beside me goes down.

Her gaze catches mine, and she quickly shakes her head no, before saying something inaudible—I assume into her earpiece. I turn just as one of her men pushes past me to take out one of my father's guards. For one second, I held on to hope that she told them not to kill me, but I don't let that thought take root.

The tension between us is still there, undeniable. But in the face of this oncoming wave, there is no room for hesitation. I need to look away. To focus. She looks away first and continues on in her quest for my father, who I've lost sight of.

I press forward, gunfire ringing in my ears, blood spraying the walls, the marble floors, my hands. The compound I grew up in is under siege for the first time I am aware of. The ease with which she and her crew penetrated the fortress is unfathomable.

This battle is about more than just survival for her. It is about revenge, power, control. And the truth, whatever that might be. The truth that keeps evading me.

As I fight my way through the halls, my mind wanders back to Spider. To the accusations. To my father's cold declaration. The battle continues on around me in slow motion. I can't shake the feeling that something deeper is happening here, something that is slipping away from me with every passing second. I need to think and it's the one thing I don't have the time to do.

She specifically said she would walk away with all of us. Including Spider. No hesitation in her gaze, no sadness in her eyes, no indication whatsoever that she even knew Spider is dead.

I turn the corner and there she is again. Kai.

Her eyes glint with an emotion I can't read. She moves swiftly, cutting down everyone in her way with the precision of a hawk.

My breath catches in my throat, my instincts screaming at me to stop her, to tell her I'll leave with her. I can't lose anyone else. Not tonight. Not ever. I start toward her, but before I can reach her, amid the madness, Blade appears.

Kai is less than three feet away from me, gun in one hand, knife in another. If I reach out now, I can touch her. I think that is Blade's knife in her hand. Despite the stench of blood and death, I can still smell her. Lavender, honey, citrus, and defiance.

She is a vision of deadly grace, cutting through the enemy ranks, our ranks, with lethal accuracy. Her eyes cold, her movements swift, her focus singular. Her men follow her lead, cutting down anyone in their path as they charge forward with a single-minded purpose. That's the entire Yakuza.

She's backed by the entire fucking Yakuza. What the actual fuck? What did I miss? When the hell did this shit happen? Where the fuck is Satō?

My heart skips a beat. Kai isn't just a threat; she is a whirlwind of destruction.

Without thinking, I move instinctively to intercept her, my gun raised, but it is too late. Her crew forms a perfect, impenetrable shield around her. No matter how many of our men charge at her, there is no slowing her and her army.

I catch a glimpse of my father again standing behind the dark wooden balusters on the mezzanine. My view of him is partially blocked by Kai and her men walking up the stairs. He stays ever vigilant, cuts through the chaos with surgical precision, and his movements are sharp and decisive. I notice the sweat on his brow. His arms look heavy with rigor; he is starting to show signs of wear.

As if in an instant, the carnage escalates. Blade is in full enforcer form, but he isn't fighting for us. He is cutting down my father's men, for Kai, as they make their way up the steps toward my father. Fucking traitor. I can't wrap my head around the fact that he isn't fighting by my side. None of this is making any fucking sense. It's as if I went to sleep and woke up in a parallel universe.

He tears through all the men on the steps like a force of

nature. His movements are almost inhuman, quick, beastly, and deadly. And he is taking out our men. His men. Men he has fought alongside for years.

The tightness in my chest is overwhelming.

I am on the verge of having a panic attack.

There is no hesitation in Blade's eyes as he cuts down anyone who stands in his way. His gaze locks onto mine, and for a moment, there is a strange, unspoken understanding between us. The lines of our allegiance are blurred. There is no longer a clear "right" or "wrong." There is only survival. Am I on the right side? I have to be. This is where we belong.

Blade isn't here for a political statement, he is here for something personal.

I guess we all are.

I fire my gun on autopilot, up the stairs in Kai's direction. I reload, and fire again. I don't hit anything. I'm not even sure I was aiming at a target. I step over pieces of the Murano glass chandelier littered on the floor and follow up the steps behind them. What am I even doing? I'm so close to Blade and Kai that I can hear them. Do I join them? Do I fight alongside my father? Everyone seems to know exactly what they need to be doing right now. Everyone except me. I'm wandering around aimlessly in the most treacherous gunfight I have ever been in. How am I even still alive right now? Is anyone even shooting at me? It's almost as if my presence here is unnecessary. Fucking figures, what's new?

"You always were a thorn in my side, Blade," Kai calls out, her voice cutting through the sounds of the fight.

Blade launches himself toward her. An unstoppable force, like a tidal wave crashing against her defenses.

Kai nods and they open to let him through. And everyone just obeys her.

Blade kisses her with such force it almost knocks her over.

A pang of jealousy rises in my gut. For one night, they were mine. For one night, they were everything I ever wanted. And now, I'm on the outside watching them like a stranger.

He whispers something in her ear and then releases her and starts fighting alongside her, protecting her six.

I'm so distracted by the weight pressing down on my chest that I almost miss it.

Kai lunges forward, and in a single motion, she strikes my dad with a katana. A fucking katana.

The entire room seems to freeze.

The Don, my father, the man who had held so many lives in his hands, the man whose power has shaped our world, is brought to his knees in front of me by the woman who dropped in on us like a nuclear bomb, leaving nothing but fallout in her wake. His life drains away as Kai's blade slashes into him from chest to gut, blood splattering across the ground in a sickening arc. The sight of exposed viscera causes bile to rise into my throat.

She filets him open the same way he fileted Akira. Blood seeps from him onto the marble floors and travels like a slow-moving river.

My stomach churns, the sight of my father's life slipping away before my eyes. The pain, the betrayal, the violence, it all washes over me like a tsunami.

Kai stands over my father's body, her eyes cold and unfeeling.

"You deserve to suffer for taking my father from me, for taking Akira from me, for taking everything I love from me" she says, her voice filled with an eerie calm, "for everything you took from Blade, for what you did to Ava, for the damage you've caused your own fucking son, and for god knows what other atrocities you've committed that we don't know about. I wanted to take my time and enjoy every fucking second of your suffering at my hands. But I love your son. So I'll settle for you to simply die."

The words cut through the air like a dagger, the final blow to a man who had ruled with an iron fist for decades.

I love your son.

Me?

She can't mean me. She means Blade, who was brave enough to stand beside her. The son who chose her.

My heart is racing, my mind screaming with confusion. This isn't how I imagined it would end. I had expected something else, something different.

I expected my father to win.

I expected her to die.

I am not sad, though, and I don't know why. Initially all the tension left my body, and then almost immediately my blood began to boil.

It is over.

Kai's gaze shifts toward me, her expression unreadable, but there is something there, something soft. Before I can process it, she is standing in front of me. All the fighting has ceased. The instant the Don fell, the fighting stopped.

Then I realize why. He named Blade his successor. Blade is standing at Kai's side. With my father dead, they all wait with bated breath to be sure. To know that their new Don has chosen a different path.

Everyone is staring at either the Don's body on the floor, at Blade covered in the blood of his brethren, or Kai approaching me.

I don't know where to look.

Blade walks up behind her. "Kai, it's done, let's go. He

knows his father killed Spider. He doesn't care. He can't be reasoned with."

Kai turns to look at him. And in what sounds like utter agony, whispers, "no."

No, I think, *turn around*. Look back at me.

"Plus, he's the Don now. He can't leave."

The words are a sucker punch. He's chosen a side. It's not mine. And he's leaving me with the fallout. Abdicating the throne and getting the fuck out, abandoning the cleanup to be done by the man who wasn't enough in the first place.

She looks back at me and asks, "Where's Spider?"

The minute I hear that name leave her lips, something in me snaps.

"Get on your knees," I demand, my voice shaking with anger and disbelief.

Kai obeys without hesitation, her head lowered. "Look at me, you cunt." She looks up at me. I register the confusion on her face but I shove the thought down.

Blade stays steady at her side. "Kai, get up, let's go."

She holds up her hand and he freezes. She trained her new puppy well.

I no longer live in a world I recognize.

Her eyes meet mine with a look of resignation. "I told you, I will always submit to you, all you ever have to do is ask."

Her words fan the flames of my rage in a way I have never been consumed with before. How dare she act like she would do anything for me after destroying everything I have ever known.

I grab Blade's knife from her thigh where she must have holstered it before grabbing a fucking katana, my grip tight. This is it. This is the moment that defines what comes next. I know what this will cost. Yet I can't seem to stop myself.

"You've destroyed everything," I accuse, my voice low but steady. "You killed my father. You killed Spider. You used us to enact some twisted revenge fantasy and you didn't care who you hurt in the process. This is your end."

Kai's lips form a faint, hollow line. "I what?" she whispers. "Killed Spider? Tor, I lo—"

I don't let her finish. I can't. My heart twists, but there is no room for mercy. There is no room for anything other than what has to be done. I am the one left standing, the one who has to carry the weight of this broken world. I am now the Don. And weak men don't survive.

I stab the cold, sharp instrument into her gut before she can finish her sentence. I can't bear to hear it. I pull out the blade gleaming in her blood. The look in her eyes is part heartbreak, part despair, part relief. I can't look at her anymore, it makes my stomach turn. My chest constricts, I am dizzy and disoriented. I focus on her blood on the knife to keep from passing out.

Her gasp is the only sound that breaks the silence between us.

Blade decks me so hard I fall to the floor, cutting myself on shattered glass.

As I get up, I watch as he reaches for Kai, lifting her in his arms. The woman who just betrayed everything he had once fought for. The woman who destroyed us.

He carries her away.

I don't stop him.

The Yakuza start to charge me. Kai raises her hand and grits out, "No, stand down." before she appears to lose consciousness. They obey her command and follow behind her as she lay limp in Blade's arms.

"Don't you dare think you've won," Blade bellows, his voice a raw cry of anger. "The next time I see you, I will kill you."

I stand frozen, watching the woman who had once been mine, now cradled in Blade's arms, who was also once mine. Her blood seeps from the wound I inflicted, staining everything it touches as she's carried out.

Blade turns the corner, disappearing into the distance, carrying Kai's body with him. The compound is in utter disarray, carnage in every direction. No piece of furniture on this first floor or the mezzanine remains intact, no wall unscathed.

I am left standing here, the weight of everything crashing down on me. I have an empire, yet I have nothing.

Blade's last words linger in the air, a promise, a regret.

The battle may be done, but the war is far from over. A line had been crossed, and the price of everything I just lost is written in blood.

CHAPTER 28

BLADE

The hospital room is eerily still, the steady beeping of the monitors the only sign of life. I don't even recognize her. She's steel strength, epically powerful, she always seemed larger than life. Yet as she lays in the bed, her face pale, framed by the harsh glow of fluorescent light, she looks exceedingly frail. Machines hum softly, tubes and wires connecting her to the fragile tethers that keep her here.

I slump in the chair beside her and drop my head into my hands. Fuck, my clothes are a mess, bloodstained, torn, reeking of sweat and desperation, and that disgusting smell of damp clothing like when it's been left in the washer for too long. I can't even feel the bruises on my knuckles, split open from the one fight I didn't win, at least not in time. I was too late.

Tor will fucking bleed for this.

Slowly, I lift my head, my eyes feeling bloodshot and hollow, but I watch her. Her lips, so often curled into a smirk, are lifeless. I can't see the fire in her piercing, violet-black eyes.

"Fuck, princess, open your eyes for me." Her hands, hands that have shoved me, slapped me, and pulled me close all the same, now lay limp at her sides. I take her hand in mine. Fuck me, I never realized how small she was. Her hands feel so cold and clammy, devoid of the usual warmth she exudes.

"God, you're a fucking piece of work, you know that?" The sound of my voice surprises me, low, gravelly, teetering on the edge of breaking. I let out a humorless laugh, shaking my head. "You never could let any of us have the last word. Always have a comeback, don't you? So get up. Tell me how much you hate me. Tell me how much you want to kill me. I can't do the silence again, princess. I need you to speak."

I stand suddenly and start pacing the small, sterile space as emotions churn in my gut, too much to keep inside. The pressure feels like an anvil crushing me. "You don't get to do this. You don't get to leave like this. Not after everything. Not after you..." My voice falters, and I turn back to her, my chest heaving with the weight of everything I never said.

"I was fucking pissed at you," I admit, stepping closer to the bed. "For a long time. At first for existing and showing me that I am still capable of feeling things. Then for the things you said, the things you did. For pushing us away, for pushing me away, for running after telling me you'd stay. But I get it now." I swallow hard, my throat tight. "You did it for your dad. You did it to protect yourself. Hell, maybe even to protect us. You did it for..." my voice catches, choking on the name, "Spider." It takes me a minute to find my words again. "You did it for Tor's mom, and Tor, who I'm going to rip to shreds for doing this to you. You did it to protect me. But that was my fucking job, princess. You took my fucking job from me, but I... I forgive you. For all of it. Do you forgive me? Fuck, princess, wake up. Please tell me you forgive me. Please."

My voice softens to a tone I never knew I was even capable of. I lean over her, brushing her hair out of her face. I cling to her hand again as if I can keep her here with me if I hold her tight enough. "But you? You had to kill the bastard yourself. You have to do everything by your fucking self."

A bitter laugh escapes me, and I wipe at my face with a shaking hand. "That's what pisses me off most, you know? You got to finish what I should've done. He was just as much mine to kill as he was yours. Always so eager to prove that you don't need anybody, that you didn't need us." A resigned sigh escapes me. "That you didn't need me." It's getting harder and harder to breathe. My voice cracks completely and something inside me breaks. "That's fine. It's fine, cause you know what? I need you." I can't believe what I'm saying. I do know I'll say anything, anything at all if she just looks up at me.

"Why did you get on your knees for him back there? After everything. After I told you he can't be reasoned with. He is a stubborn fucking bull. Always has been." I lower myself to my knees beside the bed, my hand clutching hers even tighter now. "I thought I wasn't capable of love. Not after Ava. Not after my parents. I told myself that for years. It was easier to shove everything down, turn it all off, and pretend I didn't have it in me. But then you came along and blew my life to hell. And now..."

I blink back tears. The first tears that have fallen on my face in over ten years.

My voice drops to a whisper. "Now, I'm realizing I've been lying to you. I've been lying to myself. Because I love you. For fuck's sake, Kai, I love you. I'm begging you, don't leave me. Everyone fucking leaves me. You told me you would stay. So fucking stay. You promised me you would always stay safe. So stay safe. Kai, please. Princess, please wake up."

A single tear slips down her cheek, glistening in the dim light. Every muscle in my body freezes, staring at her face, hope sparking in my chest for the briefest moment.

I stop breathing when the monitors erupt into a shrill, frantic alarm.

"No," I whisper, my voice cracking as her hand tenses, then goes completely inert in mine. "No, no, no!" I jump up, panic gripping me as the door flies open and doctors and nurses rush in.

"Sir, we're going to need you to step back," I vaguely hear one of them say, but I don't move. I can't move. I stand rooted to the spot, my eyes fixed on her as they work to revive her. Hands grab my arms, pulling me away as I shout, "Do something! Don't let her... don't let her die or I swear to god I will fucking kill you! All of you!"

I'm shoved back into the corner of the room. I can't see anything, the room is a blur. My senses are overwhelmed by the scent of sterility. I don't feel like I'm here. I hear nothing except for the quiet, ragged sobs escaping my throat. I press my back against the wall, sliding down to the floor, my head buried in my hands. "Please don't leave me, princess."

The room starts to spin. I hear frantic voices, sharp commands, chaos from her bedside. But I can't look at her. All I can do is repeat over and over again, "Please don't leave me, please." The same words I repeated for hours when I found Ava. The same words I swore I would never say again when I found my parents. And yet, here I am. Again. Begging the person I love to stay with me. Her eyes burn in my mind, her beautiful face frozen in time. And all I can think of is, how am I alone again? And I never told her the truth, I never told her I love her, not until it was too late.

I struggle to open my eyes.

Wait, am I dead?

The last thing I remember is being shot outside of the compound. Fucking idiot. I know better than to turn my back on anyone, ever. Fuck. Shit, I hope Blade got the files.

My head hits a rough surface as I jostle around in a confined space, pain ricocheting through my skull on the impact. I finally get my eyes open, but I can't get them to focus. Shit, it's so dark.

A stark pain shoots down my arm as I'm thrust against a hard surface. I can't extend my legs. Fuck me. My hands frantically scour over every available surface. The abrasive felt under my fingertips and the rounded edges in front of me confirm what I already suspected. I keep getting tossed around back here in this dark, confined space. I am in a fucking trunk.

My mind starts alternating through every possible scenario, like I'm that guy from that movie. The one who envisions infinite timelines in order to figure out which of the millions of possibilities will lead to the one outcome that doesn't end in my ultimate demise.

I need to get to Kai. That's the only thing that matters.

I still have no idea what my next move is when the car comes to an abrupt stop. I brace my feet against the side of the trunk to try and prevent slamming against the back again. I fail, and, fuck that shit hurts. At least these fucks didn't think to tie me up. I guess they thought I was already dead.

I can hear Bruno and another of the Don's men arguing outside. While it is muffled, I can make out that neither of them wants to get blood on their designer suit. Assholes. I try and listen past their bitching to see if I can get any indication as to where we are. Knowing Bruno, we're probably at the lower Hudson. The river is his favorite dumping ground. If I act dead and wait for them to dump me, maybe swimming away is my best chance. There is no world where I can fight the two of them off in my current state. I can tell by the lack of hard metal against my hip they have relieved me of my weapons. I remember the knife I keep by my ankle. Despite the pain, I contort to reach down. Fuck, they took that, too.

My chest tightens and my breath begins to pick up. Fuck, I don't think I have a way out of this. The Hudson is a tough swim on a regular day, let alone with three fresh bullet wounds. I can't even feel my left arm, though I can't totally tell if that's because I'm injured or just because I'm lying on it awkwardly.

I need to get back to the boys. To Kai. What the fuck is taking these morons so long? Then I remember I shouldn't be complaining about my last few moments of breathing. I need to fucking focus. I need to get out of here, they need me.

A gunshot sounds and I flinch. As my pulse pounds in my ears, I hear Bruno swearing and shouting.

I hear metal clink against metal and I make myself as small as I can.

Another gunshot, then another. I tense and flinch involuntarily as I count them. There's more yelling I can't make out, some more screaming. Thirteen rounds are fired, not counting the first one, and I can discern that one gun is popping louder than the other, so it's definitely a firefight, not just a barrage of bullets from one person.

The vehicle rocks around me and I can't help it, a whimper escapes me. Some muffled thuds as bodies clearly hit the ground.

Another eight rounds pop off in quick succession.

I am clenched as tightly as I have ever been, balled up in the fetal position, my teeth grinding so hard I am surprised they didn't crack. I count heartbeats, willing myself to breathe slowly. Fourteen heartbeats pass before I decide the complete silence outside is really the end of it. Nothing for the next twelve heartbeats other than the horn of a passing boat.

Well, at least I know for sure we are at the lower Hudson.

I hear a muffled voice bark out, "Throw me the keys." The voice sounds familiar. But I shake my head, that wouldn't make any sense. It's not possible.

I hear the quick clink of keys and I brace myself for what's coming.

I picture Blade and Tor in my mind. Their smiles when we were all with Kai. Fuck, I wish I could see my boys like that one more time. Happy for fucking once. And I picture Kai, my fucking breathtakingly beautiful, feisty as fuck Kai. *I love you, sweetheart.*

As the trunk opens, I close my eyes, take in a deep breath, and brace myself for the end. I'm already bleeding out and living on borrowed time. I don't want to see the ugly ass mug of whichever fucking former friendly is about to end me. I just want to see Tor, Blade, and my Kai. That's the image I want as my last one. I smile as I see the look on their faces in the limo.

I hear the man clear his throat. Fucking shoot me already. I'm ready. There is no way out of this for me.

"Hey, kid. Smiling even in the face of death, that's my boy."

I can recognize that dickhead Irishman's voice from anywhere.

I pop my eyes open and stare up at him. My father. "Dad?"

To be continued...

Mmm, that's it. You did so well... but I'm not done with you yet.

If you're still hungry for more, grab the next installment of the Edge of Vengeance series, It Begins in Us, at valentinavallay.com.

Come see where this ride takes us. I'll be waiting for you...

ACKNOWLEDGMENTS

Bro, I don't even know where to start. What started off as one girl with a dream has turned into the ride of a lifetime. We wouldn't be here today without the countless people that have been in my corner, cheering me on to completion. Yes, I see what I did there, and no, I won't be changing it.

r1k, you kept me sane when I was anything but. You weren't just support, you were the problem-solver who quietly fixed what I couldn't, carried what I shouldn't, and held everything steady so I could chase this dream. Without you, this book would still be sitting unfinished. You taught me that just because I *can* do something doesn't mean I have to do it alone, and you've proven time and again that I never have to.

To Lady and Schmunty, you taught me how to be present and embody unconditional love. This is the most invaluable gift I have ever received. And to Duke, my first ever best friend, and my best boy, you live in my heart for all eternity. I hope they have books in doggy heaven. I love you three most of all.

To my best friends, you know exactly who you are. Ale, Mo, and Nani, there is no world where I could have done this without you. From fielding a thousand text messages to reviewing countless possibilities and providing feedback, you are the foundation my world is built upon. I love you. Especially for believing in me and helping me get past obstacles I struggled with throughout this process. When my mind wasn't being the kindest of friends to me, you all always were until we got that bad boy back on my side.

To my family, thank you for championing me. No, you still can't tell your friends I wrote a book. I love you, and I know you want to be proud and share that pride with the world. This one is just for me and my readers. To my brother, you're my best friend, and your voice acting skills are insane. If I ever write a SFW book, you better get ready to get to work. To dad, thanks for not freaking out. Not that either of you will ever see this, I just wanted to say it. Also, mom, I told you not to read this. Why are you reading this right now? You should never have gotten this far. I guess we now know where I got the "you never listen to anyone, you're so stubborn" vibe from.

To my editor Gina Denny, I can't imagine getting here without you. Thank you for fitting me into your insane schedule. I leave every one of our calls rejuvenated and ready to tackle these stories with a renewed sense of direction. Thank you for teaching me how to use the em dash and ellipses correctly, for organizing my chaos, and for keeping me on track. You've become a trusted partner on this journey, selfishly I request that you never retire, I don't want to have to write a book without you.

To the voice actors that brought this story to life, your talents are immense. Eyes of Suggestion, Jaxon Jones, and MythosVA, it has been an honor working with you, thank you for bringing your unique voices to my boys.

To the incredibly talented Sakananachi and Noctornos-Arts, you made my people real. I cannot thank you enough. Some of my best memories have been conceptualizing these characters with you and seeing you make them a visual reality. I adore you both.

To Ricky Armellino and Ryan Riveros. Thank you for

jumping in to help me craft the song for a pivotal scene in the book. I remain in awe of your talent. To Eyes of Suggestion, thank you for co-writing the song with us. I had no idea how much fun writing a song would be. Thank you for lending your immense creativity to 'Stay With Me'. I can't wait to work on the song for book two with you.

To Mo, Ale, MJ, and Melly, my alpha reader team. Reading your feedback and being able to discuss the story with you was one of the most rewarding experiences I have ever been a part of. I looked forward to your commentary submissions like a Sylus girlie waiting for a five-star memory card drop. Sorry, not sorry, that I took you on a wild ride. We're in this together, from beginning to end. Are you ready for book two?

Thank you to Zito and Kytana for helping me navigate the Twitch streamer world. And Zito, my sanity thanks you for always being there when my computer or I had a meltdown to put things back in order. Too bad I don't have an on/off switch, but I can be turned on and off again, so there is that.

Thank you to MythosVA and Eyes of Suggestion for helping me iron out some dialogue to align better with your characters' voices and for going above and beyond in promoting this project. When you came on board, I was nowhere near prepared for the level of support I would receive from you two. I am grateful to you both.

To Trampoline, thank you for the immeasurable support. I was always overwhelmed, and you were always jumping in to help, well beyond the scope of what was required of you, without being asked. I don't think the words 'thank you' are anywhere near enough to capture how grateful I am. I bounced ideas off of you, and bounced back from the edge numerous times because of you. I love you.

To RMK Management Pty Ltd and especially Otto Reitano. The audiobook wouldn't exist without your time, experience, and skill. You're my hero, and you're funny as hell. Working with you has been an absolute privilege, one I wouldn't trade for anything.

To Carson Beck and soundBOX Studio Group, there is nowhere else I would ever want to record anything. You're amazing, and it is an honor and a privilege to work with you. Carson, you are the best mentor a girl could ask for as I embarked on the voice acting aspect of this journey. You're also an incredible friend. Thank you.

To Leilani O'Bity (Oldest, Bitch in the Yard) and Adriana, your brilliance is irreplaceable. I knew at some point I'd need to market this thing, but I had no idea how. I would have been lost without you. Like if y'all think I had any idea how to be an exhibitor at TwitchCon… that would be incorrect. Leilani, you spearheaded it all and walked me through each step of the way while managing a superhuman schedule. Adriana, you taught me how to do things I still can't even explain. I love you two, you're a godsend.

A special thank you to those who started along with me on this journey but ended up taking a different fork in the road before reaching the destination. To Andronicus Edits, thank you for your edits on the first five chapters. It was a pleasure working with you. To voEROS, a contributor to this story. Thank you for your contributions to the early development of the story, your participation in developing sex scenes, as well as your edits to chapters, 1-2, 8, and 21. I wish you nothing but immense success in your future endeavors.

ABOUT THE AUTHOR

I write the kind of love stories that leave bruises. Twisted, tender, and steeped in shadow, my romances explore the fine line between obsession and devotion, pain and pleasure, ruin and redemption.

By day (and often well into the night), I'm an author who breathes life into damaged characters and dangerous desires. But my world doesn't end on the page, I also stream bedtime stories and chaotic chats with my reader community on Twitch. I also co-wrote and performed the vocals for this novel's original song.

Through Patreon, I offer early access to chapters, steamy bonus scenes, voice notes that slip under your skin, and short audio dramas. And yes, when the story demands to be heard, I narrate my own work, giving breath to every broken vow, whispered promise, and dark confession.

This space is for readers who crave intensity. For those who love their stories a little messy, a little haunted, and a lot unforgettable.

Welcome to the dark side, my beloved Valentine. I've been expecting you.